Lisa M. Lane

Murder at an Exhibition

Grousable Books

Murder at an Exhibition

A Tommy Jones Mystery

Published by Grousable Books, Encinitas, California
ISBN: 979-8-9853027-4-5 (print)
ISBN: 979-8-9853027-5-2 (e-book)
Library of Congress Control Number: 2022914744

Cover illustration: The National Gallery from Illustrated London, or, a series of views in the British metropolis and its vicinity, engraved by Albert Henry Payne, from original drawings. The historical, topographical and miscellaneous notices, by W. I. Bicknell, 1846. Cover design: Sarah Lane Daymude. Cover font: Baskervville by Atelier national de recherche typographique, France.

Map of London, 1863

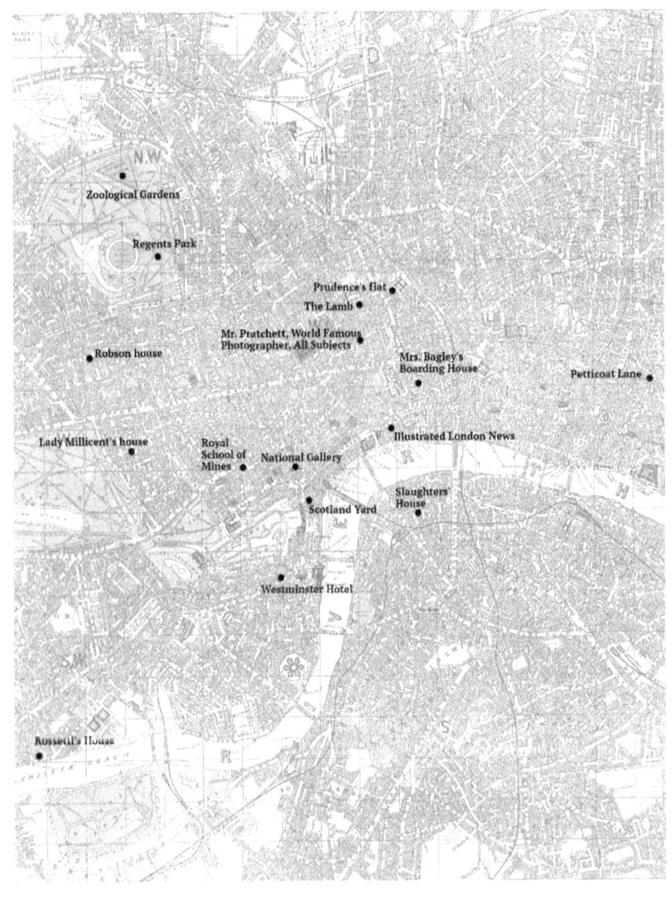

Characters

Jo Harris: magazine illustrator, friend of Ellie and Bridget
Bridget Williams: friend and housemate of Jo Harris
Mrs. Bagley: proprietor of boarding house in Shoe Lane
*Ann Little Ingram: manager, *Illustrated London News*
*Queen Bertha: a horse that won at Epsom Downs
Hugh Pratchett: photographer
Reginald MacLeish: solicitor
Samson Light: London University student, tutor to Tommy Jones
Prudence Henderson: day maid in the Slaughter household
*Hannah Cullwick: maid of all work, photographic model
Andrew Church: Samson's friend at his boarding house
Percy Fry: art student and man about town
*Margaret Dalziel: engraver, Dalziel Brothers
*T. H. Huxley: scientist and educational reformer
James Robson: art critic and collector
Cecil Robson: James Robson's son, a painter
Lady Millicent Stroud: a customer of Pratchett's and art collector
*Sir Charles Eastlake: director of the National Gallery
Smith: assistant to Sir Charles Eastlake
*Joseph Bazalgette: engineer
*Dante Gabriel Rossetti: artist and poet
*Fanny Cornforth: Rossetti's model and housekeeper
*Giovanni Morelli: Italian art critic and expert
Miriam Frankel: market woman and photographic subject
Mrs. Gretz: friend of Miriam Frankel
Angus in Holywell Street: purveyor of pornographic images
Inspector Reginald Harkness: Scotland Yard
Constable Moberly: Piccadilly Station
Detective Inspector Cuthbert Slaughter
Ellie Slaughter: Cuthbert's wife, guardian of Tommy Jones
Tommy Jones: boy who lives with the Slaughters

* historical figure

Jo knew she had seen the dead man's face somewhere before, but she couldn't place him. His body was lying curled up on the floor, as if he had fallen when the blow hit him. And it must have been a fierce blow to leave such a gash on his temple. She quickly noted the position of his body, the white hair sticking out above his ears, the cut of his coat.

On the wall behind him, the paintings for the Royal Academy Exhibition were hung close together, from floor to ceiling, the red of the walls separating them by only an inch or two. The open door behind the man's body, through which he had fallen, showed the gallery's ladders and brooms.

Although she felt sorry for the dead man—it had been a violent death, after all—Jo's instinct was to try to frame the scene, a body surrounded by painted pictures. Surely one of the illustrated magazines would want a rendering. Her fingers itched to get out her sketchbook and draw it all before she forgot.

"Miss, you'll need to leave the area," said the constable, coming up behind her. "Unless you knew the deceased?"

"No, I didn't," said Jo, still confused as to why she felt she should know him. Her memory for faces was quite good. The constable's look held both concern and condescension. She heard people talking as police ushered them out of the gallery, taking names and addresses. The constable prepared to lead her out.

"It's all right," said Jo. "I'm leaving."

"Please talk to Constable Moberly, there with the notebook. He'll need your name and address."

"Yes, of course."

There was a bench in the square across from the gallery. Jo sat down, pulled out her notebook, and sketched the scene. The man's body crumpled on the floor, the gash, his hair, the smooth brow, his loose-fitting but respectable jacket. Then the paisley carpet onto which he'd fallen, the pictures hanging low on the wall nearby. She hadn't had time to take note of the pictures themselves, but she could return for that. Something odd there, but she couldn't recall just what. Who was this man, and why did she feel she should know him?

1

"Honestly, I have no idea how you get your stitches so small and tidy," said Jo, firmly setting down her dress and accidentally jamming the needle into her finger. Bridget smiled sympathetically.

The dining room at Mrs. Bagley's boarding house was quite warm in the afternoon, but the light came in from the street so it was the best room for sewing.

"It's because you have to do so much," Bridget said. "You're having to go all round the hem. We could get you a crinoline." She looked down at her beadwork with an impish smile.

Jo growled. "Where's Esther? I'd happily pay her to do it." She sucked on her finger.

Mrs. Bagley overheard as she went through on the way to the kitchen.

"You know perfectly well Esther works at her father's shop till four," she said. "And you should hem your own dresses." She and Bridget exchanged a look over Jo's head.

"I don't think," said Jo, retrieving the errant needle from among the folds of brown fabric, "that people should have to engage in tasks for which they have no talent."

"Oh, here she goes," said Mrs. Bagley loudly from the kitchen. "Back up on her socialist pony." They heard the range door open and close. "Bridget? I think this only has a few minutes to go."

The aroma from the meat pies wafted into the dining room, deliciously scented but making the room feel even warmer. Jo could sense the beads of sweat along her hairline as she started again on the hem. Bridget rose and leaned across the table. "I'll do it for you later with the lamp, if you like." Then she went in to tend to the pies.

A waste of good daylight, thought Jo, jamming the needle in and out. *It's perfect for drawing. I should let Bridget do the sewing for me and go get my sketchbook. When* Once a Week *pays me for those bridge pictures, I could take her out for a nice coffee or something.*

In truth, she had enjoyed the bridge drawings. Usually she focused on people because that's what the publications wanted. Human interest. But the reopening of Westminster Bridge the previous May had encouraged greater interest in the bridges that spanned the Thames. Thomas Page had outdone himself with the engineering, which many had admired when his Chelsea Bridge had opened a few years before. That project, however, had been plagued by years of delays. For Westminster Bridge, Page had built it one half at a time, each direction separately, so traffic was not disrupted. Detective Sergeant Mark Honeycutt, a friend of Jo's, had told her that Danduran's diving bell had been an innovation that had made construction possible. She couldn't imagine working under water.

Jo had found it refreshing to focus on trees, and the light, instead of drawing a face. The new green paint, chosen to match the benches in Parliament, made the whole bridge shine. Jo rarely had the opportunity to draw things outdoors, and the weather had been quite perfect.

And that's what I'm good at, she thought, as the needle again cruelly entered her finger. *Not sewing, or cooking, or uttering inanities in social settings.* Sucking her finger again as tears came to her eyes, she glanced out the window. The trees on Shoe Lane were still. If she wanted to capture the Vauxhall Bridge at sundown, she'd need to go. After dinner. Because Bridget's pies were worth staying for.

Young Tommy was quite nervous. "Are you sure we're allowed to be in here?" he asked Samson. It was half past seven, and Tommy was still rubbing the sleep out of his eyes. Morning came early when you were thirteen years old.

"It's perfectly all right, so long as we're gone before the first class starts," said Samson, his curly hair making him look younger than his twenty-two years. Truthfully, he was a bit nervous himself. He'd only been here once before, and Jermyn Street was not an area he knew. But Sarah Pemberton, another external student, had an uncle who worked here at the newly named Royal School of Mines. She had arranged to borrow the key so he could bring Tommy. He walked confidently to the cabinet and carefully opened the doors.

And there it was. The J.J. Lister microscope. Its brass gleamed. Samson carefully took it out and placed it on a table where the morning sun shone on it.

"It's got an achromatic lens," said Samson. "So there's no rainbow ring around the image. Hand me that box there, will you?"

Tommy gently took out the flat wooden box. Samson opened the lid and pulled out a slide, placing it under the lens. He put his eye to the instrument and turned a few dials. Then he stepped back. "Take a look," he said.

The leaf didn't look like a leaf. The pattern of veins were so clear, you felt you could see the sap pulsing through them. Its surface seemed to be made up of very small panes.

"Can you see the cells?" asked Samson.

"The little panes?" said Tommy.

"Yes, all connected together."

Tommy gulped and nodded. "It's wonderful."

He stared and stared. He couldn't believe how beautiful it was.

"We have time for a few more, then we really must go," said Samson. "Here's a bit of muscle, from a pig." He slipped the slide in so Tommy could see.

The door at the far end of the room opened, and a man entered. He was in his late thirties, had a shock of dark hair, a determined face, and intimidating sideburns. Samson and Tommy froze as he approached them.

"I assume," he said, not unkindly, "that you do not have permission to be here."

"No sir," said Samson, standing up to his full height. "But I wanted my pupil here to have an opportunity to look through a superior microscope."

The man smiled. "And whom might I be addressing?"

"Samson Light, sir. I'm a physiology student, external, and this is Tommy Jones."

"I am also named Thomas," said the man, reaching out to shake Tommy's and then Samson's hand. "Huxley," he said, "I teach here, and donated this microscope."

"It is most wonderful, Mr. Huxley," said Tommy sincerely. "I had no idea nature could be so beautiful."

Huxley took a slide out of the box, holding it up to the light. "Ah yes," he said, "these are the biological slips." He looked at Samson and Tommy with interest. "Most of the students here study geology. You two are more interested in botany and animal physiology?"

"Indeed, sir," said Samson. "We study life."

Huxley nodded, his bushy eyebrows lowering, making him look hawk-like.

"Well said, young man," he said. "Well, I'm certainly not going to report you. I have been trying to get the School here to add physiology to the curriculum. I also teach at the Royal College of Surgeons. Perhaps I shall see you there someday..I'll remember your name, Mr. Light."

"I hope to be there some day, sir," said Samson. "It is an honor to meet you."

"Likewise, young man." He began walking back toward the door, and spoke over his shoulder. "Put it away carefully, please. I'll be back in a few minutes to set up on my own."

Samson and Tommy left without being seen by anyone else. As they began walking toward Piccadilly, Tommy breathed a sigh of relief.

"Who is Thomas Huxley? He seemed rather important."

"He is a geology professor who is trying to make way for anatomy and physiology to be taught more regularly. He wants to train young men like me to teach, and be doctors, and scientists. I can't believe we got to meet him." Samson was a little red in the face.

"He was very kind, wasn't he?"

"Yes, he was. He also happens to be one of the examiners at the University of London, although I think his double professorship means he probably won't be doing it by the time I take my exam. But just to meet him! Did you know they call him Darwin's bulldog?"

"No! Why?"

"He debated Bishop Wilberforce three years ago, just after Darwin's book came out. You must have heard about that. And now he has his own book, saying that ape brains are more similar to human brains than they are to other primates."

"Are they?" asked Tommy, fascinated.

"Well, he dissected the brains himself, so he should know."

Bridget arrived at work a little late because she was thinking and walked more slowly. Mr. Pratchett, World Famous Photographer, All Subjects, had been expanding his business. She'd been working there for almost two years. Today she'd brought some of the buns she'd made because she knew how Pratchett loved her baking, and she had something in particular to discuss with him.

Passing the cake shop on her way to Theobalds Road, she stopped and looked in the window. The cakes were beautifully designed, with smooth fondant and decorations of flowers. She'd much rather work in a bakery, creating lovely confections. But cake shops were for experts, usually men, and the other kinds of baking were too horrible to contemplate. Bread, she knew, was made in underground rooms with dark ovens. The dough was kneaded, or even trodden underfoot, by men covered in sweat, flour, and dirt. No wonder Dr. Dauglish had invented his mechanized process for making aerated bread. You'd never eat bread if you thought about how it was made by hand. And thanks to Dauglish, people did think about it, and bought his bread.

Food was Bridget's passion, but photography was her job. Hugh Pratchett liked her, she knew, because of her excellent visual sense and her care with equipment. She was also detailed with the tinting, especially on the tintypes. And patrons sitting for their portrait trusted her kind and gentle manner.

She arrived to find Pratchett, as usual, in the middle of a half-finished project, his tufts of white hair sticking out madly above his ears.

"I can smell them from here," he said, sniffing the air appreciatively but not looking up. "Buns, is it?"

"Yes, indeed," said Bridget, amused as always by his extraordinary sense of smell. "Yesterday's, I'm afraid, but still sweet and tasty." She put the paper-wrapped package on the counter.

"How are the stereoscopic views coming along?" she asked as she hung her hat on the peg and put her business apron over her pale blue skirt.

Pratchett peered up at her. It always took a minute for his eyes to refocus.

"I'd say they're coming along well. But some are just a little off."

"How off?" She looked over his shoulder at a double image of the pagoda in Cremorne Gardens.

"The positioning is correct, but when you look . . ." He slipped the image into the stereoscope and handed it to her.

The effect just wasn't quite right. Her eyes tried to align the two images, but one seemed sharper than the other.

"I see what you mean," she said. Pratchett looked weary, she thought, his eyes rheumy. "Is it worth the trouble, do you think?"

"I'm starting to think not," sighed Pratchett. "The London Stereoscopic Company produces many hundreds of these, using their own photographers. And they've become so cheap that no one wants any of quality." Bridget nodded in sympathy.

He opened a drawer to put the double image away.

"Mr. Pratchett," said Bridget, "before Miss Peyton arrives, I'd like to ask you about something." Miss Peyton was sitting for her portrait at eleven o'clock.

"Yes, Miss Williams?" He looks a little wary, she thought. He thinks I'm going to ask for more money.

"I've noticed a number of gentlemen customers come in, and they always ask for you," she began. "They say I cannot assist them."

Pratchett looked at her for a moment.

"And you're wondering why?" he asked.

"I think I may know," said Bridget. "I wonder are you selling photographs of women? Perhaps in less reputable costume or poses?" She was proud of herself that she had at last asked the question aloud.

"Miss Williams, I hardly think it suitable to discuss . . ."

"I want to make sure, Mr. Pratchett," she said, "that these women are being photographed with their own consent and agreement?"

Pratchett considered her, with her earnest look and determined brow. "Yes, Miss Williams. I can assure you that they have agreed and are being paid for posing, rather than paying me."

Bridget swallowed. "So the gentlemen pay you?"

"Yes, Miss Williams. And since we are being indelicate, I may venture to say they pay me quite a lot. In fact, without them, I would not be able to keep the shop open. You've noted, I'm sure, how few of my new ventures have become profitable." He gave the drawer of stereoscopic photographs a baleful glance.

It was true that the shop had been in some distress. Photography studios had opened all over London in the last few years. Some specialized in the old-fashioned daguerreotypes, others in tintypes or, as Pratchett did, the newer glass positives. These cost far less to produce, but people also paid far less for them.

"What happens after you sell the photographs? To the women, I mean?"

Pratchett looked confused. "Nothing," he said. "The man takes the print with him, that is all."

"So you only pay the women once?"

"Well, yes. If they pose once, I pay them. If they return and their pictures have been popular, I pay again for a different sitting, different poses."

Bridget frowned. "There seems something wrong in that," she said, "but I cannot think what it is at present. I hope we can talk about this again?"

"If you like, Miss Williams. But not with sitters in the studio, please."

"Of course," agreed Bridget. "I'll get ready for Miss Peyton."

She went into the studio at the back, making sure the draperies on the high windows were wide open to let in the light. As she set up the upholstered chair, the Doric column, and the aspidistra for a bit of foliage, she could hear the paper wrapper rustling. Pratchett must be tucking in to the buns.

⁂

"Skylights," Jo's father had said back then. But young Jo hadn't been listening. She was looking. Throughout the Dulwich Picture Gallery, the light from above seemed to flood in, illuminating all the paintings.

"There are roof lanterns up there, and the glass panels," her father explained. He was enchanted by the architecture, which had inspired him as a young man.

Jo had remembered to ask, "You were here when you were young, weren't you, Father?"

"I was the same age as you are now, about sixteen or seventeen, when this gallery opened to the public. I couldn't get in before that. It was only open to Royal Academy students."

They were standing in front of Caracci's *Magdalen*, number 274. The Magdalen seemed to be lost in thought, rather than penitent, Jo imagined. She looked closely at her face. The figure looked like a real person, not at all idealized. She noticed the way the face was drawn, showing the various folds and imperfections. I will draw like that some day, she thought.

"And that is why you became an architect," said Jo. Her father had told her many times.

He nodded and peered at the Magdalen's cloak. "I was inspired by this building, the work of John Soane. He was the son of a bricklayer, too."

She always remembered her father fondly. He had been an enthusiastic but not very successful architect. He hadn't known anyone, and the Harris family had no connections. But he had made sure his only daughter had drawing lessons and classical tutoring. He knew she would make her own way, and she had.

Jo had returned to the gallery on this particular Saturday to improve her trees. Moving from work to work, she sought out trees that were particularly well drawn. When she came to one, she would sit on the floor with her sketchbook and try to copy it. Some days there were so many students on the floor she couldn't find a spot, but today it wasn't crowded. She found the Magdalen again in the late afternoon, remembering the tree at the back. She thought of her father as the skylight illuminated the page in her sketchbook. The bag he had given her was tucked under the sketchbook, helping her balance it. She began copying the tree.

"The woman looks blotchy," said a voice nearby. A large man was crouching next to her, looking at the Magdalen. "And everything behind her looks like a hazy afterthought. Look at those clouds."

"I'm working on the tree," said Jo.

The man turned to look at her. He had extraordinary eyes of deep brown tinged with melancholy, and his wavy hair was thinning but still framed his face. He smiled above his bushy beard. "Why?"

"Because I'm bad at trees." Jo couldn't help smiling back. He seemed to radiate energy.

"How do you know Caracci's any good?" he said, looking back at the painting. "I'm bad at drawing breasts, but I certainly wouldn't copy those."

Jo looked up at the Magdalen's breasts. They were exposed, since her cloak wound around the lower half of her body. But they looked small and round and unnatural. And blotchy.

"Better to do life drawing for that, I should think," said Jo.

"Much better," said the man, and she could sense that he wanted to lower his eyes to her chest, but didn't. Instead, he bent slowly and sat down cross-legged next to her. He held out his hand. "Dante Gabriel Rossetti," he said. "You will have heard of me."

Jo shook his hand and frowned. "No, but you obviously think I should have."

At his crestfallen expression, she smiled. Everyone had heard of Rossetti.

He smiled back with a twinkle in his eye and looked over at her drawing. "Hmmm. You aren't a mere art student."

"No, I'm an artist," she said, "and illustrator."

"What do you illustrate?"

"Magazine articles and stories, mostly. I have not yet explored engravings and other media, as your Pre-Raphaelite Brotherhood has done."

He nodded, more serious now. "We have changed art for all time."

Jo couldn't help smiling. Mr. Rossetti had extraordinary confidence.

"By example?" she asked. "Or are you a teacher?"

"Both. I happen to be a teacher also, at the moment. At least, I teach at the Working Men's College. But we're changing art through our work, and how we live."

Jo looked back up at the tree. Her focus was gone now, and it was getting late. She'd been here since the gallery had opened that morning. She began to put her sketchbook away.

"I am so sorry," said Rossetti. "I have broken your concentration. Please forgive me." He rose carefully, his ample girth making him somewhat awkward. He tugged down his waistcoat.

"No, it's all right," said Jo, standing also. "I should be going anyway." She noticed he was looking at her clothes, the fall of her dress. She saw approval there, rather than the disdain she often saw when people realized she wasn't wearing a crinoline. Of course, his clothes were rather outrageous, she thought. The fabric of his jacket was decorated in a colorful swirling pattern.

"Are those birds?" she said, looking more closely.

"Yes, it's a new design for fabric," he said proudly. "Morris and Company. Do you like it?"

"Very much," she said, and looked up into his eyes. Goodness, if she were so inclined . . .

"I'm going to get some air, Mr. Rossetti," she said.

"Dante, please. I'll accompany you, Miss . . . ?"

"Harris," she said. "Jo Harris."

They walked out of the gallery into the sunlight. Rossetti put his large-brimmed hat on and stuffed his hands in his pockets, then looked at her with a confused expression.

"Yes?" she asked, working the strap of her bag into a more comfortable position on her shoulder.

"You have no parasol."

"No, it's far too hampering. I need both my hands."

"Ah, yes, for sketching." He had clasped his hands behind his back as he walked beside her.

"To get myself on the omnibus," she said.

He laughed. "Right. And no hat or, God forbid, a bonnet."

"No." She raised her face toward the sun.

He looked her up and down. "Nor, if I'm not mistaken, a corset."

Jo stopped and peered closely at him, lowering her eyelids. He stopped also and stood with his legs apart. Like a Colossus, she thought. "Omnibus," she said, and turned to continue down the path.

He fell in alongside her. "Have you ever posed for an artist, Miss Harris?"

"Good heavens, no. I belong behind the sketchbook, not in front of it."

"Perhaps," he said, "I could draw you, and allow you to draw me. Would that be fair?"

To capture those eyes would be quite something, thought Jo. The deep sadness in them, masked by humor. A confidence that undoubtedly hid some sort of sensitivity, or fragility even. She wondered whether she could do it.

"That would be fair."

"Excellent." They were approaching the omnibus stop. "How can I find you?"

Jo was twenty-nine years old and knew better than to allow a man, even a famous man, to know where you lived. "I'll find you," she said.

"Please do. 16 Cheyne Walk, Chelsea. You can come to the house. See my menagerie."

"Menagerie?"

"Exotic animals. I love them. Although I'm not terribly good at keeping them alive. Or we could meet at the Zoological Gardens." His eyes sparkled. "Let's do that. Name a time."

Jo could see the omnibus coming up the road. The horses looked fresh and ready for a five-mile haul across the river. "Next Saturday, one o'clock?" she said.

"Yes. Shall I bring a picnic?"

"Let's each bring something to share." She held out her hand. "Nice to have met you, Mr. Ro— Dante."

He took off his hat and swept it down as he bowed over her hand. "And you, Jo."

❧

Samson Light and Tommy sat at the kitchen table, since the light was better there in the afternoon. Ellie was upstairs with Prudence, freshening the bedrooms.

Samson pushed the book toward Tommy. "You see here there are two types of muscle, smooth and striated. The one we saw from the pig was smooth."

Tommy took a note in his book. "Do they do different things?"

"They do. Striated muscle is voluntary and works on command." He kicked Tommy under the table.

"What did you do that for?" Tommy yelped.

"That's my voluntary muscles. But smooth is like your stomach. It contracts involuntarily, and for longer. But heart muscle is different. It looks striated but is involuntary."

"Well, I hope so," said Tommy, ignoring his kicked leg and making another note.

"And all non-heart striated muscles are connected to the skeleton." Samson showed a drawing of the skeleton.

"That makes it easier," said Tommy. They heard Ellie and Prudence coming down the stairs. Samson rose when they entered the room, but Ellie waved him to sit.

"All right, you two," said Ellie, coming over and rustling Tommy's hair. "Who wants tea?"

"Yes, Mrs. Slaughter. I would love some," said Samson. Prudence went to the corner of the kitchen and was gathering her bag and changing into her outdoor shoes.

"How about you, Prudence?"

"No thank you, Missus. I need to get home and make some toast and cheese for Mother." Ellie noticed Samson watching Prudence change her shoes. Must keep an eye on those two, she thought.

"All right. Well, be sure to take her a slice of apple pie from the larder, and tell her I hope she feels better soon."

"Thank you, Missus." Prudence wrapped the pie in a towel and glanced gratefully at Ellie, then gave Samson a quick, shy smile. "See you Thursday."

Monday and Thursday were the afternoons Samson came to the house to tutor Tommy. Not coincidentally, they were also the days Prudence came to clean. Tommy had insisted that Samson, a young man, should not come when Ellie was home with just him. Tommy was only thirteen, after all, and Ellie was a married woman and Tommy's guardian. So Samson and Prudence came on the same days.

Ellie made the tea as Tommy closed his notebook.

"Is that all for today, Samson?"

"That's all for today." He began stacking his books and tying them together. "Can I help, Mrs. Slaughter?"

"You can bring the biscuits from the larder, Samson. Bring the big tin. I expect the Inspector any minute."

The larder was dark and cool, but Samson knew the biscuit tin. This was their ritual. He'd stay for tea, hoping for a chance to talk to Detective Inspector Cuthbert Slaughter. Ellie's husband was with the Metropolitan Police, the detective division, and worked out of Christchurch Station. He had seen Samson's advertisement in *The Times* and had taken him on to tutor Tommy.

They heard the door open and Cuthbert moving outside the study, removing his shoes and putting on his house slippers.

"Hullo!" Ellie called, as she put the pot on the table.

"Hullo," said Cuthbert, coming into the kitchen. "Good evening, Tommy. Mr. Light."

He enclosed his wife around the waist and snuggled her neck. Ellie laughed.

"What's that for?" she said, smiling up into his eyes.

"Just a good day," he said. "I hope you had a good day too?"

"I did, as a matter of fact," she said. "The house is clean, and the women's committee meeting for tonight was cancelled. I have an evening to do some embroidery."

Cuthbert nodded. "Good," he said. "I'd love to put my feet up." He sat down at the table and looked at the stack of books tied with a string. "Anatomy today, then?"

"Yes, sir," said Samson.

"And how are your own studies going?"

"Very well, sir. I think I'm ready for the first Bachelor's of Science examination questions, but not for the practicals."

"The practicals?"

"The laboratory work, sir. Getting time with the equipment has been difficult. But I think I found a solution. I've ordered some specimens and shall work in my room, using a board and my scalpel."

Practical is the word for it, thought Slaughter. Such a resourceful young man was an excellent mentor for Tommy.

Tommy, although not his and Ellie's natural child, was their joy and their responsibility. They'd been granted guardianship of him after Tommy was thought to be culpable in the murder of a man who worked at the gasworks. But he wasn't. His parents having died, the best place for the lad was right here. He was thriving, and Cuthbert wanted to make sure he could study what he wanted.

Tommy wanted to be a doctor, so studying animal physiology was the logical place to start. And Samson was a natural teacher.

"Well, if you need any help or some space to work . . ." Cuthbert glanced over at Ellie, who nodded, "you're welcome here. Just so long as Tommy can watch."

"Thank you, sir," said Samson, as he finished his tea. "I'd better get back to my rooms to study."

"Take a few candles from the larder," said Ellie. "Just to give your eyes a break from your lamp."

"Thank you, ma'am," said Samson. "See you Thursday, Tommy. Be sure to study those diagrams."

⁂

"Oh, the puff paste is as light as air," sighed Mr. Pratchett contentedly. Bridget had brought in a meat roll recipe she'd been trying, made with chicken instead of veal. They were baked the day before, but no need to share that. The women at the boarding house had been grateful but unimpressed, so she'd brought them to work.

"So, Mr. Pratchett," said Bridget. "Tell me again about this latest scheme. The idea is to photograph art?" The shop was quiet this morning. It often was. Traffic was light on Theobalds Road, even for a Tuesday.

Pratchett licked his fingers and nodded vigorously, the white hair above his ears wagging wildly. "Yes, it's just the thing. Photographing art."

The light came in through the front window of the shop, and Bridget could see the dust motes in the air. She should wipe down the photography equipment in the window today.

"Why," asked Bridget, "would anyone want a picture of a picture?"

"Not just pictures of pictures," said Pratchett. "Other art too. Did you know, only a couple of years ago, the director of the British Museum had many of the archaeological items carried up to the roof to be photographed? The South Kensington Museum even sells photographs of its collection. And you may recall that Prince

Albert, may he rest in peace, wanted all of Raphael's works photographed."

"But why?"

"To share art with the people! Reproductions are often the only way people can see great art. Not everyone is in London. Not everyone can go to galleries. And some art is privately held. Who will ever see it?" Pratchett raised his hands in the air, as if asking an eternal question.

"They can see it in the illustrated magazines," argued Bridget. "The wood engravings show the shading and nuance better than a photograph. And engravings work on the printing press."

"True, true," said Pratchett, helping himself to another meat roll from the bag. "But in an engraving, the engraver adds his own touches. It's not a true reproduction. A photograph is the truth!"

Bridget thought a moment. Certainly these were good arguments for photographing art. But still . . .

"Look," said Pratchett. It was his favorite introductory word. Look! Appropriate for his profession. "Here's another reason to try it. More and more galleries are having exhibitions and issuing catalogs, catalogs filled with reproduced photographs. There is a lot of money to be made."

Later that evening, Bridget shared the idea with Jo during dinner at the boarding house.

"Pratchett says there is a lot of money to be made," said Bridget, offering Jo a roll from the basket.

"I'm sure there is, but he always says that," said Jo. She was thinking about trees and breasts and Rossetti. Mrs. Bagley and the other women at the table hadn't noticed she was distracted, busy with their roast mutton and greens. Bridget seemed determined to get her attention, so Jo obliged. "So, he would sell these photographs through print shops, like lithographs and other reproductions?"

"I assume so," said Bridget.

"And you think he can produce the images cheaply enough?"

"Yes, so long as he stays with the collodion positives and doesn't try to get fancy."

"Where does he want to start photographing?"

"He's to start at the Royal Academy Exhibition first, then the main gallery. Sir Charles Eastlake wrote to him. They're both members of the London Photographic Society. Mr. Pratchett wants to do most of the work on a Sunday, when no one is there. He even said he'll let me do the photographs for the lesser works."

There was conversation at the other end of the table, but Esther was near them and overheard. "That Mr. Pratchett," she said, helping herself to buttered carrots, "it seems like he always has a scheme. Do any of them succeed?"

Bridget and Jo shook their heads. "They never seem to," said Bridget. "He's a dreamer. The shop's full of photography paraphernalia, old and new. He does have paying customers who want their portrait done. Some even come in off the street. But he's tried everything: making picture frames from bamboo, printing stereoscopic pictures, even hand carving tripods with spikes for outdoor work. Nothing he does seems to sell very well."

"He could always go underground," said Esther. Her curly head leaned over the table so she could see Jo and Bridget.

"What do you mean underground?" asked Jo.

"You know, less reputable subjects. There's a market for pictures like that in the places I used to work. Spitalfields, Whitechapel. Working people, ladies of the night, opium dens . . ." The others at the table were starting to listen. Esther stopped and shrugged.

"And women," Mrs. Bagley added. "Pictures of naked women sell well. On Holywell Street."

Across the table from her, Annie, who worked at a clock shop in Holborn, blushed furiously and concentrated on her food. Mabel handed her the jug of water.

"I happen to know he does some of those," Bridget said. "I wasn't supposed to see but I did. Gentlemen come in the shop and buy them from him. He assured me he pays the women who pose."

There was a collective groan around the table. "Oh, that's right," said Jo, "probably a pittance for taking their clothes off. Then he can sell as many prints as he wants."

Mabel, who wrote puzzle questions for *Every Boy's Magazine*, chimed in. "What they need is royalties. Like writers get every time their work is republished."

"That's what I was trying to think of!" said Bridget. "A way for them to get paid whenever their photograph is sold on. Royalties. That's what I need to talk to Mr. Pratchett about."

⚜

James Robson looked askance at the painting as the students awaited his verdict. His gray bushy side whiskers drew down as he frowned.

"This one, I'm afraid, is not one of Turner's best," said Robson. "Notice how everything is red and orange. There is little variation of color except in the waves, which look feeble and disjointed. As a mood piece, of course, it is excellent. But I'm afraid Mr. Ruskin was quite wrong in thinking it a masterpiece."

The students, if they were shocked, endeavored not to show it, but rather nodded to each other and prepared to move on.

"Who is that?" Tommy asked Samson. They were across the room.

"That's James Robson. He's an art critic and teacher."

"What is an art critic?"

"Someone who tells people what art is good and what isn't."

Tommy frowned and motioned around the National Gallery.

"They let him teach here?"

"Oh yes," said Samson. "He's donated several of the paintings, as a favor to the nation."

"Some favor," grumbled Tommy.

They were standing in front of a still life, and Tommy was struggling to understand what any of this had to do with the science Samson was supposed to be teaching him.

"What am I supposed to be looking at again?"

"The composition and the attention to detail. But there's more to a still life than that."

Tommy looked closely at the dead fish and the melon that looked like it would roll off the table, then over at Samson, who pointed.

"Notice how nothing on the table really looks fresh. What might be a theme for this picture?"

Tommy looked again. The grapes did look like they'd been sitting out a while. "That somebody needs to clean the table?" He knew he wasn't being helpful, but he enjoyed having Samson on now and then. He could be so serious.

"Decay," said Samson patiently. "There's a theme here of decay. That everything gets old and dies. And that wealth and prosperity may end."

"Why would anyone want to show something so miserable?"

"The Dutch became very rich off of trade, over a century ago. Maybe they knew their success could end. Maybe they felt a little guilty about all the money they'd made."

"Was any of the wealth made from slaves?" Tommy was interested in slavery. He'd learned about it from the Inspector's sergeant Mark Honeycutt, who came from America. Plus, Ellie and Jo Harris promoted abolition of the slave trade in their work at the Women's Reform Club.

"Yes, I'm afraid so. Dutch ships carried slaves from Africa to the Caribbean."

"Then they had something to feel guilty about!"

"Indeed," said Samson, "but it's also important what they did with their wealth."

Tommy looked again at the melon in the painting. "I'm hungry," he said. "Is it all right if we have our lunch now?"

Samson laughed and led him out into Trafalgar Square. Tommy was a thoughtful and curious pupil but he was also a thirteen-year-old boy. He'd grown up in a workhouse and had come to live with Inspector Slaughter and Ellie several years ago after some sort of danger that Samson hadn't quite understood. But one wouldn't know it from the way he behaved, Samson thought. Tommy was very good, Samson suspected, at modeling himself on those he admired.

Tommy liked the open square because it was always changing. The day was bright, but not too hot to sit in the sun. There were several dozen people in the square. Men in tall hats rushed by on their way to meet other important people, old couples walked arm and arm enjoying the bright day, and a beggar with no legs below the knee sat next to his upturned cap on an old blanket. There were a few coins in the cap. Carriages clattered up the street from Whitehall and over from Pall Mall. Tommy and Samson went to sit by the fountain.

"Missing those lions," said Samson, getting the lunch out of his bag.

"Must be here somewhere," said Tommy, as he took a sandwich from Samson and grinned. The joke never got old. Everyone knew that the famous painter Edwin Landseer had been commissioned to create four huge lions for the base of Nelson's Column. But even though he'd been hired several years before, the lions hadn't appeared.

Once they had eaten, Samson folded up the wrappers and put them in his bag.

"Now I need to return to Bloomsbury, and you need to return home to change for work," he said. "Do you need fare for the omnibus?"

Tommy didn't like Samson to give him money. He knew Samson didn't have enough, even with Inspector Slaughter paying him for tutoring.

"No, I'll just run down Strand to the bridge. I'll be home in no time." Then he thought to be polite. "Thank you for showing me the paintings."

Samson smiled. "I know they don't make much sense now," he said, "but art is the way that people understand the world."

"Jo Harris says that too."

"Yes, your friend Jo would know. I'd like to meet her. Perhaps she could come back here with us some time."

Samson stood up and put on his hat.

"See you Monday!" He adjusted his bag on his shoulder and headed across the Square to catch the omnibus.

By the time Tommy got home, it was almost two in the afternoon. Ellie wasn't there, and he knew Inspector Slaughter must be at the station. Prudence was blacking the stove, her dress and double apron tucked under her knees as she knelt in the kitchen. A cloth covered the stone floor, and the blacking box was next to her. Her work gloves were filthy, and Tommy could see the blacking had smeared on one wrist. She must have wiped the hair out of her eyes because there was another black mark on her forehead.

"Don't you come in here, Tommy Jones," she said when she saw him in the doorway. "I'm almost done and then I need to burn it off."

He looked toward the back door in dismay. "If you need your boots, you can just go around through the alley and get them."

"All right," he said, but he also needed his old clothes so he could go to the gasworks. He ran around through the alley, opened the back door, grabbed his clothes and boots, then went back around again so he could change in the bathroom. He put his good clothes, which he'd worn to the Gallery, in the bedroom upstairs. He didn't actually sleep in the bedroom. He preferred his bedroll in the kitchen.

"Bye, Prudence!" he shouted into the kitchen, and went out the front door to earn a few coins helping out at the gasworks.

"Who can eat when there are wombats to be seen?" cried Rossetti when he saw Jo sitting near the Zoological Gardens entrance with her picnic basket. He had the same floppy hat, carried in his hand despite the sunny day, a satchel over his shoulder, and an excited expression on his face.

"Not a typical greeting," said Jo, laughing. "Do you ever practice the social niceties?"

"Goodness, no," he said, grabbing her basket and heading toward the entrance. "If I practiced them, I might get good at them."

He stepped up to the booth and plopped two shillings on the counter. "Two, please," he said. The girl at the booth was pretty, with blonde waves framing her face. She blushed at his smile.

"Oh, no, Mr. Rossetti . . ." began Jo, reaching into her bag for coins.

He held up his hand. "No," he said, "I'm paying. I invited you! Come along now." He took the tickets and turned around, away from the entrance.

Jo strode to catch up. "But the entrance is behind us," she said.

"We have to go in the exit to get to the wombats. They're nocturnal," he said, as if that explained everything. No one was guarding the exit, so they waited for a woman and a young child to come out. The woman was explaining, "Yes, and it's so nice that all those animals came here to visit us from faraway Australia . . ."

They turned left and walked past the deer enclosure, the superintendent's office, the elands, and the giraffes, to a small building at the end of the path.

"Here it is," said Rossetti with a flourish. He opened the door for her. "It may take a moment for your eyes to adjust."

It was dark and cool in the building, and there was a little table near the door. The zookeeper rose from behind the table and said quietly, "Welcome to—oh, Mr. Rossetti! How nice to see you again."

"Thank you, Gerald. May I introduce Miss Harris, a fellow artist?"

Gerald was older, perhaps in his sixties, with a placid face and small, kindly eyes. He moved slowly to come around the table.

"Pleasure to meet you, Miss Harris. I assume you would like me to bring out a wombat, Mr. Rossetti?"

"Yes, if you would, please," said Rossetti. "Whichever one seems most willing to be moved."

Gerald went into a room down a short corridor. Jo's eyes were beginning to adjust to the gloom.

"You see," said Rossetti quietly, "they hunt at night, and sleep during the day. So they have to bring them out specially for us. They have three here. The Common Wombat and the Black Wombat just arrived in March from Australia."

"You know a great deal about wombats, Mr. Rossetti," said Jo, amused.

"I love them. They're so unique and beautiful. And from so far away."

Gerald came from the room carrying a large animal in his arms.

"Still sleepy, I'm afraid, Mr. Rossetti, Miss Harris. But lovely all the same."

The wombat was about the size of a dog, and it had four legs, but there the resemblance ended. Jo thought it looked like a furry pig, or even a chubby rat, or some sort of small bear. It blinked sleepily but seemed not to mind them.

Rossetti was enchanted. He handed the picnic basket to Jo and reached out toward the wombat with his arms. "May I?"

"Of course, Mr. Rossetti. Watch those claws, though."

The animal was transferred to Rossetti's arms like a giant baby. "Oooh, look at you, sweet thing. Your small rounded ears. This one's the Common Wombat, Jo. Isn't he marvelous? Do you want to hold him?"

Jo shook her head. It was a fascinating creature, but it was more delightful to watch Rossetti's face. He looked about ten years old, as if he had just been given the most wonderful present in the world.

"Here, I'll put him down so you can see him walk," said Rossetti. Jo stepped back a bit.

The wombat stood for a moment where he'd been put, blinked, waddled forward a few steps, and then settled comfortably into a ball and went back to sleep.

"Nocturnal," said Rossetti.

"I had better put him back in his pen, sir. Better the soft hay to sleep on than the hard floor. If you don't mind?"

Rossetti leaned over to help Gerald lift the creature from the floor. The zookeeper called back as he went down the corridor, "Perhaps he'll be more awake next time. Enjoy the zoo, Mr. Rossetti, Miss Harris."

"Goodbye, Gerald," Rossetti called down the hall. He held the door open for Jo, and they emerged squinting in the harsh sunlight.

"So, our picnic! I'm ravenous. What have you brought?" He was leading them toward the shade of a large tree near the giraffes.

"Bread, ham, cheese, and beer in bottles. What have you brought?"

Rossetti looked sheepish and patted the pockets on his coat. His face lit up as he pulled out a packet. "Sweets!" he said. "I brought peppermint humbugs."

Jo laughed. He'd obviously forgotten to bring any food for their picnic. She sat on the grass under a tree, smoothing her skirts. Dante flopped down beside her and reached for the basket. "I'll serve," he said, seriously.

She watched as he got out the food, itching to pull out her sketchbook. "May I draw you a little now?" she said. "I don't want you to lose that expression." There was still a bit of boyish wonder around his eyes and mouth.

"Work before food? If you must. But I intend to eat first." He took a hunk of cheese and bread and opened both bottles of beer, putting one beside her. She took out her graphite pencil and sketchbook, flipped to a blank page, and sketched quickly. He observed her closely as she worked. "Tell me about yourself," he said. "You draw for magazines. For how long? Have you ever done anything else?"

"I've been drawing since I was a child," Jo said as she sketched. "My father taught me, then I took classes. I never thought of being anything other than an artist, but I did have to work for a time for my uncle, doing accounts for his business in the City." The curve of his cheek, the line of his hair. "I did my drawings in the evenings and began selling them to magazines by the time I was nineteen. What about you?"

"You've got the most lovely skin," he said. "I don't know how since you don't wear a bonnet."

"What about you, I asked."

"I'm a Rossetti," he shrugged. "We paint; we are poets. My father was an Italian nobleman, a critic, and a poet. He died almost ten years ago now. My mother Frances, my two sisters, my brother—we are all very close. Have you ever written poetry?"

Jo shook her head. She had captured the slant of his brow, the darkness around his eyes, but the boyishness had faded, replaced by intensity.

"You should," he said. "Poetry and art go together. Words and images. Poetry should inspire art. Great art should inspire poetry."

"Well, this," she said, "is not great art. I just want to capture your eyes. They are extraordinary."

"They are," he said. "I've made several self-portraits. I am quite attractive."

"Humility," said Jo, "does not seem to be one of your attractions."

"Faith in oneself," said Rossetti, "is so much more important! Where would we be, what wonderful things would have ever been created, if we were occupied in being humble?" He finished his bread, took a large slug of beer, and pulled his sketchbook out of his satchel. "My turn," he said, "but could you tilt your chin up a bit?"

"In a moment. Almost done," said Jo, refusing to let him rush her. Much of his energy, she thought, comes from impatience. He must have been impossible when he was younger.

He remained silent, observing her as she finished. As soon as she blew away the last bits of graphite, he began to sketch. She tilted her chin up.

"Yes," he said, "I want more of your neck." Jo laughed.

2

"So, the women need to get royalties," Bridget explained, as she set up the upholstered chair and the potted aspidistra. "Whenever you sell a picture with them in it, they should benefit too."

Pratchett was only half paying attention as he set up the camera. "That would cost me."

"It would," said Bridget. "But it's only fair. You're making money off of their bodies."

Pratchett winced. He wasn't sure about young women these days. They seemed to say whatever was on their mind. Luckily, they could still cook. But Bridget hadn't brought in anything today, and he was getting irritable.

"I'll think about it."

Bridget decided not to press the issue. "Who are we setting up for?" she asked.

"A very important woman," said Pratchett. "Lady Millicent Stroud wants a portrait in her new hat."

"Lady Millicent Stroud? Isn't she a member of the Women's Reform Club?"

"I believe she patronizes it, yes. But she isn't one of you young radicals."

Bridget didn't think there was anything radical about trying to do some good in the world. She wasn't a full member of the Club, although she did volunteer when Jo or Ellie needed some help.

"She wants her portrait just because she has a new hat?"

"It is not for us to judge the needs of our clients," sighed Mr. Pratchett. "All that matters to us is that she wants a lovely picture of herself, looking elegant in her hat. So, we must make sure we light the hat as well as her face and clothes." He went over to the window and tugged the curtain open a bit more. The afternoon sun made the room glow. It was the perfect time for a picture.

They heard the shop door jingle as Lady Millicent entered.

"Hello?" she called, in a deep, commanding voice. "Is anyone about?"

Bridget snorted quietly and glanced at Pratchett, who was desperately trying to smooth the white tufts above his ears.

"Yes, Lady Millicent. Just coming!"

Bridget finished adjusting the pillow on the chair. She heard Pratchett say, "After you, Lady Millicent."

Lady Millicent Stroud entered the portrait room rather as a ship sails into a harbor. Her maroon walking-out dress was exquisitely tailored, the piping on the edge of the jacket a smooth black satin. The shape of the crinoline was quite hidden by the layers of fabric in her skirt, which belled out a little further than was truly fashionable. Bridget decided to move the aspidistra away from the chair to make more space.

"Is that where I am to be seated, young woman?"

"Yes, Lady Millicent." She saw Pratchett glaring at her over Lady Millicent's shoulder. "If you wouldn't mind, please."

Lady Millicent nodded, her large hat with its sweeping brim bobbing a bit over her eyebrow. She handed Bridget her parasol as if it were suddenly distasteful, and sat down. The chair creaked loudly. Lady Millicent rose abruptly.

"Your chair is defective," she said, turning to Pratchett. "It would be better if I stood. Don't you have one of those Doric pillars or something?"

Pratchett bowed slightly and said, "Of course, Lady Millicent. Bridget?" But she was already fetching the pillar.

Pratchett scurried across the room to look quickly into the camera. "Yes, yes, would you just lean your elbow there on the pillar, and perhaps touch a finger to your cheek? That will tilt the hat to perfection."

"But I have nothing to do with my other hand," declared Millicent. "It's just . . . hanging here."

"Would you like your parasol?" suggested Bridget, and received a frown in reply.

"No, no," said Pratchett, "perhaps a fan would be better?"

"A fan!" cried Lady Millicent. "An excellent idea! But I didn't bring one. Surely you have one?"

Pratchett looked somewhat frantically at Bridget.

"Shall I go to Mrs. Randolph's shop and borrow one?" offered Bridget. "I'm sure she'll have black if she doesn't have maroon." Lady Millicent tipped her nose in the air and turned away, as if the details were none of her affair.

"Yes, go, Bridget," said Pratchett. "And do hurry."

"May I walk you to the omnibus stop, Miss Henderson?" asked Samson Light.

"Thank you, Mr. Light," said Prudence.

It was a warm Southwark evening, and they had just left the Slaughters' house. Other day workers passed them on the pavement, some in conversation in pairs but most walking alone with their heads down.

Samson felt a bit shy, which he knew was silly because Prudence was a kind person. But she was also innately sensible. He'd watched her pluck a chicken even though she wasn't a cook, and scrub the stone floor even though she wasn't a charwoman. She did what needed to be done, without any fuss. And sometimes her tongue could be sharp. But right now, her straw blonde hair was peeking out of her bonnet and glinting in the evening sun.

"How is your mother feeling?" he asked.

"I think she's a little better, but she's still very weak," said Prudence. "She does better with a bit of company."

"There are some illnesses," said Samson, "where it's better for the patient to be left alone, and others where company is desirable." Company is desirable? He sounded like a schoolteacher. He looked over and admired the wisps of Prudence's hair and the smooth round line of her cheek.

"I'm sure that's true," said Prudence.

They passed a cart where a woman sold bread, no longer fresh as in the morning but good enough to sell to workers on their way home. "That reminds me," said Prudence. "I need to help Mrs. Slaughter to make bread on Monday."

"She usually does it herself?" asked Samson.

"She likes to, but sometimes she starts and then I finish."

They walked a bit in silence.

"I took Tommy to the National Gallery," said Samson. "Do you like looking at art?"

She paused and thought, her nose crinkling a little.

"I think so," she said. "I've been to the British Museum and seen the statues. From Greece, I think they were. But I've never been to the National Gallery. Is it very big?"

"Oh yes, very. It occupies the whole western side of the building. And it has so many paintings." He swallowed and mustered his courage. "I'd be delighted to take you sometime, on one of your days off."

Prudence looked up at him. Her eyes seemed very blue, he thought. Much bluer in the open air than in the house.

"That would be very nice of you, Mr. Light."

"Samson, please."

She smiled. "Samson."

He said goodbye to her at the omnibus and could not resist a little bow as she waved at him from the window. He smiled to himself as he made his way across Blackfriars Bridge. Then he suddenly remembered that to get home, he would have taken the same omnibus. He walked another half mile and caught the next one to Bloomsbury.

Samson's rooms in Gower Street were in a house full of students like himself who had moved to London to study near the University College. He was too late for dinner, but Ellie had made sure he'd eaten before he left. His fellow student Andrew Church was at the dining room table and was looking at what appeared to be chunks of minerals scattered on its surface. Mrs. Ellis would not be pleased, thought Samson.

"You're looking at rocks?" he asked, leaning over his friend's shoulder to look.

"No, not rocks," said Andrew with exaggerated patience. "Look closer. They're fossils."

Samson leaned in and saw little shapes pressed into the rocks. "Fancy dress rocks! Where did you get those?"

"I was allowed to borrow them for tonight," said Andrew. "The man at the collection said I could, seeing as how I'm a reliable young man."

"Little does he know," said Samson, patting Andrew's shoulder.

Andrew laughed. "Well, he doesn't know everything, that's certain. But I'm careful with fossils."

"You are a friend to every rock you've ever met," said Samson. There was a bowl of apples on the table. He took one and bit into it.

"They're fossils. I'm a friend to every fossil. How is your pupil doing?" asked Andrew, drawing the whorl of a nautilus into his notebook. He wrote *Cephalopoda—Ammonoidea* next to it.

"Very well," said Samson. "He's quite knowledgeable for a child who's lived in a workhouse, and he's a quick learner. I like him very much."

"And the money's good," said Andrew.

"You're being a Scot again," teased Samson as he munched his apple.

"Nothing wrong with a bit of money," said Andrew, not looking up. "Your people know that."

Samson laughed. Their argument about Scottish versus Jewish predilections went back to the day they met. Both men were sensitive about their heritage, and both liked to make fun of their own background before other people had a chance to do so. It had made them instant friends.

"I'll leave you to your rocks," said Samson as he headed upstairs to wash and study in his room.

"Fossils," muttered Andrew. "Fossils, dammit."

"*Signore* Morelli, I am so pleased to meet you." Sir Charles Eastlake, director of the National Gallery, extended his hand. His intelligent face and balding head conveyed an air of concern and goodwill.

"And I you," said Giovanni Morelli. "*Piacere.* I am always happy to travel to England and see your galleries." Morelli had only a touch of gray in his dark, wavy hair, and his regular features looked slightly weather-beaten. He did indeed look happy, and not at all tired from his travels. But he also had a look of determination and stood in a way Eastlake could only describe as confrontational. He was a revolutionary and an Italian patriot as well as an art expert.

"I understand you are only in London for a few weeks?"

"Yes, I have not quite a month to visit London. I plan to enjoy your National Gallery and the Dulwich Picture Gallery. Then I have two private collections to view before my return to France."

"Ah, yes, I had heard that the Louvre had requested your services. As for us, we are delighted to have you for however long you want to stay," said Eastlake, as he accompanied Morelli to his office. "I assume our man Smith found you good rooms? I asked him to make arrangements at the Westminster Palace Hotel."

"Yes indeed, I am very comfortable. And so close to your seat of government. I feel very much at home."

"Yes, your work for Italy's new government is well-known here." Sir Charles knew better than to be nervous about it, but he was very much aware of Morelli's active participation in keeping the finest Italian art inside Italy. This was despite the fact that the year before, Morelli had sold the gallery a valuable Italian painting, Lorenzo Lotto's *Portrait of Giovanni Agostino della Torre with his son Niccolò*. It had cost Morelli only 124 Napoleons, but the gallery had paid 400. Morelli had nevertheless considered it a gift, to introduce the British people to the art of Lotto.

"We thought that as a scientific man," said Sir Charles, "you would appreciate the latest advances at the hotel. I have not experienced it myself, but they tell me the hydraulic lifts take you up to the top floors with little noise or fuss."

He opened his office door and escorted Morelli to a green velvet chair in the large room. The walls were paneled in oak, and the beige carpet was thick. Several paintings hung on the wall, each in a unique gilded frame. Instead of sitting, Morelli went over to the smallest painting.

"Ah, I see you have a Gillot," he said.

"Yes, a gift from James Robson," Sir Charles said. "I assume you know him?"

"The art critic? I know of him," said Morelli, taking a very close look and frowning.

"I see that famous frown," said Sir Charles, "but do not be concerned. We have had it authenticated by experts."

Morelli looked up and smiled. "*Naturalmente*. If it were an Italian painting, I would be the expert you would want." Not very humble, thought Sir Charles. Although he believed Morelli was from Sicily, Sir Charles was reminded of the pride that had been the Roman Empire.

Morelli was younger than Eastlake by at least twenty years, and yet, as he sat down, Sir Charles could not help noticing that Morelli was a little stiff in one knee. He handed him the catalog of the National Gallery collection, and asked, "Shall I send for some tea, or would you prefer coffee?"

"Coffee, if you please," said Morelli. Sir Charles went to the door and asked Smith to bring coffee.

"While you're in London, and here at the National Gallery, can I interest you in attending the Royal Academy Exhibition? It is here, of course, in our eastern wing. I would be delighted to accompany you."

Morelli was looking through the catalog. "I would prefer to leave the new works until the last. Since I am here to concentrate on what you call Old Masters, I may not have the time."

"Yes, of course," said Sir Charles.

Morelli stopped on a page and pointed to a listing. "I would very much like to see *Doge Leonardo Loredan*, by Bellini. You acquired this some time ago?"

Sir Charles had expected this work to attract his guest's attention. "Yes, almost twenty years ago now. It is beautiful. Shall I have Smith show it to you? You will find the Titians in the same room." Morelli stood as Smith, blond and trim, came in with the coffee. He looked surprised.

"I'm sorry, Mr. Morelli, do you not want the coffee?"

"Later. I want to look at your Bellini first." Smith nodded respectfully and followed. One never knew with foreigners.

The Royal Academy Exhibition had been open for less than a week, but the new carpets were beginning to show its popularity. Hundreds of people came every day to view and argue about the new works. *The Eve of St Agnes*, by John Millais, was a particular attraction. It wasn't as though moonlit scenes hadn't been painted before. But here the angle was from above, the woman was indoors, and she almost seemed trapped in the grid of moonlight coming through the window. The work was dark and yet she was light somehow, and you could sense an eerie quiet.

It was quiet now, as the gallery was closed on Sunday. Mr. Pratchett and Bridget had been admitted by Matthew, an older guard who'd been given strict instructions to keep a watchful eye on the paintings. The photographers could move them to get better light, but they needed to be careful. Sir Charles Eastlake had instructed the guards personally. It was different now, Sir Charles had warned them. People insisted they be admitted when the gallery was closed. The artists themselves would sometimes want to touch up the varnish. Well, at least they didn't do what Turner had done almost twenty years before, touching up the painting itself. The frames were part of the art, so extra care was required and sometimes carvers would ask if they could fix something. Engravers needed to sit with a piece for awhile to copy the image for the illustrated magazines. And now there was photography.

Sir Charles had been not only president of the Royal Academy, but also president of the Photographic Society even before he became director of the National Gallery. He keenly felt the responsibility for the gallery to photograph its collection. And in the eastern wing, even though the Royal Academy Exhibition was temporary, several items were worthy of photographic preservation. Certainly, Sundays were busier now than they used to be, but the guards could manage it.

Bridget was carrying the camera and Pratchett hauled the box of plates and a mirror for adjusting light. The tripod legs kept tangling in Bridget's skirt, and not for the first time she envied men their trousered way of life. But it could be worse. If Mr. Pratchett weren't an active and enthusiastic member of the Photographic Society, they'd still be using the wet collodion process. She'd have to cart in an entire dark-room to process the plates on the spot, or run outside to prepare and fetch each plate. With dry plates, they could take them back to the studio for processing.

They entered the Middle Room, and Pratchett set down his box, taking out the list.

"We're not doing too many, but it will take some time," he murmured.

"How many is not too many?" asked Bridget.

"Twenty-five. But only six here in the Exhibition. The rest in the National Gallery, in the western wing." He nodded toward the archway into the gallery proper.

Bridget sighed. This would take at least four Sundays, maybe more.

"How do we reach the top ones?" she asked. The paintings covered the wall from just above the floor to those hung very high up. The higher works tilted outward from the wall so the viewer could see them better. Jo had told Bridget that the ones very high and very low were liked the least by the Council that decided which works to accept. Artists dreaded being "hung high."

"We're to tell the guards which paintings we need taken down for next Sunday," said Pratchett, looking up the wall nearest him. Bridget looked up at the skylight and noted how the light patterned the floor. She set up the camera so that the paintings could be displayed in the most even light in the room. Then she moved the easel Matthew had left in the corner.

"Let's get started," said Pratchett, reaching for the Millais, number 287. "Did you bring anything for lunch?"

∗∗∗

Samson Light had arrived early at the Slaughters' house to collect Tommy for the lecture. Perhaps Prudence would still be there.

"Come in, Samson," said Ellie from the parlor. "Help yourself to some tea. I'm afraid Prudence already went home to her mother."

Mrs. Slaughter was an observant woman, thought Samson. She came into the kitchen as he was pouring himself a cup of tea.

"Milk's in the pantry," she said, tying on her apron. "I know your lecture is at seven, so we'll eat early. Tommy should be home from the gasworks in a few minutes. I know he's very excited to go with you tonight."

"Thank you for the tea, Mrs. Slaughter," said Samson, "and for encouraging Tommy to go with me. I've heard that Thomas Huxley gives excellent lectures, but I've never had the pleasure of attending one."

"And I'm glad Tommy's stopped working at the theatre," she said. "He found it exciting, but it took him so far south. And he was never home in the evening."

Samson nodded and took a sip. "So many educational opportunities are available in the evening now. Lectures for working men and women are so helpful."

"Do they make the language simpler or anything? To help those who have less education?" Ellie Slaughter had been lucky enough to have been educated by her father in Yorkshire.

Samson thought a moment. "No, I don't believe so," he said. "I've been to several now, and they've been intellectually very stimulating. I always take copious notes." He took his notebook out of his pocket for emphasis.

"Oh! I'd better get one for Tommy." She went into Cuthbert's office and got a small notebook and a pencil, then put it on the

35

kitchen table. She was just taking the chicken out of the oven when they heard Tommy burst in the front door.

Without looking up, Ellie called, "Shoes off! Jacket outside!"

"Yes, Mrs. Slaughter," Tommy called back, going back out the front door and around the alley to the kitchen. He hung his jacket on a hook just outside the door and put his shoes beneath it.

"He always reeks when he comes back from the gasworks," she explained to Samson, who wrinkled his nose. "Don't worry—I have a fresh jacket for him upstairs, and a clean shirt."

"I'll go upstairs and wash my face. Then we can eat and go!" said Tommy as he sprinted up the stairs. Ellie put the chicken and potatoes on the table. "Get me the jug of water, will you, Samson? I'm going to eat later with Cubbie." Samson got the water, thinking how much he liked it here in this kitchen. The Slaughter home was always so welcoming. It got lonely at the boarding house in Bloomsbury.

Ellie retreated to the study to finish working on the proposal for a Working Women's College. Tommy and Samson had a quick and quiet dinner, then took the omnibus to Theobalds Road. They walked through Bloomsbury, up Lambs Conduit Street, and round the corner of The Sun pub into Great Ormond Street. People were filing into the lecture hall. Some were carrying copies of Huxley's recent book, *Evidence as to Man's Place in Nature*.

"He's like a famous actor, isn't he? People are coming who really admire him," said Tommy, impressed.

The Reverend Mr. Maurice mounted the steps to the stage, his sharp eyes taking in the crowd. He pushed back his wispy hair from his forehead and held up his hand to quiet the audience.

"Welcome to the Working Men's College for our lecture this evening. If you are familiar with our work, we welcome you back. If not, know that we have classes of all kinds for skilled working men, including courses in Latin, painting, and science. We have been serving the needs of working men for almost a decade." There was a smattering of applause. "Tonight, we have a very special guest: Mr. Thomas Huxley. He will be speaking this evening on 'Man's Place in Nature'. May I ask that you keep the center aisle clear, please, as our own Mr. Porter shall be using a magic lantern to show the drawings. Thank you. Professor Huxley?"

Professor Huxley took the stage, his leonine head nodding to acknowledge his audience.

"Good evening," he said. Tommy sat up straighter so he could see.

"It is a great pleasure to talk to you this evening about some of my current work on the nature of man. I believe most of you have heard of the recent work of Charles Darwin and may know already that I am a great proponent of his theory of evolution by means of natural selection." There were nods around the room.

"Tonight, I would like to demonstrate to you some of the similarities between man and what we call the man-like apes: gorilla, chimpanzee, orang, and gibbon." An image appeared behind him of the skeletons of these creatures, drawn as if they were walking in a line, with man at the front. "They are all without a tail and have the same number of teeth as human beings . . ."

After the lecture, Samson and Tommy's notebooks had many pages of scribbling, and a few sketches from the magic lantern slides.

"That was so interesting!" said Tommy, as they walked back toward Samson's boarding house. "I had no idea we might have evolved from monkeys."

"Not monkeys, Tommy. Apes. Monkeys have tails and cheek pouches."

"Yes, but it's still amazing. The skeletons! Can we go and see an actual skeleton, Samson?"

"Of course. I'll take you to the zoology collection that Grant created. How about next week?"

"Oh, yes, please!"

They had reached the corner. "If I give you money for a cab, Tommy, you promise you'll use it to get home?"

The corners of Tommy's mouth turned down. Cabs were a waste of money when you knew your way on foot. But he didn't want Samson worrying about him.

"All right," he said, taking the coins and looking around for a cab. "If you want me to."

Smith had waited patiently as Giovanni Morelli examined the Bellini and took a few notes in his little book. Exquisite leather cover, thought Smith. Tuscan.

"Now the Giorgione, I think. *A Man in Armour.*" Morelli raised his brow as he looked at Smith.

"Of course, sir. It is in the next room."

There were quite a few people in the National Gallery that morning. Smith made a path through them for Morelli, and quietly asked the couple standing in front of the painting if they would mind stepping aside. They did so without comment, although they looked curiously at Morelli as he came forward and took a lens from his waistcoat pocket.

"I have had this work described to me," he said. "But it looks far different than I expected." He gestured with the lens. "The armor is not as vivid as I thought it would be, not as defined. But the proof," he said with a meaningful glance at Smith, "is always in the hands."

Morelli's eyes glinted as he moved forward for a closer look. Smith's eyes widened, and his concern was noted by a young page coming through the gallery, who approached Smith quietly.

"Sir, is there something wrong?" He noted Morelli peering closely at the painting, and Smith's discomfort.

"I'm not sure," Smith whispered back. "Would you mind very much fetching Sir Charles?" The page moved discreetly but quickly toward Eastlake's office.

Morelli put his notebook in one pocket and took a larger notebook from another. He began to sketch the hand holding the spear. Then he stopped, stepped back, and looked more broadly over the whole painting. He tilted his head to one side, muttering something in Italian. Visitors were beginning to notice his behavior.

Still with his eyes on the painting, Morelli edged closer to Smith.

"How was this work acquired?" he asked.

Smith began looking through the catalog as Sir Charles approached. The knot of people stepped back so he could join Smith and Morelli in front of the painting.

"Signore Morelli," said Sir Charles, calmly but loud enough for those nearby to hear, "what do you think of our Giorgione?"

"I think," said Morelli, "that it is not a Giorgione."

There were murmurs among the people in the room.

"I have seen this figure," said Morelli, "at the Cathedral in Castelfranco. That is a Giorgione. But here, look at the structure of the fingers. Compare this in your mind to the hand of the man with the stick in his *Tempest*. Someone has tried here to imitate Giorgione, and even evoke some of Titian's style about the head." He looked at Sir Charles. "This was painted by someone who studied Giorgione's work at the cathedral. But it is not by Giorgione."

"Good heavens," said Sir Charles. "You're not saying it's a forgery?"

"No, my friend. A simple misattribution. The painter was likely working shortly afterward, in the sixteenth century, and in Italy. Perhaps even in Castelfranco itself."

The observers muttered and nodded. A simple misattribution.

"Thank you, Signore Morelli," said Sir Charles graciously. "We had no idea. It was bequeathed to us, so we had no opportunity to ask questions of the donor."

"Do not trouble yourself, Sir Charles. Giorgione is one of the most difficult artists to attribute correctly. It is becoming my life's work to study his hand, how he used light, how he rendered flesh. And my methods are scientific, based on minute observation of the human form."

"Yes, of course. I'm very grateful to you." Sir Charles glanced at Smith. "I was about to take some lunch at a cafe in St Martin's Lane. I would be delighted if you would join me?"

Morelli nodded, and Smith followed the two men back to the office, frowning. It would take days to revise the provenance and the plaques.

As yet unfinished, the sketch was nevertheless stunning. The woman appeared to be praying. Even with broad strokes in charcoal, her upturned face was angelic, her hands open in front of her. A bird with a poppy in his beak was dropping the flower into her hands.

"My mourning is no secret," said Rossetti softly. "Everyone knows I am not the same man since she died."

"This is your wife?" Jo asked.

"Yes, this is Lizzie. I began sketching it before she died. I may never finish it. I was thinking of Beatrice as a supplicant. But now it seems better as a sublime moment, like a trance."

"And the poppy?"

"She died taking too much laudanum." Rossetti looked down at the paints and brushes on the table, not at Jo or the drawing.

"This is Dante's Beatrice. Your Beatrice." The bird was death, she knew. She looked closely. It was the most detailed object in the picture.

"Yes, she was my love, my muse. The reason for my life and my work."

"It is incredibly sad," said Jo. "I have seen the sadness in your eyes. I thought I guessed. But now I know." She turned to face him. "I am so sorry."

He looked up at her, his eyes tender and filled with pain.

"We weren't suited. I destroyed her, when I should have supported her work. She was so fragile. I burned her up."

Jo walked slowly over to a smaller table, glad for once that her dress was too long. The sweeping sound across the floor seemed to move time ahead of the sadness.

"You prefer watercolor to oils?"

"I shouldn't," he grumbled. "It seems a painter is only taken seriously if he works in oils. But I much prefer watercolor. I can get just the amount of transparency I want, just the right amount of detail. Here, you can see what I mean."

Rossetti reached for a stack of sketches and pulled out a watercolor that was clearly an Annunciation. It was about two feet tall but less than a foot wide. The Mary figure occupied the lower half of the rectangle. She had been sitting reading her book, but now her palms were upward, and she looked over her shoulder at the angel. The angel filled the upper half, leaning over a wall of flowers to give Mary the news. The dove representing the Holy Spirit was bright with a gold glow around its head, and she looked up at Mary. The flowers leaned in on the scene, giving it a feeling of closeness that was almost suffocating.

"It looks as if the Virgin is trapped, rather than grateful for the news that she's going to give birth to Jesus," said Jo.

Rossetti grinned. "You have it exactly! Look—have you seen my earlier work on the subject?" He went to a drawer and took out a magazine engraving. It showed a young Mary sitting up on a couch or bed, foreshortened toward the viewer. The angel, his back turned toward the observer, pointed the lily toward her. The Virgin looked downward, as if she would rather be anywhere else.

"You did this before the watercolor?" asked Jo.

"Long before. The original painting of this was exhibited at the Royal Academy over ten years ago, in the second year of the Brotherhood. The critics didn't like it. James Robson said she looked like a miserable child, attacked by a lily. He missed the point entirely."

Jo compared the two. "Your more recent work is so much more lush."

He smiled. "I have been working on adding more romance, to draw the observer into the setting. Learned that from my friend Hunt."

Jo looked again at the engraving of Mary on the bed. "Who modeled for this?" The sitter's face was so sensitive that even in the engraving, she seemed pale and fragile.

"My sister, Christina. She let me sketch her in different positions until I found what I wanted." Rossetti turned toward Jo. "You'll meet her at my garden party, in a fortnight's time. You will come, won't you?"

The sadness in his eyes was now lit by enthusiasm. Of course she would come.

3

"Mr. Pratchett?" Bridget looked around the shop, but it didn't seem like Pratchett was there. She put the bag of fresh cream rolls down on the counter. She had let herself in with the key. Maybe he just hadn't come in yet.

She put on her apron and went to the back studio to open the curtain and let in some light. Despite the warm weather, she'd had to use her umbrella on her walk from the omnibus stop, and now the rain was tapping at the window in the studio. Mr. Pratchett wasn't back here either.

The sign wasn't turned to "in use" on the dark-room door, so she took a peek inside. Pratchett must have come in last evening, because there were freshly developed albumen prints hanging on the rack. She might as well check these before Pratchett arrived. There was a full set of the six pictures from the Royal Academy Exhibition. She took a few of them off the rack out into the bright studio and set them on the table, pulling out a magnifying glass. There was a stack already on the table of the pictures they'd taken from the main gallery, including several Turners, a Caracci, and Botticelli's *Adoration of the Kings*, which Sir Charles Eastlake had wanted photographed carefully. It was his prize acquisition, and he had requested additional prints for his personal file. Settling onto her stool, Bridget pushed away the National Gallery items and looked for any areas of fogginess or blur in the ones from the Exhibition.

Oh, good, she thought. Millais' *Eve of St. Agnes* looked excellent. Any fuzziness was part of the artwork, not the photograph. A. Cooper's *Cromwell at Marston Moor* looked good, as did Richard Redgrave's *Sunshine*. Bridget wasn't a fan of Redgrave. She'd been much bothered by his painting *The Outcast* when she'd been younger. It showed a young woman with a baby being cast out of the house by her father, while the family cowered or frowned. A sister kneeled, begging the father not to do it. The viewer could see it was snowing outside. Surely the young woman and her child would die out there. It had given Bridget nightmares.

She went through all six pictures, then got out the Exhibition catalog to begin tagging them. All went well until she got to #299, *The Enchanted Frog-Prince*. It was listed in the catalog as being painting by a Mrs. F. L. Bridel. She knew this was actually Eliza Fox, who had married a Mr. Bridell, with two Ls, a few years before. Jo had taken Miss Fox's classes, which she had taught in her father's house. Bridget had heard the stories. Her classes had been the only place where female artists could draw nude models. Miss Fox had been active in the Society for Female Arts and had helped petition the Royal Academy to provide training for women. You'd think they could get the artist's name right. Or was this some kind of punishment? Bridget felt angry just thinking about it.

Perhaps that was why she failed to hear the door of the shop open as she returned to the dark-room to prepare the plates for their next trip to the National Gallery. She laid out the collodion, water, silver nitrate, and gutta-percha, referencing the list Pratchett had tacked onto the wall. As she lit the lamp to begin her work, the door of the dark-room slammed shut behind her. She heard a scraping noise and a key turn in the lock.

"Mr. Pratchett?" she called loudly. He must have come in and not seen her enter the dark-room. She waited a few seconds but the door remained closed.

"Mr. Pratchett?" she called again. There was no answer. She heard the back door to the alley slam shut, and she tried to push the door of the dark-room open. She was locked in.

"Well, I don't know where she is," grumbled Mrs. Bagley, her hands on her hips. "All right, I guess I'll have to make the dinner myself." Jo stood in the kitchen, trying not to look helpless.

Mrs. Bagley began to bang the pots around.

"Maybe the omnibus didn't come," said Jo, trying to be helpful without actually providing kitchen help. She really needed to be finishing her sketch of the facade of the National Gallery. *Once a Week* wanted it for the review of the Royal Academy Exhibition. Plus her feet hurt, and she wanted to take off her boots and sit down.

But truthfully, she was worried. Bridget was never late, not only because it was her responsibility to cook, but because she loved doing it.

She still wasn't home by the time dinner was finished, and now even Mrs. Bagley was worried. Jo went upstairs and fetched her bag.

"I'll go and find her. She must have been held up at the studio. Mr. Pratchett can be demanding."

"You be careful," said Mrs. Bagley. "Maybe something's happened."

"Like what?"

"Like a fire or something. There was a fire up on Theobalds Road a few weeks ago. The building burned to the ground in minutes. And you know all those chemicals that photographers use."

Jo knew. Photography shops, art studios, bakeries, all were in danger of catching fire. But there were other dangers, too. She put her police whistle and her hatpin in her bag with her sketchbook and went to catch the omnibus.

The premises of Mr. Pratchett, World Famous Photographer, All Subjects, were dark. Jo peered in the front window. It was odd. The drapes were still open. Usually they were closed at night so the cameras and stereoscopes weren't on display, tempting a burglar. But there was no movement within. She tapped on the door. Still quiet.

She wanted to walk around the back, but the gas streetlights only lit Theobalds Road, not the alley behind. She peered down the alley and saw that the hat shop had a light on in the back room. The glow was enough that she could see her way to the back door of the studio.

As she passed the lighted window, she saw two women at the rear of Mrs. Randolph's shop, working by lamplight. One was sewing a veil, and the other pinning and gluing flowers on a hat. Jo wondered how much they were paid, whether working this late helped them make enough money to feed themselves and their families.

The back door of the studio was locked, and all seemed quiet. Jo pulled the hat pin out of her bag. Should she? What if no one were inside, or a policeman saw her?

When she'd been a child, her father had locked up his special drawing pencils in his desk drawer. It was a simple lock, just a matter of getting a pin inside at the right spot and pushing the edge of the latch. She'd done it more times than she'd care to admit, borrowing the pencils, then carefully returning them to the drawer. It was only when she got older that she realized her father must have known, because his pencils would have been worn down.

Even in the dark, the task was easy. The lock clicked, and she cautiously opened the door. The curtains were open in here too. Very strange. Bridget had told her they always closed the back studio at night. She decided it was silly to be in the dark and felt around for a lamp, almost knocking it over. She felt around on the same table for a box of matches and lit the lamp. The light made strange shadows on the high windows.

"Hullo?" she called. "Is anyone here?"

Nothing. She stepped further into the room.

"Hullo?"

This time she heard a scraping sound nearby. There seemed to be a small room of some kind against the far wall.

"Hullo?"

She heard a faint cry from behind the door of the small room. "Bridget?"

The cry came again. She got closer to the door and put her ear near the crack. "Is that you?"

"Jo?" she heard Bridget cry.

"Yes! I'm right here. Are you locked in?" she tried the door.

"Oh, I can't believe you're here! Thank goodness! Yes, I've been locked in." The voice was faint, but Jo could hear her.

"Where's the key?"

"It's not in the door?"

"No," said Jo. "Other ideas?"

"On the work table? Or there is a spare key up front in the shop, under the counter."

Jo found the key in the shop and opened the door. Bridget looked terrible. Her hair was mussed and her dress wrinkled. She put her arms around Jo.

"Oh, thank you, thank you, dearest friend. You came to find me!"

Jo held her back and put a hand on her friend's pale cheek. "What on earth?"

"I was in the dark-room. Someone came in and locked me in. He left through the back door."

"How long have you been in there?"

"Since this morning."

"Have you had anything to eat or drink all day?"

Bridget shook her head, the tendrils of hair that had come loose brushing her shoulders. "There's water in the dark-room, but it isn't clean for drinking." She sat down on the stool.

"Is there anything to eat here?" Jo asked.

Bridget pointed toward the shop. "There are some cream rolls on the counter."

Jo went to get the buns and bring some water from the kettle. "Do you need to go downstairs?"

"No." Bridget blushed. "I . . . used the developing pan."

They sat at the table as Bridget ate the buns and drank the water.

"When you weren't there to make dinner, we knew something was wrong," said Jo. "Who do you think did this?"

"I have no idea."

"Not Mr. Pratchett? Wait, why wasn't he here to let you out?"

Bridget shook her head, and between bites said, "He never came in. I can't believe that he would have done it."

"Where would he have gone?"

"I don't know. I've been thinking about it all day. We don't go back to the National Gallery till next Sunday, so he wouldn't be there."

"Do you know where he lives?" asked Jo.

"Yes, but I've never been there. He has a small flat in Harpur Street." She suddenly looked very tired.

"Let's get you home. We'll see if we can find him in the morning."

Cecil Robson took out a fine sable brush and a tube of ochre. It was lazy, he knew, to use paint in tubes. But it was such a good invention. No need to mix pigments and oil in a bladder, only to have it dry out or separate after an hour. There was nothing wrong with convenience. He touched up the earth around the base of the tree, adding tiny dashes of yellow-brown. More depth, he thought. Well done.

The studio was large and light. Built onto the house originally as a conservatory, it served very well for painting. He'd pushed the plants over to one side. The little orange tree was suffocating under a palm. If Mother had been alive, she would have frowned at that, he thought. She had loved plants. And she had not been fond of art as a way to make a living. Cecil has been sent away to school, and then on the Grand Tour. He'd returned, not with a love of classical literature and language, but with the desire to become a commercially successful easel painter.

He had overheard her talking to Father one evening.

"He cannot make a living as a painter," she had said. The sound of thread pulling in and out of fabric emphasized her words.

"Perhaps he can. He has some good technique," his father had said.

"We shall end up supporting him till the end of our days. How will we manage that with Edith the way she is?" Edith, Cecil's sister, was in a sanatorium, and likely would remain there her entire life.

"We shall manage," said his father. "I don't want him forced to do what he doesn't want to do. He will be a serviceable artist. Just so long as I don't have to critique his work." He had heard the tapping of his father's pipe onto the dish.

"James," his mother had said, "perhaps he should learn a trade."

There had been a pause.

"No son of mine," said his father, "is going to be forced into trade. I will not have him turn out like my father."

And that had been the end of it. Grandfather had been in trade, importing and exporting. The old man had read little, and thought art was a waste of time. His son James, however, had spent much of his life in the arts, drawing and now writing about them. He had loved the old man, but felt he had led a life without any deeper meaning. To James, meaning, morality, and religion—these were everything. God's work was not import and export. His son could follow his heart.

Cecil worked quickly, and finished the area around the tree by lunch time. He had written to Christina yesterday, but had received no reply. Irksome, he thought, as he ate the egg he hadn't bothered with at breakfast. She was beautiful, and intelligent, and talented. He caught sight of himself in the sideboard mirror. He had taken much trouble lately with his hair, brushing the dark waves back from his forehead and letting them curl behind his ears. He was considering growing a goatee. Yet Christina looked at him with that blank disarming stare. Perhaps her look hid deeper feelings?

James marched into the dining room just as Cecil was finishing his coffee.

"Good afternoon, Father," he said.

"What? Oh, good afternoon, Cecil. Done painting for the day?" He was looking around for something to take with him, his portfolio under his arm.

"Perhaps," said Cecil. "Or perhaps I shall just work on something different. Or go to the gallery." Cecil's father paid the rent on an atelier in Portobello Road.

"Good lad," said James, grabbing a roll. "I'm off to the British Museum Reading Room. Then I have a meeting with Mr. Hall before going to the club. I shan't be home till late."

"Mr. Hall?" asked Cecil. "Isn't he that Irishman?"

"Yes," sighed James. "He may be an Irishman, but he's editor of the *Art Journal* and a man to be respected."

"But Father," said Cecil, "he hates the Pre-Raphaelite Brotherhood, and everyone thinks he's a sanctimonious hypocrite, always looking down his nose."

"Cecil, that's unfair. He's a highly moral gentlemen and does not deserve the ridicule he receives from others. It's that damned Mr. Dickens. Twenty years ago, he wrote one of those novels, and made everyone think he modeled that reprehensible character on Mr. Hall. Reputation, my boy, is very hard to earn and so easily lost. Remember that."

Father ended every conversation with a lesson.

⁂

Bridget was wearing her best frock for the outing to the Royal Academy Exhibition and stood looking at a painting showing people in a castle room.

"I don't understand," she said to Jo. "This painting looks every bit as good as anything next door in the National Gallery."

Jo looked in her catalog. "It's by Mrs. E. M. Ward." She looked up at the painting. "Oh! That must be Henrietta Ward. Her husband is Edward Matthew Ward. He paints too, but hers are better." She flipped through the catalog. "She's got several paintings in the Exhibition. Likes doing history subjects. This one is *Queen Mary Quitting Stirling Castle*. So that's Mary, Queen of Scots."

"She looks so determined and yet so sad," said Bridget. Working in photography had given Bridget a keener eye, thought Jo.

"She won't see her baby again, but he'll grow up to be King James."

Bridget nodded. "I like that it's set in a bedroom, rather than at court."

"Why?" asked Jo.

"It seems to make a domestic scene more—I don't know—noble or something. It's fancy, but there's a cradle, and a cup, and the rug. You can imagine being there."

"That's what makes Mrs. Ward so good," said Jo. "It's a shame they had to hang it so high up."

They tried to look at the painting below it, but they were getting crowded out by other visitors.

"Why do they cram so many paintings together on the wall?" asked Bridget.

"To get as many in as they can, I suppose. It does make it all look like wallpaper, doesn't it?"

The room was getting unpleasantly full. People were straining to see the pictures near the ceiling. A man's hat fell on Bridget as she took Jo's arm to leave. Bridget turned to return the hat to its owner, and a young man with wavy hair retrieved it from her gratefully.

"I'm sorry, miss," he said.

Bridget smiled. "It's no matter," she said as she turned back to Jo.

"Allow me to introduce myself," said the young man. He tried to bow but was nudged by a woman behind him who was using her parasol to work her way through. "I'm Cecil Robson, the painter." He looked as if he expected her to recognize the name.

"Bridget Williams," said Bridget, reaching to shake his hand.

"I have two paintings in the Exhibition," said Cecil. "Perhaps you've seen them?"

"I apologize, sir, but I'm not sure." Jo was pulling her away, not realizing Bridget was talking to someone. "I must stay with my friend."

"I'll accompany you both," said Cecil, trailing behind.

They came out into the courtyard, and Bridget inhaled the fresh air with a sense of relief. She then introduced Cecil to Jo. He seemed a nice enough young man, thought Jo.

"Mr. Robson's a fellow artist, Jo," said Bridget.

"Nice to meet you," said Jo.

"And you, Miss Harris," said Cecil, looking around the courtyard. "I see a vacant bench over there. Shall we sit?"

The courtyard was cool, the stones chilled by the shade. Bridget pulled three flattened handkerchief squares from her bag.

"Oh dear," she said, "Our lunch has been squashed."

"It's just bread and cheese," said Jo. "It will be fine. Won't you join us, Mr. Robson?"

"No, thank you. You didn't plan for guests, and I ate earlier." He watched as they shared the bread and cheese.

"Miss Williams, are you also an artist?" he asked.

"Oh, no," she said, trying not to talk with her mouth full.

"She is, though," said Jo. "She's an artist with making food."

"A fine talent," said Cecil. "You must think in three dimensions. I'm afraid I am no good in the round. I'd make a terrible sculptor." It was funny, thought Jo, how he can sound humble while his tone reeks of self-appreciation.

"Jo's being silly. I'm a photographer's assistant, but I would like to have my own bakery someday."

"Well, to be a photographer's assistant, you must have a good eye," said Cecil. He's flattering her, thought Jo. What an upstart. And she's smiling at him. Well, he's attractive, if in an oily sort of way.

"I don't know about that. I am starting to think the job can be dangerous," said Bridget.

"How so?" asked Cecil, with a look of surprise.

"I was locked in the dark-room recently by someone who came in the back door."

"Who?"

"I have no idea."

"Goodness," said Cecil. "Why would someone do that?"

"I think they wanted to steal. I went in yesterday morning and several things were missing."

Jo had gone with Bridget to the studio first thing that morning. Pratchett had been there already and was horrified to hear about what happened to Bridget.

"I'm so sorry you were alone, Miss Williams," Pratchett had said. "I was called away to Bromley to visit my brother, who is not doing well. I completely forgot to tell you, or to ask you to take over the studio."

"How is your brother now, Mr. Pratchett?" Jo had asked him.

"Better, I think. Of course, with consumption, one is never sure whether being better means anything."

Jo had made her excuses and left. Bridget had gone into the back, where Pratchett had clearly not tidied up yet. The work table had paper and pens scattered about, and an inkpot was overturned. The stack of photographs from the gallery looked askew, and Bridget looked through them. That was when she discovered several were missing. Pratchett was not pleased.

"Why would anyone take his photographs of paintings?" asked Cecil.

"I have no idea," said Bridget.

Cecil looked at Bridget with kind eyes. "I am very sorry you were subjected to such a thing," he said.

"Thank you," said Bridget. "Jo came and rescued me." She looked over at her friend in appreciation.

"She was locked in there all day," said Jo, shaking her head and digging in her bag. "Bridget, I'm so sorry, but I forgot to bring us anything to drink."

"Allow me," said Cecil, rising and doffing his hat. "There is a tea shop around the corner in Piccadilly. I would be delighted to take you there."

"I'm not sure we have time," said Jo, watching even more people entering the Exhibition.

"Of course we do," said Bridget. "Thank you very much, Mr. Robson."

Jo entered the office at *The Illustrated London News* with some trepidation. She had made an appointment with the art editor, Mason Jackson. The message had said nine o'clock, and although that was early for a Saturday morning, Jo had been there on time. She knew the address by heart: 198 Strand. Everyone knew where the popular journal had its offices.

A clerk was sitting at a large desk, just removing his materials from the drawers. She was about to speak to him, when Mr. Jackson himself came in the door, removing his hat and nodding to her quickly.

"Miss Harris, I assume?"

"Yes, Mr. Jackson. Thank you for seeing me this morning."

He looked into her eyes with a piercing stare, then opened the door of the inner office. He was a small man, with a round head and small round spectacles.

"It will have to be rather quick," he said. "I have a meeting with Mr. Lash in twenty minutes."

Jo followed him into the office. Jackson removed his jacket and slung it on the back of his desk chair, then sat down abruptly. He looked over a few papers lying on top of a pile on his desk. Not being invited to sit, Jo stood.

"Harris, Harris . . . oh yes, you drew for us once before?"

"Yes, just once, in March. All your artists were assigned to the royal wedding, and you were kind enough to commission me to draw a picture, for the piece about Mr. Harvey's death."

"I remember," Jackson said. "That one, as I recall, was from a photograph?"

"Yes, it was."

"But I remember you do draw well from life?"

"Yes, I do."

"And you have no plans for today?" His tone was brusque.

"None whatsoever," she said, quite sure she could cancel her lunch with Bridget, and that Mrs. Bagley would understand if she couldn't be there for house duties. Saturday was cleaning day at the boarding house.

Jackson stood and was searching his pockets. He pulled out some coins and gave them to her.

"Ten o'clock train from Waterloo to Epsom. Need a drawing of that damned horse."

"Which damned horse would that be?" asked Jo. He looked at her sharply.

"The one that won at Oaks yesterday. Queen Bertha its name is. Forty to one odds, and it won. No one has a drawing of the damned mare."

"I can do that," said Jo.

"Good. We only have today. Scott will take the beast back up to Yorkshire tomorrow to his stables. I'll need the drawing by Monday morning so we can meet press time." He began looking around for his hat.

"You left it by the front door," said Jo, adjusting her bag over her shoulder.

"Ah yes. Thank you. Oh, usual pay, Miss Harris. Whatever I paid you last time, plus two shillings. If you do well, I may have more for you in future." He went toward the front door and grabbed his hat.

"Thank you for the opportunity, Mr. Jackson."

He nodded and went off down the Strand. To make the train, Jo would have to head directly to Waterloo Station. There was no time to notify Bridget or Mrs. Bagley. They'll understand, she thought.

The train ride took almost two hours, and she kept wondering whether she had brought enough with her. Sketchbook and pencils were in her bag. She had no food, but Jackson had given her enough money for both a return ticket and some lunch.

When the conductor came around, she asked him directions from the station to Epsom Downs racecourse.

"If you want to go to the racecourse, don't get off at Epsom. Get off one stop earlier, at Tattenham Corner. That'll put you near a nice tea room, and a shorter walk down the road."

Jo thanked him and, following his directions, reached the stables. There was quite a lot of mud, and although her boots were sound, she found her skirt to be a problem. Even hemmed it was always a bit long. The skirt was getting filthy. Perhaps they won't notice, she thought. I really only need to talk to stable hands anyway.

She approached the first one she saw, a lad of about twelve mucking out a horse stall.

"Good morning, young man," she said.

"Good morning, miss." The boy had blond hair and his brow looked misshapen and scarred, as if he'd been kicked in the face when he was younger. Perhaps by a horse, she thought. He'd be interesting to draw.

"I'm looking for Queen Bertha?"

"Yes, miss. Go to the end of the block, then turn right. Second stall."

Jo dug in her pocket for one of Jackson's coins and gave the boy a penny. He nodded, put the coin in his pocket, and resumed his work.

Queen Bertha was a huge horse. At least, she looked huge to Jo, who was no horsewoman. While she enjoyed walks, Jo was not otherwise fond of the outdoors, and people who knew horses tended to be quite different from the people she knew. The mare moved around the stall quite a bit, shuffling her hooves. Jo was accustomed to drawing at the Old Bailey and in the street, so she could manage the movement. But Queen Bertha looked different from London horses. Her neck was longer and her legs thinner. Perhaps racehorses were different from the working kind.

There was nowhere to sit, so she balanced her sketchbook on the half door and began to draw the horse and its stall. Queen Bertha didn't seem to mind. At one point, Jo even fancied that she posed for the picture.

Before she'd half-finished, a man in a tweed cap and houndstooth jacket approached her.

"Here, who are you then?"

"I'm sorry." Jo transferred her pencil to her left hand so she could hold out her right. "I'm Jo Harris, from *The Illustrated London News*."

It was the first time she'd been able to say this. The only other drawing she'd done for *The Illustrated London News* had been created privately. Since then, she'd only been able to say she was from *Once a Week* or another lesser illustrated paper. The reaction now was quite different. The man actually smiled as he shook her hand.

"Are you now? Come to see our Bertha, have you?"

"Yes. We heard of her great victory."

The man puffed up. "Forty to one, she was. Most amazing thing I've ever seen."

"Are you her owner?"

"No, no, John Scott is her owner. I just run the stables here."

"Well, thank you for allowing me to capture her for the newspaper."

"Happy to do it, miss, happy to do it. Can I bring you some tea, or something to eat?"

Goodness, this was much better than working for the other pictorial magazines.

"If it isn't too much trouble, that would be lovely."

He touched his hat and went off around the corner. Jo drew the horse as best she could.

Samson came downstairs and stretched his arms up. The desk and chair in his room were hard, and he thought he might fetch himself some tea. Mrs. Ellis always left the things out for "her boys," as she called them.

"There's a parcel for you," said Andrew, looking up from a book. "I put it in the kitchen because it smelled terrible."

His dogfish! He'd had to do a lot of talking to get it without paying. The fish monger in Covent Garden made his living selling fish, not giving them away. Samson had asked for one that was too old to sell, thus the smell. To do the dissection he'd have to take it up to his room. Mrs. Ellis would not be pleased. He'd find some twine and hang it out his window, like he'd done with the rabbit.

"I'll put it out back," he said, wrapping paper around it. There was a small ash bin by the back door, for the boys who went out to smoke. Mrs. Ellis didn't like it, but she had a pipe every evening herself. He tucked the fish inside and closed the lid firmly to prevent night animals getting to it. Perhaps he could get his board and some pins and do the dissection outside, near the back wall. There should be enough light if he worked in the late afternoon.

Once he'd dissected the dogfish, Samson hoped he could move on to a larger rabbit before the weather got too warm, and then the frog. Those three, he knew, would teach him all about vertebrate anatomy.

Even with the wrapping, his hands smelled like fish, so he washed before getting the tea out of the larder.

"Would you like some tea, Andrew?"

"I'd like something stronger," muttered Andrew.

"What?"

"Tea's fine. Thank you," said Andrew. "Say, you want to go out tonight? I'm meeting Percy and his girl down at The Lamb."

Samson brought his tea over to the table. He had a lot of studying to do, of course, but it would be nice to do something else for a change. And he'd never been to The Lamb.

The Lamb was in Conduit Street, not quite a mile from the boarding house across Russell Square and further on past where Huxley had lectured. Samson noticed a woman with a basket standing in the gutter under a streetlamp, her vegetables and onions for sale even at that late hour. "She's always here," said Andrew, noticing Samson's gaze.

The pub was crowded and noisy even for a Saturday night. Andrew saw Percy hail them from a table near one of the front windows and waved frantically back.

"Why don't you go up and get us some beer?" he said loudly to Samson. "I'll go and say hello. Get us a seat."

"What will you have?" asked Samson, dismayed that this meant he'd have to pay.

"Whatever's cheap!" said Andrew, grinning. He pushed off through the crowd.

Samson elbowed his way to the counter and ordered two pints by holding up two fingers and mouthing "beer" to the old publican behind the bar. He waited and listened to the two men arguing loudly next to him.

"It's not right, I'm telling you. Hacking shouldn't be allowed." The man pounded the bar for emphasis.

"Why not?" said the other, his words slurring, "all's fair in love and football."

"Look, if you let the players kick each other, it's not football anymore, is it? It's a blood sport!"

The publican handed Samson his beers, and he pushed back through the crowd. There were men and women, many of them who worked around University College: porters, grocers, booksellers. Some had obviously been imbibing all day, but others were just meeting friends.

Percy Fry was squeezed into a corner with Anne, his girl. Samson had met her only once before. She had an open round face and her smile showed yellowing teeth, but her blue eyes were intelligent and didn't miss much. Her plump figure took up most of the bench. Percy was her opposite, with lanky dark hair and a lean face. His great passion was neckcloths and cravats, and the one he was wearing tonight was emerald green with gold thread shot through. Percy claimed to be studying art, but everyone knew he was just living off his father's money and spending time with Anne.

Percy was holding forth about photography as Samson sat down, handing Andrew his beer.

"It is an art form," said Percy, "because it requires composition, an artistic eye, and a sense of the dramatic."

Andrew was shaking his head. "It's a documentary process," he said, "not art. It simply reproduces what's in front of the camera."

"Maybe it's both," said Anne.

"It's art, and that's why the various photography groups have exhibits," said Percy.

"It's documentation, based on an understanding of chemistry," said Andrew.

"It's art, because it preserves for all time the nobility of man's place in the world."

Andrew took a drink. "It just captures reality."

Percy leaned forward. "It also captures dreams."

"What sort of dreams?" asked Anne. This is what she loved about Percy, that he'd go off into his imagination.

"Some dreams, my dear, that might be too shocking for you," he said.

"Too shocking for me?" she laughed heartily, her blue eyes twinkling, "I've spent the last two years shocking you!"

Percy blushed. Samson realized they must be talking about something conjugal. He wasn't easily shocked, but that aspect of life he knew little about. Too much time with his books, he supposed.

"All right, then," said Percy, "I'll show you something. Something very special." He reached into his pocket and took out three photographs, mounted on paperboard like *cartes-de-visites*.

"Oh," said Anne, "whose *cartes* have you got? Queen Victoria? Some Indian nabob?" She tried to peer over his shoulder.

"No, these are bigger, like cabinet cards. And they have nothing printed on the back, see? That's because the photographer doesn't want to be known. At least, not publicly."

He pushed the beers aside and laid one of the cards down on the table. It was a picture of a young lady, bent over a table. She was looking over her shoulder at the camera, a highly provocative look, her skirt raised so you could see her bare thighs. Andrew and Samson swallowed.

"Now look at that and tell me it's not art," said Percy.

"It's a tart leaning over a table," said Anne, laughing. "What's on the other two?"

Percy laid them down too, as if making his final point. One showed another young lady, this one with dark hair, squatting over a chamber pot, her skirt pulled up over her knees. She was leaning forward, and one breast had tumbled out of her chemise. Andrew inhaled sharply.

The third card showed a lovely blonde woman, on her knees.

"Oh my God," Samson said, standing suddenly and knocking against the table. Percy quickly removed the cards while Andrew and Anne grabbed for the beers before they slid off the table.

"What's wrong?" said Percy.

"Nothing," said Samson. "I'm sorry." He took a breath, trying not to stare at the cards in Percy's hand. "I've . . . I've had a long day studying, but I just remembered an exercise I didn't finish. I think I'd better go."

"Goodness, Samson. I hope you're all right?" Anne looked concerned.

"Yes, I'll be fine. I'll see you all another time. Thank you for inviting me," he said to Andrew, who nodded, looking confused.

"Maybe he's never seen pictures like this?" he heard Percy say as he pushed his way toward the door.

He's right, of course, thought Samson, as he walked home, grateful for the cool night air on his face. I've never seen pictures like that.

It was quiet in the National Gallery, and Pratchett was planning the photographs for the third set of pictures, which he and Bridget would shoot next Sunday. It had been a long morning photographing the second set. Two of the plates Bridget prepared had been unusable. It wasn't her fault, he reflected. Anthony, the junk man, just hadn't scraped off enough of the old chemicals to make the plates viable.

Pratchett knew he should not be using refurbished glass plates for a job this important. It was a good thing there had been only two bad ones. The rest had worked well, and they had managed to complete most of this wing of the main gallery. He took out the list Sir Charles had given him, flipping it over to the back. He let out a groan.

How could they have missed one? Two full Sundays they'd been photographing, and the Royal Academy Exhibition pictures had been done first thing. But here it was, and they'd missed it: another Millais, *The Wolf's Den*. Animals, Pratchett thought. I don't like paintings of animals. It was in the West Room. That's probably why we missed it, he thought. Usually, the less important works were closest to the entrance. He assumed it was back further to draw people in through the rooms. At any rate, he'd better go and take a look. If it was up high, he'd need to request that it be moved.

Bridget had already left in a cab with the box of exposed plates and the camera, so Pratchett took up the list and the catalogue, walking across the vestibule between the National Gallery exhibits and the Royal Academy rooms. The galleries were eerily quiet, and his shoes echoed on the marble. There had been two guards on duty, but they'd gone outside to the Square to chat and watch people.

Pratchett entered the Royal Academy Exhibition rooms and felt himself surrounded by paintings. It's a shame Sir Charles wanted so few of them photographed. Pratchett was quite enjoying himself. He felt very important working in the galleries when they were closed to the public, setting up his equipment, adapting with the available light for the best possible image. This project would be good for his little shop, too, and his reputation. Perhaps he could move upward in the London Photographic Society, after this commission for Sir Charles, the president. Discharging this duty well was crucial. He sighed. He should never have bought reused plates.

Number 498. He checked his catalogue. Should be right here. But he didn't see anything with animals. Oh, there it was. Children, not animals, with wolf skins, playing a game. Quite handsome, the children, and a lovely composition. It would be easily taken down, since it was hung just above eye level. Sir Charles must really like Millais, thought Pratchett.

He strolled back to the National Gallery side, checking his list. Two of the paintings he needed were in this room just next to the vestibule, then one more in the third room beyond—

Pratchett stopped in surprise. A man was trying to reach a painting down from the wall. It was the Carracci that he and Bridget had photographed two weeks ago, *Susanna and the Elders*. It wasn't a large painting, a little over four feet by three, but it was hung with the hook high on the wall, and the man was short. He was tugging on the hanging wire. Was this someone who worked for the museum? Surely not. Museum staff wore respectable clothes, and this man wore a rough jacket and a tweed cap. Maybe he had been sent to move the painting? But no one who knew anything about hanging paintings would tug at the wire like that. You could damage the wall.

At that moment, the man looked up and saw him. He let the painting fall back, and stared at Pratchett for a moment. His eyes, Pratchett thought. Malevolent. This man, small and spry, means to hurt me. The man approached him, walking quickly. Pratchett wanted to run but froze, not really believing the man would harm him, here in the gallery. He could feel his mouth open in shock just before the man's fist connected with his nose. He fell back, then grabbed his handkerchief as his nose started to bleed.

No longer frozen, Pratchett turned and ran out to the vestibule, desperately holding his handkerchief to his nose. He glanced at the front door, but the guards couldn't be seen outside, and he knew the door was locked on Sundays. The Exhibition—sometimes artists came in to touch up their work. Maybe someone would be there. Run, he thought to himself. Find someone!

Pain exploded on the side of Pratchett's head. He felt nothing more.

4

"Just let me show you this one," Rossetti said, taking Jo's hand and pulling her into the East Room. "It's Hunt's. I want to know what you think."

It was late afternoon, and the Monday crowds were just starting to thin. Rossetti turned toward a particular painting, just a little above eye level on the wall. It was a child, dressed like Henry VIII in the Holbein painting, legs apart as if he straddled the world. But instead, he held what looked like a croquet ball, with the game around him.

"Isn't it strange?" said Rossetti. "You need a minute or two to see its beauty."

"Your Mr. Hunt," said Jo, peering closely at the painting, "he's the same artist who did *The Light of the World*?"

"The very same, almost ten years ago now." Jo could see the style was similar, but the subject completely different.

"I wouldn't say his style has matured," said a voice behind them. Jo turned to see Rossetti grinning at Mr. James Robson.

"Mr. Robson! What a delightful surprise," said Rossetti, shaking his hand.

"Indeed, Mr. Rossetti. A more pleasant place to meet than the Working Men's College, don't you agree? If a little more busy."

"Much more pleasant. Mr. Robson, may I introduce Jo Harris? She's also an artist, and a very good one."

James Robson bowed slightly and reached out to shake Jo's hand.

"Enchanted to meet you, Miss Harris. Are you a painter as well?"

"No, I am a sketch artist for magazines," said Jo. "Pleased to meet the great art critic. I believe I met your son when I was here before."

"Have you indeed?" Robson was not a tall man, but he was slim, and his large head and sweep of dark brown hair gave him a definite presence.

"You don't like Hunt's new painting, Mr. Robson?" asked Rossetti.

"It's a beautifully detailed work, but not in the same class as the one you mentioned, *The Light of the World*. That was a noble work of sacred art. I cannot fathom the message behind this one."

The three of them looked again at the painting. The child's angelic face had a slightly stubborn look as he gazed at the viewer. The stance was as defiant as in the Holbein, and the background, a lovely formal garden, was painted with meticulous detail.

"The boy is king of hearts because he's adorable. Anyone would love him," said Rossetti.

"How do you know it is a boy?" asked Jo. "Couldn't it be a little girl?"

Robson scoffed. "It is a boy, the kind of boy who will inherit everything, not just hearts," he said, then looked around. "I must go and find Sir Charles. Shall I see you later at the college?"

"Yes, indeed. Class tomorrow," said Rossetti.

"Goodbye, Miss Harris." Robson doffed his hat to her, then disappeared in the crowd.

"I had no idea you knew James Robson," Jo said.

"Of course! He helped me when I was a budding painter. And now we both teach at the Working Men's College. He does drawing, and I do painting."

"He seems nice, but I'm sure the students like you more," said Jo.

"They do, but not because of my unmistakable charm. I let them use color."

"Robson doesn't?"

"No. We were both supposed to teach visual art on canvas. But he has them draw and sketch and shade, for hours on end. They often go through the whole class having never used any color."

"What do you do?"

"Color, day one! Life is not colorless. And they get more enthusiastic when they are allowed to be colorful."

"That must be a metaphor, too," said Jo with a smile.

"Yes! Life without color is not worth living." Rossetti tugged down his peacock blue and green waistcoat. "Shall we move into the other room?"

Jo began to follow him, but the crowd was pushing against her, parting to let two men carry a large ladder across the room to a door built into the wall. The first man opened the door and Jo heard a shriek from one of the women, then a scream from another. She saw over the heads that the door was open, and several people were gathered around it.

"He's dead!"

"Who is he?"

"What happened?"

"Is there a doctor in the room?"

"He's dead, surely."

Two ushers arrived and asked the crowd to move back. One left to call for the police. The workers helped clear some space, laying the ladder down as a kind of barrier. A man in a very tall hat, evidently a doctor by his manner, pushed through the visitors and knelt next to the man whose body had fallen from the little room where the ladder was stored. There was a hush in the gallery as people craned their necks to see. Whispers went to the back that the doctor had pulled a handkerchief out of his pocket to cover the man's face.

Jo could hear one of the ushers encouraging people to leave the room. There had been an accident and the police were on their way. If you please, ladies and gentlemen. There is much to see in the Middle Room. Gentlemen began escorting ladies back toward the archway into the gallery.

"I'd love to take a look," said Rossetti quietly at her elbow.

"Me too," said Jo. "Let's step to the side here and wait."

Most of the crowd had left the gallery within a few minutes. Jo and Rossetti could see the body lying on the floor with its face covered, the presumed doctor kneeling beside it. The far door had been opened and the police were just arriving outside. Jo and Rossetti walked up quietly to take a look.

"Do you know who it is?" Rossetti asked the doctor.

"No," he said, and then, "Oh! You're Gabriel Rossetti, aren't you?" He looked surprised and pleased.

Rossetti smiled. "I am. Do we know each other?"

"Not at all, but I know your work. I was at Oxford. Saw your frescoes in the student union."

Jo could swear that Rossetti flushed a little, embarrassed.

"Yes, well . . . you say you don't know who this man is?"

"I'm afraid not. But it looks like he died from a blow to the head. It's rather unpleasant, so I thought the ladies should leave." He looked pointedly at Jo.

"Oh, Miss Harris is an artist too. With an interest in anatomy," he added.

The doctor nodded. "The fatal blow appears to be here," he said, pointing to the man's temple. He raised the edge of the handkerchief. "Do either of you know who he is?" They looked at the pale face and tufts of white hair over the ears, shaking their heads. But Jo had a nagging feeling she should know. She looked around, at the carpeting, the edge of the door, the pictures hanging low near the floor by the body.

Rossetti joined her on the bench outside as she sketched and tried to remember.

"You think you know him?" asked Rossetti, watching her draw.

"I'm not certain. I don't think I've ever seen him, but I feel like I should know who he is."

"Perhaps someone has described him to you?" Rossetti reached into his pocket, took out a pencil, then leaned over and drew a slightly different jawline on the victim.

"Yes!" she said, ignoring his infringement on her sketch. "He's been described to me by Bridget." She thought a moment, then slapped her hand on the bench as if making a decision. "I think that's Mr. Pratchett, the photographer."

"But you can't be sure?"

"No, I have never seen him. But she talks about him a lot. The tufts of hair, the placid face. She works in his photography shop every day, and they've been taking photographs at the National Gallery on Sundays. I think that's him."

"Should we tell the police?" asked Rossetti.

"I can't be sure. I think I'll tell Bridget first, and maybe wait for the morning papers. If it's him, the police will know. Bridget told me he always carries his calling cards in case he meets a potential customer."

Neither of them noticed the small, spry man in a tweed cap leaving the gallery.

Inspector Reginald Harkness was not having a good day. It had begun when he'd been unable to find his new collar. A household search had been performed at Craven Street, and it had been the new maid who had discovered the collar in the dustbin. The culprit was clearly Muggles the terrier, but that discovery did not make the situation any better and Harkness ran late to the station wearing his old collar.

The late morning had been taken up with meetings at 4 Whitehall Place, which was responsible for all the Metropolitan Police stations in Greater London. Here also were the offices for cab licenses and other duties. Harkness was more comfortable in his job at the back of the building, where the public entered the police station from Great Scotland Yard. After a constable brought his meat pie for lunch and accidentally dropped it on his trousers, creating a gravy stain, Harkness was just sitting down to an unsatisfying afternoon of paperwork. A number of items the new clerk gave him were illegible and had to be redone, including the lists from the Prisoners' Property Office. It was really quite a lot of bother for a Tuesday.

The death of an unknown man at the Royal Academy Exhibition was reported late in the day. Harkness decided it was best to walk. It was less than half a mile, it wasn't raining, and Whitehall was crammed with traffic. Carriages with diplomats, ladies making calls in Westminster, M.P.s going to Parliament for the evening session, carts with various goods, all made their way up and down the street with little care for the width or extent of the vehicles clogging the road.

Making his way around to the far wing of the National Gallery, Harkness entered to find several constables, two Exhibition ushers, and any number of ordinary people milling about.

"What's all this then?" Harkness demanded of Constable Moberly, who was standing by with his notepad. "A murder?"

Moberly nodded. "Yes, sir. I've secured the area, sir."

Harkness looked around at the dozen or so people still chatting in groups, and frowned.

"I've taken down the names and addresses of witnesses," Moberly said. "I take it you're Inspector Harkness of Scotland Yard, sir?"

"Detective Inspector," grumbled Harkness. He went over to the lifeless form and looked under the handkerchief at the victim's face. "And no one knows who he is?"

"No, sir. A doctor was here. He covered his face."

"Did you get the name and address of the doctor?"

"I did, sir."

Harkness observed the dead man's clothes, his fingers, the gash on his head. "Craftsman of some sort," he declared. "Not an aristocrat or working man or scholar." He sniffed. "Something with chemicals, though. Who runs this place?" he asked.

"Sir Charles Eastlake, sir."

"But he directs the National Gallery," said Harkness.

"Yes, sir. He's also in charge of the Royal Academy Exhibition. I've sent a constable to fetch him. He's apparently at a hotel in Whitehall visiting with some art expert."

"I see." The wagon had arrived and two assistants were bringing in a cart for the body. "You're from the Piccadilly station?" he asked Moberly.

"Yes, sir. Shall I tell the carters to take the body to the coroner, sir?"

"Not yet," said Harkness. "I'd like to speak with Sir Charles, but I suppose we'll have to wait till he arrives. He might know who the man is."

"I might indeed," said Sir Charles, coming up to the officers. "You're Inspector Harkness, I believe? I'm Charles Eastlake." He looked worried despite his calm voice. He held out his hand.

"Good afternoon, Sir Charles," said Harkness. "I believe we've met before. At the opening of the Metropolitan Railway a few months ago."

"Oh yes!" said Sir Charles. "Indeed." His eyes were hooded, his brows knitted together in a look of concern. "Shall I look at the body now?"

Harkness leaned over and pulled back the handkerchief. Eastlake straightened up immediately.

"Yes, I know who he is. That's Hugh Pratchett. He's a photographer I hired to take some photographs of works in the Exhibition. And in the National Gallery."

"Was he taking pictures in here, Sir Charles?"

"Yes, but not today. He and his assistant were doing the photographs on Sundays, when no visitors are here."

"So, he wasn't hired to be here today?"

"No."

"Have you any idea why he might have been here?"

"None at all, Inspector," said Eastlake, shaking his head sadly. "The poor man. He was a member of the London Photographic Society, which I chaired some years ago. An enthusiast, always willing to try the latest method."

"Right," said Harkness to no one in particular. "Please give your address to—"

"Moberly, sir," said Moberly.

"—Constable Moberly, Sir Charles, in case we need to speak with you again. And if you have the photographer's address, that would be very helpful."

He left Eastlake talking with Moberly and went to examine the closet more closely. The body had been removed, but the door was still open. The door fitted perfectly into the wall, so normally no one would have noticed it. He examined the edge of the door and the frame, noticing a few hairs near the latch, white and frazzled like the victim's. There was no lock on the door. Moberly had come over with his notebook.

"Let's talk to the ushers," said Harkness.

The ushers were not helpful. They had seen nothing and knew nothing about Pratchett.

"It was difficult to see anyone in particular," said the tallest of the men. "It's been quite crowded with visitors."

"Moberly, are you willing to accompany me back to Scotland Yard, or are you supposed to return to Piccadilly station?"

"I've been told to be at your service," said Moberly.

Will Carney squeezed his tweed cap between his small but strong hands. He did not like being questioned. Often he didn't know the answers, and even when he did, he didn't phrase things like he meant them. He shifted from one foot to the other.

"So, you say there were a great many people about when the body was discovered yesterday?"

Will nodded. "There were, but the ones working at the gallery asked everyone to leave. The police were coming, so I left quick."

"And why were you at the Exhibition?"

"I was studying the galleries, to see how I could try to steal the painting again."

The gentleman nodded. "I'm afraid that won't be possible. Thanks to your mistake, they will have more police, and perhaps others in plain clothes, around the gallery. We won't be able to take it now."

Will couldn't see the gentleman's face clearly. The warehouse room was dark, but they had met here once before, when he was hired for this job. Water lapped against the side of the building. Limehouse docks was not the gentleman's turf, Will was sure, but no one would ever know about their meetings. He paid well, so Will did his bidding as he did for other gentlemen who had troubles that needed fixing.

"What about the girl at the photography shop?"

"I did like you told me," said Will, twisting his cap some more. "I locked her in that little room at the back of the shop. She didn't even know I'd been there."

"And the pictures?"

Will pulled the large envelope from his pocket. "Right here," he said.

"Put them on the floor please. You'll find a packet with money on your way out. If I need you, I'll send a message."

"Right," said Will, and put the envelope down. He saw the packet through a bit of light coming through a crack near the door, took it, and left.

The gentleman picked up the envelope and pulled out the pictures, taking them over to a shaft of light coming through the dirty window at the back of the warehouse. He looked through the photographs. Yes, this was the one. At least the photograph wouldn't be a problem.

"And then the police came and tended to the body," said Jo. Ellie Slaughter shook her head. They were in the Slaughters' kitchen in Southwark.

"Well, it's obviously out of Cuthbert's jurisdiction, but perhaps he can help," she said.

Tommy had made the tea, and proudly, if carefully, brought it to the kitchen table. Samson moved the papers aside. The two had been working at the kitchen table, with Samson demonstrating exercises for Tommy.

"It's all right, Tommy. We'll take our tea in the study so you two can work quietly," said Ellie, pulling out a smaller tray for the teacups and pouring tea for her and Jo. Upon entering the study, they settled in the two upholstered chairs so they could talk. The late afternoon light made the room warm and cozy.

"The death of Mr. Pratchett is very strange," said Jo.

"It is indeed. Did he have any enemies, do you know?" asked Ellie.

Jo shook her head. "I have no idea. I never met the man." She took a sip of tea.

"Oh, biscuits," said Ellie, glancing back toward the kitchen. "I don't want to interrupt them. Cubby usually has a tin in his desk somewhere."

She pulled out a drawer, then another. "Aha!" She opened the tin. "Only two left. Better than nothing." She handed one to Jo.

"But the really strange thing is that it might be connected to what happened last week."

"What's that?" asked Ellie, noticing the biscuit was rather stale.

"Someone came into the shop Wednesday morning and locked Bridget in the dark-room."

Ellie looked confused. "What's a dark-room?"

"It's a little enclosure at the side of the back studio. It's where they use the chemicals to develop photographs in the dark."

"Why in the dark?"

"Because the plates are sensitive to light. Open the plates in bright light and you can erase the whole picture."

"I see. How did she get locked in?"

"She says she was working in the back room on some photographs from the Exhibition—"

They heard the front door open, and Detective Inspector Cuthbert Slaughter was heard taking off his boots. He came into the study, looking pleasant if a little weary. Ellie jumped up and gave him a kiss. He smiled when he saw Jo.

"Miss Harris! What a pleasure to see you."

"And you, Inspector." Ellie went quietly into the kitchen to fetch him a cup of tea.

"We had hoped to have you to dinner last Saturday, but Ellie said you were out of town?" He took off his jacket and sat at his desk, propping open a drawer to put his feet up.

"Yes, I had to draw Queen Bertha."

"And who is Queen Bertha? A distinguished visitor from some foreign clime?"

Jo laughed. "She's a horse. Won an important race last Friday, but the odds against that were so high that *The Illustrated London*

News didn't have a drawing of her in the files." She knew she'd mentioned the newspaper hoping for accolades, but she was among friends. Ellie put the cup of tea on the desk.

"*The Illustrated London News*! Well, that's wonderful. Even if it was a horse." He took out his pipe and began packing it.

"I'm afraid it wasn't my best work," said Jo. "The horse looks a little stretched, and the stable looks more like a room."

"Well, if the horse is that little-known, it won't matter."

"Jo was just telling me about the death of Mr. Pratchett at the Royal Academy Exhibition," said Ellie.

"Oh yes," said Cuthbert. "I heard about that. Scotland Yard case. Detective Inspector Harkness, I think."

"But there's more," said Ellie. "Bridget was locked in the darkroom just a few days before, on Wednesday."

Cuthbert lit his pipe and puffed.

"Is that connected?" he asked.

"We don't know," said Jo, "but it's very strange. I was just explaining to Ellie. Bridget went to work in the morning as usual, but Pratchett wasn't there. She was working with some photographs of the Exhibition in the back and went into the darkroom to make prints. Someone came in the back door and trapped her in, then locked the back door when he left. He must have taken the key. I went looking for her and got her out, but she'd been in there all day." She stopped, aware if she went on, she'd have to explain how she opened the back door.

"That," said Cuthbert, "is most mysterious. Was anything taken?"

"Yes," said Jo. "Several of the photographs of works in the National Gallery."

"That's all? No photographic plates, or cameras, or money?"

"Nothing else."

Cuthbert puffed a bit.

"I suggest," he said, "that you let Detective Inspector Harkness know about this. It does seem likely that there's a connection."

"I've explained to Jo you can't help, since it's in Scotland Yard's jurisdiction," said Ellie.

"I cannot interfere with the investigation, no," he said. "But I'm happy to put in a word with Harkness if he proves reticent to talk with you. He's a good man, but he can be gruff and impatient, especially with women."

"So that's why I'm concerned," Jo explained.

She and Bridget were sitting in Inspector Harkness's office at Scotland Yard. He and Constable Moberly from Piccadilly had been talking together when the visitors were announced. Hearing that the women had information about the murder, they'd been ushered in immediately.

Harkness's office was wood-paneled but not fancy. The desk was large and dark, an inheritance from the previous Inspector, who had been moved to a lesser position in Croydon. He'd taken to drink, they said. A glass panel in the door allowed the Inspector to see the desk of the station. He had noted Jo's height and lack of crinoline when she came in, trailed by a flustered Bridget. Harkness knew about that sort of woman, he thought as he took in Jo's dress and manner. They believed themselves independent, but in a pinch, they were nervous and unsure. She probably held a job, too. Something artistic, or maybe a governess. And the little one looked like a typical victim, peering about with her mouth open like she'd never been in a police station.

"You're concerned because your friend here locked herself in a room at a photography studio operated by Hugh Pratchett?" Harkness asked.

"No," explained Jo for the third time. "I'm concerned because she was locked in by someone, someone who left by the back door."

"And locked it," said Harkness.

"Yes, he took the key."

"And you know it was a man?" he said, turning to Bridget.

"No, I don't."

"How did you get out of the room?"

"I came and found her," Jo said, "when she didn't show for dinner. We live in the same boarding house."

"And you say you discovered something missing." Harkness leaned forward, tapping his pen on his finger.

"Yes," said Bridget. "Some photographs. Of paintings at the National Gallery."

"And that would be the same National Gallery next to the Royal Academy Exhibition where Pratchett was found dead on Monday?" Jo and Bridget nodded.

"Were either of you at the Exhibition on Monday?"

"I was," said Jo. "But not Bridget. I was with a friend. We gave all the information to the police."

"I have the information, sir," said Moberly from the corner.

"I see," said Harkness. He rose from his desk, stroked his mustache for a moment, and walked around toward them.

"Well, ladies, thank you for coming in today." It was clear they were being dismissed.

Jo stood. "What are you going to do?" she said, firmly.

"We will investigate the murder with all the resources at our disposal," said Harkness in what he hoped was a reassuring tone. Always good to be reassuring with women.

"And Bridget's being locked in? Will you be sending a constable to investigate the studio?"

"We will be sending a constable because that was where Mr. Pratchett worked, so there might be clues about his murder," said Harkness.

"What about the man who locked Bridget in?" Jo was standing her ground, even as Harkness was clearly trying to usher them out.

"We will search for footprints, or any other clues, won't we, Constable?"

"Yes, sir."

"And if we have any more questions, we'll contact you. Please do not worry. Good afternoon, ladies."

There was nothing more to do but leave. When they stepped out into the courtyard, Jo spoke.

"That was infuriating," she told Bridget, "He treated us like we were simpletons."

"I certainly don't think he believed I was locked in the dark-room," said Bridget, shaking her head.

"And he didn't seem to care about the pictures," said Jo.

"Maybe he has some idea who killed Mr. Pratchett and doesn't need our testimony?" Bridget asked.

"I doubt it. I think he sees us as two unimportant females, making up a story."

They began walking toward the National Gallery, then behind the building and up toward Holborn.

"We know someone locked you in the dark-room last Wednesday, and stole some of the photographs," said Jo.

"Yes," said Bridget.

"And that Mr. Pratchett was killed in the Exhibition room on Sunday, then discovered on Monday."

"Right," said Bridget. She was struggling to keep up with Jo's long legs.

"And that Pratchett took pictures of women to sell to particular men."

"Which we didn't mention," said Bridget.

"Fine," said Jo, determined. "Then if the police won't listen, I will investigate myself. Or at least try to discover who locked you in. I suspect if I sort that out, I'll find the murderer."

Bridget glanced up at Jo with admiration. "Do you think you can, Jo? That's really quite splendid of you."

Prudence was having trouble concentrating on the mending, and she knew why. Samson had not come to the Slaughter home on Monday. He had sent a note saying he was ill. Tommy had been very disappointed since they were supposed to go to the Grant Museum. But today was Thursday, so surely he would be here?

Prudence hadn't realized how much she counted on him being here. He was only in the kitchen or study, and he was here to tutor

Tommy, not to see her. But he had taken to walking her to the omnibus stop each time. And then there was last Thursday.

Her mending fell into her lap as she thought about it. It had been a clear, cool evening, a gentle breeze wafting in the London streets. Samson had ridden the route with her, squeezed against her hip in the crowded omnibus, past what she knew must be his stop. He had alighted, then turned to help her off and walked around the corner toward the flat she shared with her mother. She had not invited him in. The flat was small and her mother would be tired, awaiting her dinner.

The fading sun had caught Samson's curls, and she saw the evening light on the planes of his face. He was, she thought, so handsome. He was a man who was going somewhere, and here he was spending time with a housemaid. She had blushed thinking about it, and he had seen her face when she did. Reaching for her hand, he had pulled her gently round the side of the house into the passageway. He had kissed her, and she had reached up and run her fingers through his curly hair. His arms around her waist, the warmth of his cheek—

"Prudence? Are you in here?" It was Ellie, come to fetch her to clean the upstairs bedrooms. "There you are. Samson's all settled in the kitchen with Tommy, but they'll have to move so I can make the bread. Let's do upstairs, and then we'll ask them to move in here."

"Yes, ma'am," said Prudence, folding the mending and putting it back into the basket. As she headed toward the stairs, she glanced shyly into the kitchen. Samson was facing the door and looked up immediately. His look was perplexed, not the open bright look he usually gave her when he caught her eye. Perhaps he was working on a particularly difficult science problem with Tommy. She went upstairs and tidied the bedrooms, scrubbed the floor of the bathroom, and shook out the curtains, leaning out the window.

By the time she and Ellie got back downstairs, Tommy and Samson were moving their papers into the study. "All yours, Mrs. S.," said Tommy. He's become quite cheeky, thought Prudence, since studying science. Prudence stole a quizzical look at Samson, but his expression was blank.

When the bread was in the oven and the lessons over, Samson went to put on his shoes without coming into the kitchen. Ellie called out to him, "Samson? Would you like to join us for something before you go?"

"No thank you, Mrs. Slaughter," he said, not looking up. Prudence stood in the kitchen doorway. Why wasn't he speaking to her?

She came up to him as he finished tying the laces. "Samson?" she said.

He took a breath as if preparing for something, then looked up into her face.

"Yes?" he said.

"Shall I get my coat to walk to the omnibus?"

He paused, as if thinking what to say. Finally, "If you like."

Prudence felt his mood in the pit of her stomach. She went and got her coat, and said a hurried goodbye to Tommy and Ellie.

Samson had gone outside, and she found him waiting on the pavement, looking down at his shoes. Prudence's mother had talked to her about the moods of men. Don't wait, she would say. Find out what's wrong.

"What's wrong, Samson? Can I help?" she asked, falling into step beside him.

He said nothing for over a minute. Then he stopped suddenly at the corner and looked at her.

"Pru," he said, "I know I'm not a man of the world. I don't know a lot of things that other fellows know." He paused. She couldn't tell whether he was angry or embarrassed.

"Like what?" she asked, gently.

"About women," he said quietly. She waited.

"Pru," he said again, "I saw . . . I saw . . ." She waited as he took a breath and started again.

"Pru, I know you've had a difficult life. Or I think you have, knowing how it's been with your mother. And I know you don't have much money. So I wonder . . . have you done something for money that . . ." He hesitated. She caught his eye, and he said directly, "that you wouldn't want your mother to know about?"

Prudence's eyes opened wide. He knew about the pictures. How would he know about the pictures? She stared at him. She realized she was blushing, and that it was part fury and part humiliation. She turned and walked away from him, her heels snapping on the pavement as she hurried toward the omnibus stop. At first, she couldn't figure out why she couldn't see where she was going very clearly. Her eyes had filled with tears. She walked faster.

Her face burned as she thought about Samson, then Hugh Pratchett. How could he? He'd promised that only his most elite, most secret clients would see those pictures. It was a year ago. She'd needed the money, desperately. She couldn't pay the doctor and her mother needed laudanum. She lay moaning in agony most nights. The surgery had been successful, they said. But the pain. And the cost.

Hugh Pratchett had known her brother, before he went off to war. He offered her money, quite a lot of money, if she would pose for him. Privately, he said. She'd been up nights, deciding what to do. Her mother was in pain. And if this man thought she was lovely enough for men to pay for her photograph. . . .

The studio had been bright and comfortable, not at all what she'd expected. She'd come very early in the morning, before work. Pratchett had told her to bring a robe or gown, and to wear her very best underthings. She had brushed her hair till it shone. Then she'd taken off her clothes and adopted the poses he told her to. His voice had been gentle, and he touched her only to move a limb into better light or tilt her chin. She'd walked straight to the apothecary's with the money and been home with her mother's salvation before she awoke.

Suddenly she stopped. Who was this Samson to judge what she'd done? It had been unthinkable to do anything else. Was it wrong? Her mother was alive still, and she suffered much less because she had posed for Pratchett. Some of the money had been set aside, and she'd been able to purchase almost as much laudanum as her mother needed, so long as she rationed it carefully.

Samson was behind her now. She turned, ready to tell him exactly what she thought of his judgement of her. Then she saw he was crying too.

"Please forgive me, Pru," he said. "I'm so sorry. I was shocked when I saw the pictures. But who am I to say what you should do? You have your own life, so many things I don't know about."

"That's true," she said, calmly.

"I was so angry," he said, "so angry. When I calmed down, I asked questions, especially of Andrew." He stopped and looked down at his shoes. Then he said quietly, "I know who took the pictures."

She put her fingers to his lips. Whatever he was going to say, she didn't want to hear it.

"Samson," she said. "I'm going to go home now. And when I see you on Monday, we're not to mention this again. Is that all right?"

He nodded, her fingers still on his lips.

She turned and walked to the stop. He did not follow.

Detective Inspector Harkness was becoming quite annoyed with the many tasks he had to do, and so he grumbled to Constable Moberly.

"And they won't allow me two constables to collect evidence at the café robbery in Leicester Square, or give me extra men for this murder at the Royal Academy Exhibition. And very little of the additional money I was promised in Parliament will ever see its way here. So you see why I am in ill humor?"

The constable nodded. "Yes, indeed, sir," he said. David Moberly was in his mid-fifties, and had seen any number of Inspectors in ill humor. He had also heard many complaints about insufficient resources. It usually meant more work for him, but he liked the work. His wife was long gone, and his daughter was living with her banker husband in Chelsea.

"May I suggest, sir, that I be allowed to assist? I'm assigned to you for whatever you need."

Harkness glanced at the pile of papers. "Yes, Moberly, let's put you to work. The murder is the most important case, to my mind. But the problem is that the gentleman who was robbed in Leicester Square is an M.P., so the press . . ." He began searching the pile.

"Here's the list of witnesses at the Royal Academy Exhibition. You took their statements at the scene, but now that we know who the victim is, we need to question everyone again. Who was connected to this Hugh Pratchett? And what about Sir Charles Eastlake? Wait, no," Harkness stopped. "I'll have to talk to Sir Charles. Can't send a constable for that."

"No, sir," said Moberly agreeably. "Shall I visit Pratchett's place of business, sir? Take a look around, see if I can find something."

Harkness groaned. "Oh, God, yes. I can't believe we haven't done that yet. Go, Moberly, go. Accomplish something, and I'll see that your station hears about it. But Moberly?"

"Yes, sir?"

"Make sure you report only to me, please. Can't have people thinking I'm not investigating a murder, even if he was just a photographer."

"Understood, sir. I'll report back this evening."

5

"Whatever could it mean, Jo?"

Bridget and Jo sat at the kitchen table in the boarding house, looking at the letter. They had finished the washing up and were sharing a glass of port before bed. It was Jo's special bottle, one she had bought after her horse picture had been published. Mrs. Bagley shouldn't know about it, but she had already gone to bed.

"It sounds as though this solicitor wants to see you," said Jo. She read the note again:

Dear Miss Williams,

As solicitor for the recently deceased Mr. Hugh Pratchett, I would like to meet with you regarding the terms of Mr. Pratchett's will and the disposition of his property. Please come as soon as is practicable to my office at 24 Red Lion Square.

Sincerely,

Reginald MacLeish, Esq.

"Yes, but why? Surely I have nothing to do with Mr. Pratchett's will. He must have family."

Bridget was getting insistent, and Jo put her finger to her lips so she would lower her voice. If Mrs. Bagley found them with the port, they'd have to share.

"Has he ever mentioned family?"

Bridget frowned. "Well, no."

"All right then. Shall we go to see him tomorrow morning? I don't have to be at *The Illustrated London News* till afternoon."

"Oh, you'll come with me, Jo? Thank you," said Bridget.

"We'd better get some rest," said Jo, finishing her port and corking the bottle.

Red Lion Square wasn't far from the studio in Theobalds Road, so the women walked from the boarding house in Shoe Lane down High Holborn. Since it was Saturday morning, there was not much activity in the road, and they managed to get to the square without getting too muddy. Number 24 looked like many of the other businesses around the square, with a set brass plaque near the door. Reginald MacLeish, Esquire, was on the second floor.

"Do we knock or go in?" Bridget whispered as they stood outside the door on the landing.

"I'm going in," said Jo. They entered a tiny front room with a chair, a small table, and an aspidistra near the window. Across the room was an inner door, slightly ajar.

"Mr. MacLeish?" called Jo.

"Come in, come in," called a voice from the inner room. "I'm here."

Mr. MacLeish was a tall, kindly-looking man with round spectacles and a sober expression. Jo's fingers itched to draw him. He'd make a good undertaker, she thought. Or policeman. Or doorman. His collar was a little frayed, and his coat was a little faded, but of good quality. He smiled and motioned them to two moth-eaten chairs in front of his desk.

"And whom do I have the pleasure of greeting?" he asked.

"I'm Jo Harris," said Jo, "and this is Bridget Williams."

Mr. MacLeish's eyebrows went up as he looked at Bridget. "You're Miss Williams of Pratchett's photography studio?"

"I work there, yes," said Bridget, a little embarrassed by the unwavering gaze.

"I see," said Mr. MacLeish. "You're very young," he said quietly.

"I'm twenty-six," said Bridget. "Does that matter?"

MacLeish shook his head. "No, I suppose it doesn't." He stood up and went over to a cabinet in the corner, removing a folder of papers which he brought back to his desk. He chose a tri-folded document and opened it to read, looking at it closely.

"The estate of Mr. Hugh Pratchett," he said slowly, "was not large. Basically it consists of a few pieces of furniture from the flat, a silver picture frame, some homely items, and the contents of the photography shop. This would include several cameras, photographic chemicals, furniture and cabinets, various pieces of equipment . . ."

"Excuse me," said Jo, "but why are you telling us this?"

"Oh," said MacLeish, looking up and removing his spectacles. "Because he's left it all to Miss Williams."

Bridget's eyes flew open in surprise. "To me?" she squeaked.

"Yes. All of it goes to you."

"But Mr. MacLeish," said Jo in a reasonable tone, "surely Mr. Pratchett has family?"

MacLeish shook his head mournfully. "No," he said, "Hugh Pratchett had no family. His parents died, both of them, back in '39. His wife died shortly after his son was killed in the Crimea. Both his parents had no siblings. There are no cousins or relatives of any kind."

Bridget stared at Mr. MacLeish, then looked over at Jo. "I don't understand," she said. "Why would he leave his things to me? I've been working there for less than two years. He never said anything . . . ."

"Miss Williams, the will is perfectly legal. Since it refers to you as *Miss* Williams, it assumes you are still unmarried. Is that the case?"

Bridget nodded, dumbfounded.

"Then you own it all legally and in full. But please allow me to advise you?" He looked questioningly at Bridget and Jo. They nodded in unison.

"Now, first, there may be the matter of a few debts. Nothing serious, you understand. But you will need to go through any bills at the studio and make sure they are paid in Mr. Pratchett's name. As I understand it, there shouldn't be much there for you to worry about, but I'd manage those first."

Jo retrieved her sketchbook from her bag and started taking notes on the back cover.

"Next, you'll need to contact the landlord of the flat in Harpur Street. The leasehold on the property is managed by Mr. Jamison. He has several properties in this area. You'll need to pay him a shilling a week to remain, or you can sell all the furniture and abandon the flat. It's up to you."

Bridget had recovered somewhat. "How long do I have to decide?"

"Until the end of the month. Pratchett already paid the rent for June."

He returned to the cabinet and took out an envelope.

"Last, you'll need the keys. The police gave me these, which were in his pocket." He took out two keys and handed them to Bridget.

"I assume one is for his flat and one for the studio," said MacLeish. "You'll need to decide what to do about the flat, too. The landlady lives in the building, a Mrs. Drummond, but I don't know the amount of the rent. You'll need to talk to her. Do you plan to move into the flat?"

"I have no idea," said Bridget. "I have to get accustomed to all this. To keep the flat I would take over the rent?"

"That's correct," said MacLeish, "if Mrs. Drummond allows you to do so. As a single woman." Another reminder, thought Jo, that if Bridget had been married, even inherited property would most likely become that of her husband.

"And if I don't want to?"

"You can move out Mr. Pratchett's things and return the key. Only his personal property comes to you, not the flat itself."

"Anything else we need to know?" asked Jo.

"I don't believe so. Of course, I am at your service if you need anything," he said. The women rose, so he rose too.

"Thank you, Mr. MacLeish," said Bridget, holding out her hand. "I have no idea what I'll do with a photography studio, but I'll think about what's best."

Bridget unlocked the door to the photography studio in Theobalds Road. There were several letters on the floor in front of the door, so Jo picked them up. The interior was dark and quiet.

"No one's been in here since we went looking for Mr. Pratchett," said Jo. "That was almost a week ago. I don't suppose the police have bothered to search the place."

"Everything looks the same out here," said Bridget. She put the food they'd brought on the counter and went to the back room. "Here too," she called back to Jo.

Jo stood at the counter and looked through the post.

"Shall I open these?" called Jo.

Bridget came in from the back and smiled. "I didn't know whether you meant the post or the food."

"I'm not hungry yet," said Jo. "But they're your letters now, aren't they?"

Bridget shrugged and took a few from Jo. "Let's both read them. Should I open the drapes at the front, or will people think we're— I'm—open for business?"

"Are you?" asked Jo.

Bridget knitted her brow. "I'm not sure. There are several jobs I could finish, and I could collect the money. I don't know if I'd want more commissions."

She looked around the studio. "Do you suppose this would make a good bakery?" she asked.

Jo tried not to laugh. "Oh dear, really? Yes, that would be your dream. But no, you'd need ovens and everything. Wouldn't it be better to sell off this place and find a bakery to run?"

Bridget shrugged, "Yes, I suppose so. Let's go to the back where we can sit down. I'll leave the drapes closed."

The light was better near the table. Jo moved the stack of photographs.

"I suppose you should look at these later, to see what might need to be photographed again."

"Why would I need to do that?"

"For the ones that were stolen. Sir Charles Eastlake will still want the pictures, won't he?"

"Oh yes, but that's not a problem. I just need to print some more."

Jo looked puzzled. "You don't need to retake them?"

"No, not with the process we're using. The plates are still there. I just need to create prints. I haven't taken the plates to be scraped yet."

"I didn't realize you could do that," said Jo. "Make several prints from just one plate."

Bridget was looking at the post, opening each letter. She took a one-pound note out from one of them.

"Oh good. Mr. Morris is paying the money owed for his family picture. I can close that account."

Jo opened one. "This is a bill for chemicals, it looks like." She put it in a stack.

"This one's from . . . oh! Cecil Robson. Isn't that the young man we met outside the gallery?"

"Yes," said Jo. "What did he write?"

Bridget removed a five-pound note from the envelope and folded open the letter. "It's payment for 'special photographs'," she said, and her brows knit together. "I don't recall us doing any photographs for Cecil Robson."

"Could Mr. Pratchett have taken them without you? Or put them somewhere else?"

Bridget thought. "Oh no," she said, and her hand covered her mouth. Jo looked at her quizzically.

"Maybe it's for *those* pictures."

"What pictures?"

"The ones he took of women."

Jo could feel herself starting to get angry. "The boudoir pictures you told us about?"

Bridget nodded. "I supposed that's the polite name for them. I did talk to him about them. How the women should get paid royalties, not just a one-time payment for sitting for the picture."

"Well, yes," said Jo, "but what about the ethical implications of such a thing?"

"He didn't understand that and didn't want me interfering. So, I focused more on getting the women who posed treated fairly."

Jo thought for a moment. "Presumably, Mr. Robson is paying for pictures he already collected. Are there more? Pictures that someone might be coming for?"

"Perhaps. I'll need to go through everything, including the drawers Mr. Pratchett kept locked." She held up the keys the solicitor had given her. They were too large to fit cabinet drawers. The rest of the post contained requests for appointments. Those could wait.

"We need to go to his flat anyway. Perhaps the keys are there."

"Let's go there now, to see what furniture and things we'll need to manage. Then we can come back here, eat lunch, and start opening drawers," Jo suggested.

"All right," said Bridget. They went through the front of the shop, but as they opened the door a large woman wearing a fox stole barged in.

"Lady Millicent!" said Bridget.

"Oh," said Lady Millicent Stroud, looking down her nose at Bridget, "You're the woman who helps Mr. Pratchett. I remember you. Where is he, for goodness sake? I've been here twice and everything has been closed up." She glanced over at Jo, obviously surprised by her presence.

Bridget said, "I'm sorry to tell you this, Lady Millicent, but Mr. Pratchett has . . . passed."

"Passed? Passed?" Lady Millicent seemed confused and pushed past Bridget into the room. "What do you mean, passed?"

"He's died, Lady Millicent. Last Monday. They found his body at the Royal Academy Exhibition. The story was in the newspapers."

"Oh! I read about that. I had no idea it was *this* Mr. Pratchett," she said, puffing herself up at the unsuitability of bodies lying around in galleries. "What a horrible thing. How sordid." She stood in the room, haughty but uncertain.

"Yes, Lady Millicent. Have you come for your photograph?"

"Yes, of course. No point in having a photograph taken if the hat is out of fashion by the time it's seen!" She looked to Jo for affirmation, received none, and looked away.

"I have them for you here," said Bridget politely, going behind the counter and opening a drawer. She took out a packet wrapped in a ribbon, with a note on top. Reading the note, she said, "That will be ten shillings, please."

Lady Millicent looked annoyed, as she took the packet. "I don't have such money with me. You will need to send someone to my house to collect it. Number 5, Grosvenor Square, Mayfair. Come around to the back, and the housekeeper will assist you. Good day."

She turned and swept out the door.

"Well, she is quite something," said Jo, laughing. Bridget laughed too.

"Indeed she is," she said, and they went out, locking the shop door behind them.

When Jo and Bridget returned to the photography shop, they carried only a small metal box, a diary, a lamp, and a small china dog. Everything else, they'd told the landlady, could be given away or sold.

For all the gadgets and equipment that filled his shop, Mr. Pratchett had lived very simply in his rooms. Meeting the landlady, they understood why. She ran a clean house, she told them. No nonsense in the rooms. She went in with her own key to clean, and to make sure nothing was amiss. Every day.

"At least Mrs. Bagley doesn't enter our rooms," Bridget said as they walked back to Theobalds Road. "I can't imagine not having any privacy at all." She had clearly decided not to keep the flat.

Jo thought about her own box of drawings under her bed, and how she'd feel if Mrs. Bagley, or anyone really, saw her special pictures. She had a drawing of Nan that anyone with sentimental feelings would recognize as the portrait of a lover. She still took it out now and then, just to see Nan's face. Nan had died over a year and a half ago now.

They put Pratchett's things on the counter and Bridget opened the metal box, which contained three keys, some coins, and a few small photographs. The photographs were well-aged and seemed to be of older people who looked like Mr. Pratchett. There were two large spare keys, one each for the front and back door of the shop, and a small drawer key. Bridget fitted it into the locked drawer under the counter.

The pictures did not shock either of the women, except that there were so many of them. Each model appeared in several poses, some very similar. All the pictures were cabinet or *cartes-de-visites* size, and all featured women in various positions and stages of undress.

"These are the women you told us about at dinner," said Jo. "Do you know any of them?" She held one up to the light. It was rather dim and showed two women in their chemises, one bending over in front the camera as if tying her boot, the other looking boldly into the camera with her chemise bunched up in her hands as she lifted it to expose her legs.

Bridget shook her head. "They must have come here on days when I wasn't working. See the column, and the aspidistra? Those are from the portrait room in the back." She showed Jo a card where a woman wearing just a corset and stockings had wrapped herself provocatively around the column.

"Maybe the women entered through the back door so they wouldn't be seen from the street," said Jo. She picked out another photograph featuring what seemed to be an older woman facing away from the camera, her thick dark hair trailing down her back, and her raised skirt showing plump and perfect thighs.

"Look, there are pieces of paper in here too," said Bridget, taking them out of the drawer. "This one's a list of people." She peered at it. "Looks like the women who posed in these pictures, possibly. Initials only, but with addresses." She handed it to Jo, who was still distracted by the photographs.

"Should we give this to the police?" asked Jo.

"That would expose these women to their inquiries."

"Looks like they've been exposed to more than that," said Jo in a dark tone.

Bridget looked at the list. "Perhaps we should talk to these women first," she suggested, "Then if we find anything, we can share the information with the police."

There was a pause as both women thought. On the one hand, the list was evidence, but it might or might not be related to Pratchett's death. Bringing in the police would be seen by some as the right thing to do, certainly, but what of these women's private lives? Looking at Jo, Bridget deliberately folded the list and put it in her bag.

"What's the other one?" asked Jo.

"It's a list too, but I can't make out of what." The second list was handwritten, but the letters seemed random. "Was Mr. Pratchett tricky enough to create a code?" she asked Bridget.

"He used scientific lettering for some of the chemicals," she said, "But I haven't seen anything like this." Jo looked at it carefully. There were definite patterns, but she couldn't discern them.

"I know who should see these," she said. "Tommy Jones, the Slaughters' lad. You remember how helpful he was last year?"

"When you almost got killed?" Bridget's eyes were wide. "Of course I do. He knows the streets, but do you think he would be able to decipher a code?"

Jo shrugged. "I have no idea, but it's worth a try. He's a clever boy." The clock on the wall of the shop struck one. "Oh! I'm sorry, Bridget, but I must go. I have an appointment with the editor at *The Penny Illustrated Paper*, then I'm meeting Rossetti to draw in Cremorne Gardens."

Bridget laughed. "Rossetti? Cremorne Gardens? Are you and he having a dalliance, Jo?"

Jo grinned and winked at her. "But of course!"

The offices of *The Illustrated London News* on the Strand also managed the weeklies bought up to prevent competition for readers, such as *The Penny Illustrated Paper and Illustrated Times*. Jo was hoping to get more work with the smaller papers. Mason

Jackson, the art editor who had given her the Queen Bertha assignment, had written her a note suggesting she come by the office and inquire about work on the other papers, with a Saturday visit preferred.

Jo arrived at the office, went in, and looked around for Jackson or anyone she knew. It was lunch time, and the office seemed empty until a woman wearing a chatelaine tied around her waist came into the outer room. Her dress was a deep blue, and her hair blonde and plaited. Her square face looked placid and controlled. She was clearly in command here, and she looked up at Jo with a curious expression, brows knitted together.

"May I help you?" she asked, politely but with a tinge of cold reserve.

"Yes, ma'am," said Jo. "Mr. Mason Jackson suggested I come by to see if there was a need for my services in illustration, perhaps on *The Penny Illustrated Paper and Illustrated Times*."

"I see," said the woman, straightening a stack of papers on the front desk. "And your name is?"

"Jo Harris."

The woman thought a moment. "You're the artist who did Queen Bertha?"

"Yes."

"Jo Harris, yes. That was not a very good picture of a horse," the woman said.

Jo looked at the floor and sought refuge in honesty. "I agree," she said, "I do other subjects far better."

The woman gave a slight smile. "I'm Ann Little Ingram," she said, holding out her hand. "Pleased to meet you."

Jo had heard the name. This was the widow of Herbert Ingram, the publisher who had run all these papers. He had died almost four years ago and, although his brother had offered to take over the business, it was his wife who had taken charge of everything. She had done exceedingly well, increasing circulation and out-maneuvering the competition. And yet most people either didn't realize Herbert Ingram was dead, or assumed the brother was running the papers.

"The horse stall was well done, even if the horse was a little odd," said Mrs. Ingram.

"Yes, I do buildings quite well, and other structures. I've been working on some of the newer bridges." Jo looked her in the eye, knowing she needed to sound confident about her work.

"Do you prefer drawing architecture?"

"Not at all. My best work is drawing people. Facial expressions, personality as shown through their portrait. Despair, pain, confusion, amusement. Hard to manage with a horse."

Mrs. Ingram gave a small smile and nodded. "I would like you see your work myself," she said. "We have quite a stable of artistic talent here, Miss Harris, and I am always looking for people who excel in a particular niche. Would you be willing to come back and talk with me again? I am busy this afternoon, but what would you think of Tuesday, later in the day?"

"Yes, of course. I'd be delighted," said Jo. Her heart was beating quickly at the possibility, however vague, of working for Ann Ingram and her magazines.

"There is simply no point in going before ten o'clock," said Rossetti. "After the fireworks. All the young innocents and noisy families have gone home, the working couples dance, and the rest of us walk and enjoy the gardens. And it's almost a full moon tonight!"

They had arrived by three-penny steamer, at Rossetti's insistence, so they could see Cremorne's twinkling lights from the water. Jo had been here once, with Nan, but she tried to put the evening out of her mind so she could enjoy it with Rossetti. The night was cool, with a gentle breeze off the river, the moon adding a blue glow to the water. It cost a shilling at the gate, and Jo paid for her own ticket.

"During the day," said Rossetti as they walked through the trees near the entrance, "there are events and entertainments, balloon launchings and hawkers and theatrical performances. But now there is music, glorious music by players who have been here for hours, had a beer or two, and are playing just for the dancers."

Jo could hear strains of melodies coming from at least two different areas of the gardens. Men and women in casual evening dress sat on the grass on blankets, or on chairs around the many tables near the bandstand. There were groups of working people, and couples in elegant top hats and fashionable silk dresses. She could hear the sound of laughter and conversation from all directions, and she could see twinkling lights everywhere.

"Goodness, how many lamps are there?" she asked, impressed.

"They say a thousand," answered Rossetti.

"That's astonishing. How do they afford that at only a shilling to enter?"

"Thousands of visitors, with so much to spend their money on. Marionette shows, opera singers, games of chance. Once there was even a miniature railroad here, but it was removed. Oh! Let me show you the maze." He grabbed her hand and took her down a path to the maze entrance. Jo hesitated, looking up at the hedge.

"Are you afraid?" asked Rossetti, the humor glinting in his eyes. Jo shook her head. She and Nan had gotten lost in this maze, and Nan had laughed and laughed, the sound like a bell in the darkness.

The maze looked different now. Perhaps the hedges had grown or been cut differently. Colored gas lamps illuminated the turns. Jo followed Rossetti deeper and deeper along the passages, not paying attention to where she was going. She could still hear Nan's laughter in her head, a ghost from the past, as he pulled her along, faster and faster around the corners.

They arrived breathless at the center and fell onto the bench. Rossetti looked at her closely in the pink and blue glow of the lamps.

"Are you quite all right?" he asked, and although he smiled, she could see concern in his eyes.

"Yes, I'm all right," she said, with a weak smile, catching her breath.

"You've been here before?" he asked, seeking something in her eyes. She nodded.

"With someone special?" Goodness he was perceptive, she thought, nodding again.

And then suddenly he kissed her. It was a gentle kiss, not intrusive or insensitive. She felt his sympathy and kindness rather than desire. Not at all what she expected from Rossetti, given his reputation with women. He looked into her eyes and laid his palm gently against her cheek.

"This someone special," he said quietly, "is gone now?"

Jo took a breath. Would he understand? She wanted to believe he would. "Yes." Still she hesitated, then looked at him. "She's gone now. Her name was Nan. She died." She searched his face in the colored light, seeking his heart in his eyes.

He nodded as if deciding something and looked down at her hands, which were curled in her lap.

"Oh, Jo," he said, "I'm so sorry." And she knew he meant because Nan was gone, not because of anything else. She leaned forward and kissed his forehead.

"Thank you," she said. He took her hand and leaned back on the bench, looking up at the night sky. Jo did the same. The stars were dim, the moon shining bright and full. They could hear two men on the other side of the hedge, brushing against it.

"Right here," urged one, his voice husky.

"Oh, don't be silly," said the other. "We'll be seen."

"Just one kiss? Before anyone comes?"

Jo and Rossetti heard a rustle, a sigh, then footsteps as the couple came around the corner to the center of the maze. The first young man, tow-headed and in formal dress, caught sight of them on the bench. Even in the dark they could see him blush. The other, darker, was right behind him. He laughed when he saw the bench occupied. "Good evening!" he said merrily.

"Good evening," said Jo and Rossetti in unison.

"Have a bench," said Rossetti, standing and bowing. "We were just leaving."

As they exited the maze, Jo slipped her hand into Rossetti's. He took it and put it in the crook of his arm.

"Did you bring your sketchbook?" he asked Jo. She shook her head.

"I left it at the boarding house," she said.

"Well, I have mine. Let's go watch the dancing."

"I think I can do the cypher," said Tommy, looking at Jo's list. She had found him as he was sweeping the street for churchgoers near St. Saviour's Church. Tommy did this every Sunday morning, sweeping away muck and dirt so that women could cross the street without getting muddy. It was a dirty job, and you had to be quick to avoid the cabs and carts. But people tipped generously on Sunday.

Jo sat on the low wall outside the south door and watched Tommy peer at the odd letters.

"What is it, though?" asked Tommy.

"It's a list, we think perhaps of names. Names of people who ordered certain kinds of photographs."

Tommy nodded knowingly. "I know the kind you mean. All right, this figure is probably an 'e' since that's most common. This symbol is doubled, so it would be a name with a double letter. These are all the names of gents?"

Jo nodded. "We assume so," she said, looking up. She'd never really liked this church. Its edges felt crammed against the fabric of Southwark, and it had fallen into disrepair until fairly recently. But now it was being tidied up, and more people were attending services. The nave still needed a lot of work, though, and Jo found the gardens to be dark and gloomy.

She thought too about how little work she had been given lately. She should be drawing now, but who would want a picture of this spot? She flipped through her sketchbook as Tommy worked. Oh, dear, poor Mr. Pratchett. Here she had told Bridget she'd solve all of this, and she'd done so little. This list might tell them who bought the pictures of the women, but was it even related to the murder, or to Bridget being locked in the dark-room? There were things to investigate, but she really should be back in Fleet Street, stopping by the offices of every illustrated journal in the city. Mrs. Bagley liked her rent on time.

A shaft of sunlight was coming into the courtyard where they worked, but it was still very shady and cold. Jo got out her sketchbook and considered drawing the tympanum in the south portal, but it was hard to get a good angle from such a small courtyard. She felt she was craning her neck.

"Oh!" said Tommy suddenly. "This is easier than I thought. It's just 'next to' code."

"I'm sorry?" said Jo, not understanding.

"Each letter is just substituted for the one next to it in the alphabet. So this one"—he held up the first item—"Spcfsu Hsbwft would be Robert Graves."

"Oh! That is easy," she looked at the list. "Thank you, Tommy." She reached into her bag and took out a sketching pencil.

"Glad to help," he said. And it was true. Tommy liked Jo enormously. Since he'd met her the year before, he'd thought of her as one of the most sensible, smartest people he knew. And she didn't simper or act unsure like so many younger women.

Jo looked closely at the list, her lips moving as she deciphered the names. Suddenly she stopped and looked cross, her brow furrowing.

"What is it?" asked Tommy.

"Cecil Robson is on here," she said, "and so is Rossetti."

6

Ellie Slaughter was in the kitchen. It was very early in the morning, so she was startled to hear a knock at the back door. Everyone came to the front door on Palmer Street. Only Tommy went in and out the back way, and he was upstairs taking a bath before Samson came for his lessons.

Ellie opened the door to find a tall, square-faced woman with a serious expression.

"Excuse me, ma'am," she said, with a slight, awkward curtsey. "I've come to help, ma'am. Prudence asked me. I'm Hannah. Hannah Cullwick."

Ellie made sure her expression didn't change. Prudence had told her about Hannah, in confidence. She was one of the women photographed by Arthur Munby, the amateur photographer who worked at the Ecclesiastical Commission. Munby was becoming a figure in society. He had published a few poems, but mostly spent his weekends finding women who did the lowest work: cleaning fish at the market, emptying privies, mucking out horse stalls. He was fascinated by maids of all work, charwomen, any female engaged in pure drudgery. He liked to take photographs of them working, the harder the work the better. The stronger and more capable the woman was, the more he wanted her picture. Hannah was clearly strong and capable.

"Oh," said Ellie. "Is Prudence all right?"

"Yes, ma'am," said Hannah, shifting her weight to the other foot. "She's well and all. But her mum's doing poorly, and she wants to be there for the doctor. She said it's floor-scrubbing day, so I said I'd come."

Ellie frowned, concerned. Prudence had never missed a Monday or Thursday. Twice she'd ask to go home early to help with her mother, but she'd never not come in the morning.

"Thank you, Hannah. I'm Mrs. Slaughter. Do come in." Ellie stepped back. Hannah had to bend just a little to get in the kitchen door. She was wearing men's boots, and her hair was cut short. Country stock, Ellie thought.

"Do you need me to do any cooking before I start cleaning?" Hannah asked. Her expression indicated that cooking was something she didn't care for.

"No, thank you. We've had our breakfast. If you could wash up the dishes, then tidy the bedrooms . . ." She hesitated.

"You must have dirty work to be done," said Hannah. "Prudence said you haven't had a char in for a month, and I saw the alley. Looks like it all needs cleaning out back too." She looked down at the flagstones of the kitchen floor and seemed to be thinking how best to scrub them.

Ellie felt foolish for feeling so relieved. She adored Prudence, but she didn't have the strength or the time for some of the filthiest tasks. And Pru was so young. This woman was older and obviously hearty and didn't mind doing the dirty work. In fact, the expression on her face said she enjoyed the challenge. The other families along the row put rubbish in the alley, and there were food scraps and such that left quite a smell. It would be nice to have that area clean.

"I'd be so grateful," said Ellie. "I'll do the bedrooms upstairs, if you'd tackle the back entryway. But you should scrub the kitchen floor first. I'll make sure the boys have their lessons in the study, to stay out of your way."

Hannah was happily scrubbing the kitchen floor when Samson knocked on the front door. Tommy came bouncing down the stairs to let him in, scrubbed and shining from his bath. Ellie glanced over as he answered the door. He was getting so tall, but she supposed thirteen was the age for that. Cuthbert had been right to get him a tutor. Tommy was fascinated by science, and he and Samson got along so well. Samson was almost like an older brother.

"Into the study, you two," said Ellie. "I won't have you bothering Hannah."

"Hannah?" asked Tommy.

"Yes, she's come for Prudence. Pru's home with her mother."

Ellie noticed Samson's expression change. He looked a bit sad, then confused, then an emotion crossed his face that Ellie couldn't decipher. She'd known, of course, how Samson admired Prudence. She also knew it was mutual. But the expression on Samson's face made Ellie wonder whether her mother's illness was the only reason Prudence hadn't come today.

After an hour or so, Hannah had scrubbed all the way to the threshold of the kitchen door, so Ellie let the boys into the kitchen to get themselves some tea. Tommy watched Hannah from the table. She was on her hands and knees scrubbing the threshold with a brush and soapy water. When she reached back for the bucket but couldn't reach, he jumped up and fetched it for her.

"Thank you," said Hannah, looking up at him.

"I do the scrubbing sometimes," said Tommy, "when Prudence doesn't have time." He noticed Hannah's hands. They were larger than any woman's hands he'd ever seen.

"Well, you must be a strong lad then," said Hannah, and she smiled.

"I am," said Tommy, "but you look like a strong woman."

"I am," said Hannah, still cleaning. "I can pick a man up, right off his feet."

Tommy laughed, delighted. "Oh, do pick me up!"

"You? You're a slip of a lad," said Hannah. "Won't be a test at all. Now you get back to your lessons, whatever you're studying."

"Physiology," said Tommy.

"What's phis-i-ology?" said Hannah, as she shifted herself backward, moving her feet into the alley.

"The science of life," said Tommy proudly.

"Well, I've certainly seen enough of life," said Hannah. "I didn't know you could study it."

There was a cough and some rustling among attendees in the lecture hall.

"I had thought at one time that photography was an art, but now I am no longer sure."

James Robson looked out at the audience. This lecture had drawn only about a hundred people. I wonder, he thought, whether I am losing my touch or whether the Working Men's College was not the right venue for this.

"Back in '45, I was in that most beautiful of all cities, Venice. I was there to study architecture. And it was there that I first learned about daguerreotypes."

A few members of the audience nodded. Several of them were obviously familiar with photography.

"I was able to purchase photographs of many of the details I would typically have recorded in my own sketches. It felt like I was able to take home St Mark's Palace, the quaint churches, the canals themselves. So, I purchased a camera and equipment for making daguerreotypes."

Cecil looked around the room from his seat at the end of the third row. He had come to hear his father talk, not because he had any interest in photography, but because he was hoping to meet Percy Fry. He'd received a note saying Percy would be at the lecture tonight, and would Cecil like to join him afterward for supper and some entertainment? Cecil found Percy to be an amiable companion and a gentleman about town. He didn't like to miss an evening with Percy, although he did feel rather overdressed for the Working Men's College.

"I began," his father said, "traveling through France and Switzerland, taking photographs."

Cecil had to suppress a snort. His father hadn't taken any photographs at all. Rather he had a young apprentice, traveling with him like a servant, set up the camera at his command, take the photographs, and develop them.

"My intention was to save some of these glorious buildings, which I saw disintegrating before my eyes. Castles, churches, the extraordinary output of the medieval world, were crumbling into ruin. I could draw them, but the process was so slow."

A voice spoke quietly in Cecil's ear. "So, you came," said Percy. "May I?" He motioned to the seat next to Cecil, who rose so he could shuffle through and sit down. Percy was dressed for going out, so Cecil felt a bit less conspicuous.

"What did I miss?" Percy whispered.

"He liked photography back when he was in Venice and traveling in Europe. Thought it could preserve the buildings that were disappearing," Cecil whispered back.

"Ah," said Percy, "yes, an excellent use for photography. But it's also an art, of course."

Robson was speaking now about the details of various buildings.

"There was an array of sculpture and mosaics, details of moldings and capitals, and I could preserve it all with my trusty camera."

And your trusty young apprentice, thought Cecil.

"I was particularly interested in getting engravers to copy from photographs," Robson said. The audience was beginning to fidget in their seats. The photography enthusiasts had hoped for a more technical talk, or at least one that was more interesting.

"But after some years of copying the beauty and structure of historic buildings, I began to realize something important." He paused for effect. There was a rustling of paper as people looked to see whether the duration of this talk had been stated in the program. "I began to see that all I was doing was documenting. That was important, yes. But was it art?"

Percy nodded vigorously, his dark hair flopping into his eyes.

"No, my friends. It is not art. Photography satisfies the documentary, but not the artistic, impulse. Its image is too perfect, too devoid of life or humanity. At the same time, oddly, it also creates obscurity. The photographic process leads to inconsistent fogginess or haziness in the images. Details are lost. If I were drawing an archway in my sketchbook, for example, I could make sure I drew every detail as fine as I liked. But photographing it, I might discover later that some of the details were obscured. And it would be too late to correct it."

"That's ridiculous," whispered Percy. "Is he saying photography is too true to life, or not true enough?" Cecil shrugged. He was accustomed to his father's rhetorical contradictions.

"I conclude," said Robson, to a quiet sigh of relief in the seats, "that photography is simply mechanical. It can produce, once and once only, a single unique image, often imperfect, of an object. It is the engraver who becomes the artist, not only enhancing the detail, but making the image reproducible."

"Pffft," snorted Percy, "did he only do daguerreotypes?"

Cecil glanced over at Percy. "What do you mean?" he hissed.

"If you're using a collodion process, you can make as many copies as you like," Percy hissed back. "It's not a 'single unique image.'"

"And that is why," concluded Robson, "I no longer consider photography an art. Useful, yes. Technically fascinating, yes. But not art. Art requires feeling and an interpretation of nature. The camera can never do that." He paused and bowed. "I thank you," he said.

Percy and Cecil left as soon as Robson was finished, rather than waiting for questions. Percy walked quickly, and his tone was frustrated.

"I'm sorry," he said. "I know he's your father, but I never heard such rot."

"It's all right," said Cecil. "His views can be somewhat old-fashioned, even if everyone quotes him all the time." He skipped a bit trying to keep up with Percy's long legs.

"Up to the engraver," mumbled Percy. "Not that I have anything against engravers, mind you. My friend Edward is an engraver, in Fleet Street. But there's simply no need! With the collodion process, you can keep the plates for as long as you want and make as many prints as you like."

"I didn't know that," puffed Cecil. "You mean it isn't one plate, one picture?"

"Exactly," said Percy. "So you use more plates, get as perfect a picture as you can. And it's art, dammit, because it takes talent to do that, an artist's eye."

Cecil didn't know Percy well. They had met at a party given by Percy's father to celebrate Palmerston becoming Prime Minister. Robson had obtained an invitation for himself, and Cecil had come along. Percy and Cecil had ignored the social niceties, sidled off to the billiards room, and consumed rather a lot of whisky.

"Let us walk the streets and look for models," said Percy. It was one of his favorite evening activities, observing ladies of the night trying to attract customers.

"Let us get something to eat first," said Cecil.

Tuesday morning was rainy and dreary, but Constable Moberly was determined to find out more about the murder. And that involved traveling about the city, interviewing people, and looking for clues. He would have liked to go to the National Gallery, but Harkness had claimed that privilege for himself. He'll be warmer and drier than I will, thought Moberly, but I suppose that's only right.

He had no trouble finding the boarding house in Shoe Lane. The street wasn't long. But it was quite early when he arrived, before nine in the morning. He hoped to find Bridget Williams and Jo Harris there and interview them both. He knew they worked and might leave the house early. When no one seemed to be around, he knocked tentatively, then louder when there was no answer. He adjusted his new helmet as he waited in the rain. It was being trialed by the Metropolitan Police to replace the top hats which, even with vents in the top, were awkward and uncomfortable. At least this innovation was keeping the water off his head.

A large woman with wispy white hair, tied up in a loose bun, answered the door. Her hands were red, and she wore a work apron and held a kitchen towel. She looked alarmed when she saw Moberly's uniform.

"Constable?" she said. "Is something wrong?"

Moberly put on his most reassuring tone. "Not at all, ma'am. Do I have the honor of addressing Mrs. Emmeline Bagley, proprietor?"

"You do," said Mrs. Bagley, folding the towel.

"I would like to speak with Jo Harris and Bridget Williams, please."

He observed the expression on Mrs. Bagley's face. It went through several iterations, beginning with some anxiety, then exasperation, then defense.

"You had better come in then," she said, backing up so he could enter and waving her towel toward the small parlor. Moberly first placed his wet coat and helmet carefully on the rack by the door. "Wait in there, and I'll get them."

Mrs. Bagley went back to the warmth of the kitchen, where several of the women were finishing breakfast.

"Jo, there's a constable here to see you and Bridget." She said it off-hand, like it happened all the time, and went over to the kettle.

There was an intake of breath, and Esther Levy dropped her fork.

"About time," said Jo, pretending not to notice and rising from the table. "Esther, would you mind going up and fetching Bridget?"

"Certainly," said Esther, getting up abruptly.

Jo went into the parlor to find Constable Moberly looking at the pictures next to the fireplace. There was a scene of Westminster Bridge at sunset, one of a military horse being exercised in Regent's Park in the early morning, and one of a rose bush planted next to a streetlamp.

"These are lovely," he said.

"Thank you," said Jo.

Moberly looked up, surprised. "You drew these?" He knew she was an artist from speaking to her at the Exhibition but didn't realize that a magazine illustrator could create such nice pictures for the wall.

"I did," said Jo. "Would you like to have a seat?" She motioned to a large settee, covered in a print with green and white stripes.

"Yes, miss." He looked at Jo with admiration as he sat down.

"I've come about Hugh Pratchett's murder," he began. "Detective Inspector Harkness would have come himself, but he was detained." Moberly thought it was better not to explain that Harkness was feeling under-manned and irritable. "Will Miss Williams be joining us?"

"Yes, she'll be down presently." Jo had not had a chance to observe Moberly closely when she'd met him the day the body was found. He had a pleasant face and was older than other constables she'd seen. Someone one could confide in, she thought, and yet also someone who's been through tragedy. There was a sense of vulnerability underneath the quiet competence, and lines of humor around his mouth under his graying mustache. Drawing him would be very interesting.

"Miss Harris," he began.

"Jo, please," she said. "Everyone calls me Jo." Everyone did not call her Jo, and she didn't usually allow such familiarities, but she felt she could trust Moberly. He had a kind face.

"Jo," he said, "you gave me your information last week at the gallery, for which I'm grateful. But now that we know it was Mr. Pratchett who died, Inspector Harkness has more questions."

"Of course," said Jo. "And so do we, so I'm happy you've come." She looked up as Bridget entered, looking a little tired. "Bridget, come and sit next to me," she said. "This is Constable–I'm sorry, you didn't tell me your Christian name?"

"David," said Moberly. A forthright woman, he thought. He liked forthright women. His daughter was one.

"Constable David Moberly. He's here to talk with us about Mr. Pratchett's death."

"Excellent," said Bridget with a tone of relief. "We've much to tell, and ask you too."

Moberly took out his notebook, but before he could ask any questions, Bridget told him about inheriting the photography shop.

"And we found some pictures," said Bridget, "of women. Jo thinks they might be somehow connected to this."

"What kind of pictures?" asked Moberly, taking notes.

There was a pause. "Boudoir pictures," said Jo.

"Taken in a bedroom?"

"No, taken at the studio. But the women are in provocative poses and wearing very little."

"I see," said Moberly, as he took a note. He was not accustomed to talking about such things with well-bred women, even in his role as a constable. But he noticed to his relief that neither woman was blushing.

"Do you have the photographs here?" he asked.

The women shook their head. "No," said Jo. "They're at the studio."

"There's also a list, Constable, of gentlemen, possibly purchasers of the photographs. It's in a code, but Jo had her friend Tommy translate it," said Bridget. She glanced at Jo. They had talked about whether to tell the police about the lists and had decided they should. But only about the list with the customers. Not the one listing the models.

"All right," said Moberly, "I'd like to look around the studio tomorrow. Would you both be available to meet me there?"

"I'll be there already," said Bridget, "tidying up."

"I'm not sure," said Jo. "I may have to work. In fact–" she glanced up at the clock on the mantel. "I need to go now to Fleet Street."

When she stood, Moberly stood also, tucking his notebook in his tunic.

"Then I'll see you there, Miss Williams. Would ten in the morning be too early?"

"That is when I should get there," she said.

"May I say," said Jo as she prepared to go, "that we appreciate very much your attention to our evidence? I noticed at Scotland Yard that you seemed to be listening to us more attentively than Inspector Harkness."

Moberly tried not to smile as he donned his helmet. "Inspector Harkness is a busy man, miss. And he likes to leave the smaller details to the men upon the beat. See you in the morning, miss," he said to Bridget.

After Constable Moberly left and Bridget went back upstairs, Jo looked at the mantel clock again, contemplating a change of plan. She would have plenty of time to go to the National Gallery and try to see Sir Charles Eastlake. Then she could have lunch and arrive at *The Illustrated London News* to meet with Ann Little Ingram in the afternoon.

She gathered her sketchbook and raincoat, her thoughts coming quickly. It was wrong not to tell Constable Moberly that she was investigating on her own. He was trying to help. It would be all right—there would be time to work with him at the photography shop. The meeting with Harkness still rankled. It was her impression that Moberly was a kind man, a good officer, but that his superior was one of those people impatient with the intelligence of women. Not for the first time, however, she wondered about impressions. People are generally, she thought, as they appear to be. If they seem to be kind, they are usually kind. If they seem to be unpleasant, then they are.

She began walking toward the omnibus stop. The rain had lightened a little bit.

No, she knew this was wrong. People were not always as they appeared to be. She'd had that experience, trusting someone who seemed to be a friend, and was nearly killed as a result. I should learn from that, thought Jo. But I don't understand why, since I am who I appear to be, others cannot be the same. What must people hide of themselves in order to operate in the world?

A beggar was asking for money at the omnibus stop, holding out his damp tweed cap. She put in a half penny. Never more than a half penny, and she always took it from her dress pocket, never her bag. You didn't want beggars following you, or thinking they could steal more. But she did want to help. London was a difficult city in which to make a living, and so many people didn't have enough to eat, or to pay for medicines, or to help their family. She wanted to give something.

The National Gallery, facing the expanse of Trafalgar Square, never failed to impress her. The entrance was at the top of the main steps, and once inside there was a choice. To the right, a queue waited to enter the Royal Academy Exhibition. To the left were the main galleries. At the National Gallery, she went up to the entrance and spoke to the guard at the door.

"I'd like to see Sir Charles Eastlake," she said. "May I enter, please?"

The guard looked her up and down, and she could see he was deciding whether to demand that she pay for her entrance, and whether she represented a threat. Deciding both in the negative, he pointed toward the stairs.

"Office upstairs, miss."

"Thank you."

As she approached Eastlake's office, a man came out and almost bumped into her.

"Excuse me," Smith said. Then, realizing he didn't know her and she was heading into the office, "May I help?"

"Yes, please," said Jo. "I'd like to see Sir Charles Eastlake."

"Have you an appointment?" he inquired. His face was bland, and she was unable to tell whether he was being officious or just trying to be helpful.

"No, I'm afraid I don't. I'll only take a few minutes of his time."

Smith paused and took in her dress, without crinoline, and her bag. Art student? And yet she looked confident, and a bit older than the usual art student.

"May I ask what this is regarding?" Her brows knit, and he quickly added, "Sir Charles has a meeting in twenty minutes."

"I won't take long, but I do need to speak with him."

Smith decided that this woman could be Sir Charles' challenge rather than his own. He needed to plan for new placards, thanks to that Morelli gentleman, and had no time to play guard.

"Your name, please?"

"Jo Harris."

He turned, opened the door to Sir Charles's office, and leaned in the doorway.

"Sir Charles? I'm sorry to interrupt, but there's a Miss Harris to see you."

Sir Charles stood, surprised, and checked his pocket watch. "Very well, Smith. Send her in."

He came forward as Jo entered. "Miss Harris, welcome. Do take a chair." He motioned to one of the two in front of his desk.

"Thank you, Sir Charles. I am sorry to disturb you. I was here last week when Mr. Pratchett's body was discovered."

"I see," said Sir Charles. He was an observant man and could tell immediately that such a discovery would not have sent this woman into a swoon. He nodded and sat down behind his desk, assuming a concerned and interested expression.

"My friend, Bridget Williams, worked for Mr. Pratchett," she began. "There was an incident at the photography shop a few days before the body was found. I have promised Miss Williams to discover all I can about what happened."

Sir Charles leaned forward. "I understand. But Detective Inspector Harkness is leading the investigation, surely?"

"He is," said Jo. "And I have already . . . consulted with him. He was not very forthcoming."

Sir Charles leaned back and looked thoughtfully at Jo. His eyes, thought Jo, were piercing, especially considering the gentle triangular face. She'd seen a sketch of him as a young man, and that penetrative gaze had been evident then too.

"I see no harm in sharing what I know," he said. "But you were present, so you may have seen far more than I did. I arrived after the police. What could I help you with?"

"Thank you, Sir Charles. I already know you arranged to have Hugh Pratchett photograph some of the regular collection in the National Gallery, and a few select pieces from the Exhibition. I am wondering how you know Mr. Pratchett and decided to hire him? Was it to do with the Photographic Society?"

Sir Charles nodded. "Yes, I explained to Detective Inspector Harkness that I knew him from the Society. Hugh Pratchett was always innovative, ready to try anything new. I sent for him several weeks ago to ask about photographing some of the paintings. We discussed which type of photograph would be best."

Jo frowned. "Which type?"

"Yes, which process. Daguerreotype, tintype, ambrotype. What would produce the best and most accurate representation of painted works."

"I assume," said Jo, "that the Photographic Society has many members from polite society?"

"Yes, indeed," said Sir Charles.

"And some members educated at university?"

"Yes."

"Then why would you hire a rather middling photographer?"

"Because of his knowledge. The most important thing to me is that these paintings are photographed well, and that the photographs last. I simply do not care about the social pedigree of the photographer. In fact," he said, lowering his voice as if in confidence, "I find the practicing photographers a great deal more use than some of the higher-class members."

"And you decided on a process?"

"Yes, the dry collodion process. Dry so there would be no need to set up a dark-room here at the gallery, and collodion for the sharpest, truest image."

Jo nodded. "The incident I referred to involved the theft of some of those photographs. I wonder, Sir Charles, can you tell me who might want such photographs other than yourself?"

Sir Charles looked surprised, his half-moon eyebrows raised up on his brow. "I have no idea," he said. "I can't imagine they're of any use to anyone other than me, or rather, to the National Gallery. We're trying to create a photographic record. Surely they're not of value to anyone else?"

"That's what I'm trying to discover," said Jo. "You see, someone locked my friend in the dark-room so they could abscond with the photographs. I'm trying to find out why, and whether there's a connection to Mr. Pratchett's death."

"Very admirable," said Sir Charles. "Do let me know if there's anything else I can do to help."

Jo looked closely at him. He seemed utterly sincere. It could not be good for him to have a body found in his gallery, even if it was in the rooms belonging to the Royal Academy. She rose.

"I understand you have a meeting. I'm grateful to you for your time."

"You are more than welcome, Miss Harris."

Jo left his office, nodding to Smith, who was returning from wherever he had gone.

"Did you find the meeting profitable?" he asked her.

"Yes, thank you. Very." She turned and went down the stairs.

She was approaching the door when it occurred to her that she was already in the building and it was not yet noon. She had her sketchbook, after all. There should be time for a sketch before she had to be in the Strand.

Ann Little Ingram was in her office when Jo arrived, hoping her belly wouldn't rumble from having forgotten lunch. She had been sitting on the floor at the National Gallery, drawing the horizontal lines across her sketch of Turner's *The Fighting Temeraire*, trying for the right shading of sun and sea. It was by far her favorite work. The ugly tugboat pulled the beautiful sailing ship, and the orange of the sunset glowed into a gloomy sky. There may not have been a storm, but the dark clouds echoed the dark smoky tugboat, making it look as though the tug was creating the darkness. The sailing ship shone white and honorable, but its day was over. The passing of sail, the passing of day, the passing of an era when ships that relied on wind ruled the waves. Instead, it was the efficient coal steam engines doing the work. It was almost two o'clock when Jo looked up, and she practically ran up the Strand to get there before the day got away from her.

Mrs. Ingram had said afternoon, but they had not set on a time. Jo knew editors could get busy. But she was ushered into the office moments after giving her name to the clerk out front. Mrs. Ingram stood behind her desk as Jo entered.

The office was paneled in wood, with glass windows so that Mrs. Ingram could see the whole room all the way to the front door. Her large desk was topped in green baize, with several brass inkwells and pens. Stacks of paper, various sizes and colors, were organized along the front of the desk. The paneled back wall featured, on either side of a portrait of the queen, front pages from what Jo assumed to be particularly important editions of the magazines. A side table displayed two gilt frames with photographs, each of a young man. Both so resembled Mrs. Ingram that they must be her sons. The only whimsical touch in the room was a pitcher with a bouquet of foxglove and daisies with honeysuckle vine.

"What an interesting arrangement," said Jo without thinking.

"Yes," said Ann, and the corners of her mouth twitched. "It's from my sons, William and Charles. They know I don't like frippery in here, but it does add some life. I should have never let them read *The Language of Flowers* when they were younger, however."

Jo looked puzzled. "I'm sorry. I know how to draw flowers, but not what they mean."

Ann came around the desk and pointed at each one. "The foxglove, although beautiful, represents insincerity. The daisies signify innocence, in particular the innocence of one's children. And the honeysuckle is devoted affection, as the vine climbs the tree."

Jo laughed. "I see," she said. Ann returned to her chair and began moving the stacks of papers to the side of her desk.

"Sit, sit," she said, motioning to the chair in front of her desk. Jo sat.

"Now, you have brought some drawings?"

Jo opened her bag. This particular bag always made her feel more confident because her father had given it to her. She took out a sheaf of about a dozen drawings wrapped between two paperboard covers with string and handed it across the desk. Ann took out a small pair of spectacles from the desk drawer and put them on.

The first drawing was of a Metropolitan Police constable, proudly wearing his uniform.

"Is this from last year? From the garroting panic?" asked Anne Ingram.

"Yes, I was trying to show the anti-strangulation collar particularly."

"Rather difficult with black on black, isn't it?"

"It is, but since the point is the height of the collar, I didn't worry about it."

Ann nodded. "I like the expression of confidence on his face," she said.

"Thank you." The next two were pictures of poor children in Covent Garden.

"You've captured the hopelessness here, I think," said Anne as she looked at the two urchins, one of whom couldn't have been older than seven.

A portrait of Cecil Price, the actor, was next, showing him in a typical pose, playing Hamlet.

"Ah, yes, Mr. Price. Very well done. You've got his air of superiority exactly."

The next drawing was a group of people outside the theatre, waiting to be let in. A publican plied his goods on a tray, while his wife tried to control a small dog on a leash. Ann peered at the dog.

"Hmmm. Animals do not demonstrate your best talent, I think," she said.

Jo frowned. She knew her animals weren't very good. But would this mean she couldn't work for *The Illustrated London News*? Ann looked up.

"Don't worry. We just won't assign you to animal stories." She smiled briefly. Jo was too nervous to breathe a sigh of relief.

Jo had included in the set of sketches two she'd done of paintings, one of Van Dyck's *Samson and Delilah* from the Dulwich Picture Gallery, and one of Andrea del Sarto's *Portrait of a Young Man*. Ann Ingram nodded in appreciation at the Van Dyck, then looked more closely at the del Sarto.

"I don't believe I know this painting? Where is it?"

"At the National Gallery," said Jo. "They acquired it just last year."

Ann looked and glanced over her spectacles at Jo. "Your work on these paintings is extraordinary," she said. "How long have you been drawing paintings in galleries?"

"Oh, since I was a child," said Jo, "I do it mostly to practice, but I thought these two were more finished than the others."

"You have a real talent for this," said Ann. "I'm not sure you realize. It's very difficult for engravers to create true copies of paintings for print. They need an especially good sketch to do it well, a sketch that is very sensitive to the gradient of light and shadow particularly."

She straightened out the stack of drawings and returned it to the paperboard covers, tying the string in a bow.

"Miss Harris," she said. Jo took a slow breath, trying to stay calm. "We have a great many illustrators working here, not only on *The Illustrated London News*, but on lesser papers. We have artists we send around the world for the news stories, and artists who work creating pictures for our more fanciful tales. What we don't have is a good illustrator of paintings. More and more people read our work outside of London, and many here in London do not visit art galleries."

She handed the packet back to Jo, stood and walked around the desk. Jo, thinking this signaled the end of the meeting, stood also.

"I do not know what commitments you may have to other journals," said Ann, "but I'd like you to consider coming to work for me. We have a studio here in the building where our artists work, but I would be hiring you primarily to copy works in the galleries: the Dulwich, the National Gallery, the Royal Academy, and private collections for which I can arrange access. You would not be paid regularly for the first year, but you would have access to the drawing studio and the other artists. I think you'll find we pay very fair prices for each good drawing."

She held out her hand to Jo with a business-like smile.

"You don't have to give me an answer today, but please think about it. I will leave your name with Jeremy Church, who supervises the studio. If you would like to join us, report to him next Monday."

"Thank you, Mrs. Ingram. It's been a pleasure meeting you, and I am quite sure I shall return," Jo managed to say as Ann opened the door to the outer office. Jo walked as sedately as she could manage out the front door and onto the Strand. But she had a hard time not jumping for joy as she briskly walked the mile to Shoe Lane, hoping she was in time to help with dinner.

Rossetti met Giovanni Morelli, as requested, at the Hat and Tun in Clerkenwell. The note had arrived at Cheyne Walk, as Rossetti had expected. Whenever Morelli came to London, he looked up his old friend. This time, the note said, Morelli had something special to show him.

The pub was in Hatton Garden, which was becoming the neighborhood for Italian immigrants and the English heart of the Risorgimento. The unification of Italy, still being fought for in the streets of Rome, was dear to most of the people here. Long ago, when Morelli was just a boy, he had met Gabriele, Rossetti's father. Gabriele had been a nationalist, famous for his poetry and his politics. Years later, Morelli befriended the son, and along with many of his countrymen, had come to England. The Hat and Tun was a meeting place for family and friends.

The main room was gaslit and welcoming, and Rossetti entered with a flourish, removing his cape. He was recognized immediately by two of his students from the Working Men's College, who smiled and nodded. Morelli, who by the look of his florid face had been there an hour or two, came up and embraced him.

"Dante Gabriel!" he cried, holding him at arm's length to look at him. "I have not seen you for . . ." He looked at the ceiling, as if counting.

"Almost two years," said Rossetti, smiling at his friend.

"Look at you," said Morelli, "your hair! How long it is! Oh, your father. He would love it." He turned to the table where he had been sitting. Two men, who had been perusing some papers, looked up when Morelli called, "Look! Friends! It's Dante Gabriel Rossetti!"

The men, both dark with sun-tanned faces, lifted their glasses and smiled.

"Let's go to the back room where we can talk," said Morelli, putting his arm around Rossetti's shoulders. But first he stopped at the bar.

"*Vino Italiano?*" asked Morelli. "They get it here specially." Rossetti agreed.

"Oh, my boy," said Morelli, once they were settled at a table in the back room, "so much is happening in Italy! I assume you read the papers."

"Not as often as I should," confessed Rossetti. "The Risorgimento is stalled, I hear."

Morelli shook his head vigorously. "It's temporary!" he cried. "*Transitorio!* Just a little problem with Rome. Vittorio Emanuele will have it all brought under control soon enough. And when he's finished," Morelli tapped himself heartily on the chest, "Italy will be a true nation. You can take it from me—they made me a Senator!"

Rossetti smiled. "I'm quite sure you're right!" He took a sip of wine and remembered how much he preferred beer.

"How is everyone at Cheyne Walk? *La famiglia?* Is little Christina still writing poetry and posing for you?"

"She is indeed. And Maria gets more pious every day. William is turning into quite a gentleman scholar. You must come to Cheyne Walk very soon. Mother will be so unhappy if you do not."

"Ah, yes, your mother. Such a wonderful woman. Her brother, not so much. Such a strange man, as I recall. Your uncle. Wrote that book . . . what was it? About creatures who live on human blood." He looked up at the ceiling, then remembered. "*Vampiri!* Vampires!" He shook his head and took a sip from his glass. "They say he poisoned himself, you know."

"Yes, but mother doesn't talk about it," said Rossetti. He didn't want to talk about it either. John Polidori had died before he was born, but he had read *The Vampyre*, as had Christina. When they were children it had frightened them.

"Of course! Not the sort of thing one talks about outside *la famiglia*." Morelli put his finger alongside his nose.

"I hear you are looking at paintings on this visit, as usual?" asked Rossetti.

"I am," said Morelli, "and there is so much to see! But wait! I told you I had something special to show you." He leaned forward. "I take it you don't come to Clerkenwell often?"

"No," said Rossetti. "I spend most of my time near the gallery or at Cheyne Walk."

"Then come. *Andiamo!*" Morelli drained his glass and put it down. Rossetti did the same—you don't waste drink, even if it's wine.

They went out into the night, and Morelli led him around the corner to Clerkenwell Road. About a hundred yards down the road, he stopped and turned toward a narrow building, glowing reddish in the gaslight. The pillars and trim were brilliant white. It looked like a bit of Italy set down in Clerkenwell.

"It opened in April," said Morelli, as if he had consecrated it himself. "St. Peter's Church. A Catholic church for our Italian community!" He opened his arms wide, displaying the building.

It truly was a lovely building, and clearly the most Italian facade in all of London. He decided not to douse Morelli's enthusiasm by pointing out that Morelli himself was Protestant. Not everyone knew this. "Well, that's wonderful!" said Rossetti.

"It is! Mazzini was here. He opened it himself."

Rossetti was impressed. Giuseppe Mazzini, the famous organizer of the Risorgimento, a man who only last year had fought beside Garibaldi, was often in London. He was in exile, founding a school and charities for Italian families. And now this church.

The night was starting to get chilly, and Rossetti's cloak was thin.

"You must come to the house, Morelli. When can you come? Mother will want to sit and talk with you."

"And feed me!" Morelli's eyes twinkled.

"And feed you, and you'll make Christina and Maria so happy. When can you come?"

Morelli thought a moment, swaying slightly on his feet. He doesn't feel the cold, thought Rossetti. I'd better help him back to wherever he's staying.

"Soon, soon, *presto* . . ."

"Where are you staying?" asked Rossetti, adjusting his friend's cloak.

"Westminster something . . . Westminster Palace Hotel!"

"Allow me to accompany you," said Rossetti, looking up Clerkenwell Road and spotting a cab.

"Of course! Their kitchen is *eccellente*. We will order some supper."

Rossetti agreed and hailed the cab. It was after nine and the sky was dark but clear, with the moon just rising.

As they approached the Palace of Westminster, Morelli pounded his cane on the ceiling. "Cabbie, stop here! Let's walk," he said to Rossetti, "I like walking past the Abbey."

The air was fresh as the two men walked past Westminster Abbey toward the hotel. They passed the Crimean War Memorial, an enormous column, without noticing anything amiss. The moon and the gas lamps shed some light, and yet neither man clearly saw the person who jumped out at them. There was the motion of a cloak or a coat, a raised arm. Rossetti was pushed out of the way and fell hard on the road. As he turned to get up, he saw Morelli sway in his cloak, then he heard a dull thud. Morelli fell to the ground. Rossetti grabbed for the attacker's legs, but the villain was agile and his heel met with Rossetti's forehead as he pushed away. Rossetti could hear feet running on the road. There was no way to catch him, and Morelli needed help.

"My friend, my friend!" cried Rossetti, crawling over to the cloaked body on the ground. "Are you alive?"

There was a grunt, and the cloak stirred. Rossetti touched Morelli's head, and his hand came back damp. He couldn't move him on his own. He jumped to his feet and yelled, "Help! Murder!"

An elegantly clad couple ran down the steps of the hotel to assist. The woman put her slender hand on Morelli's chest, to make sure he was breathing, while the man folded his cloak and put it under Morelli's head. Then two men whom they had passed next to the Abbey hurried over, one with a constable in tow.

Rossetti explained as best he could, and the men helped Morelli into the hotel. At first, they almost carried him, but after a few steps he was able to walk, albeit unsteadily and with a great deal of help. The Westminster Palace Hotel was well-serviced, Rossetti thought. They may even have a doctor.

After Morelli had been settled in his room, the constable had taken notes, and the doctor had gone, Rossetti sat next to his friend.

"I'm so sorry," he said. "I didn't see him. I didn't see who it was."

"It isn't your fault," said Morelli. He looked old and tired now, not at all his florid, expansive self. "I will live, as you can see. My head will hurt for awhile is all."

"He ignored me. He went for you. Why would anyone want to hurt you?"

"It could be anyone, my friend. I have made many enemies in working for Italian unification."

When Rossetti left the hotel an hour later, he took a cab rather than walking. The attacker could still be around somewhere, and perhaps he would want to eliminate a witness. But I haven't witnessed anything, thought Rossetti. I can't be of any use at all.

7

When Constable Moberly arrived at the photography studio in Theobalds Road, he was in a cheerful mood. He had received a note from his daughter Althea that she wanted to have tea with him on Saturday. Moberly dared to hope that she would tell him she was expecting. Perhaps it was too soon, he thought, but it's been two years, just about the time Lottie and I welcomed her into our lives. He almost missed seeing the shop as he thought of holding a baby again.

The curtains were drawn and there was little in the display window. No custom would come by with the place looking so unwelcoming. And yet, if what Bridget and her friend said was true, there should be men wanting to collect their photographs. Moberly turned the handle but the door was locked, so he tapped gently on the glass.

Bridget peeked out at him, then opened the door.

"Good morning, Constable Moberly," she said.

He noticed that her eyes still looked sleepy, but she seemed glad to see him. He also smelled something wonderful.

"Have you been baking bread?" he asked. Surely there couldn't be an oven in here?

"Sweet rolls," said Bridget. "I've been up since four so they would rise just so." She walked over to the counter and opened a bag made of paper. The scent wafted over to him.

"They smell wonderful," he said. She held out the bag to him with a smile.

He bit into a roll. Sweet and light and buttery. If only Lottie could have baked like this. Then again, if she had, he'd weigh 300 pounds and would have had to retire at forty.

"Thank you, miss," he said. He looked around the shop. Counter, cameras, and cabinets at the front, about eight steps from the front door. Portrait studio paraphernalia to the right, and a door to the back.

"May I?" he asked, gesturing toward the door and making sure his mouth wasn't full.

"Of course," said Bridget, moving ahead of him and opening the door. "Most of the shop is up here, but the studio is in the back because of the light."

He saw at once what she meant. The glass panels near the ceiling let in the morning glow. Moving toward the small room built at the side of the larger room, he asked, "This is the dark-room?"

Bridget nodded. Moberly went to the door and tried the handle. It opened and he peered into the dim room. Then he leaned back out, closed the door, and paced off the distance to the back door. He examined the lock and the catch, then leaned out of the back door to look along the passageway.

"Is everything out here as it was?" he asked.

Bridget went over to him and stepped out into the alley. There was a bin there, and a few crates.

"Yes, I think it looks the same."

He looked around. The alley was flagstone and cobble, so there were no footprints in mud or anything obvious. Not that he expected to find anything this long after the occurrence. He examined the lock from the outside. They stepped back into the studio. "Miss Williams, would you mind going into the dark-room, closing the door, and shouting out to me."

She did so, hollering out "Constable Moberly!" He heard her, but her voice was not as loud as he expected. She poked her head out of the dark-room.

"Could you hear me?"

"Only just," he said, coming over and tapping on the dark-room walls. "This room is better built than it appears."

Then he walked over to the big table, which had a few photographs on it.

"This is where the photographs were that were stolen?" he asked.

"Yes. There was a small stack there."

"Do you know which pictures exactly were taken?"

"I can make a list if you like. There were five of them, all photographs of paintings at the National Gallery."

"Not the Exhibition?"

"No, the National Gallery. We were photographing several items from each, but the Exhibition pictures are still here."

Moberly nodded, took out his notebook, and wrote something down.

"May I see the other photographs?" he asked when he was done.

She knew which ones he meant, and led him out to the counter. She showed him the metal box.

"Jo and I brought back a few things from his flat," she said. Moberly raised a brow in question. "The solicitor, Mr. MacLeish, said we should. We found the key to the drawer in this box." She took it out and unlocked the drawer, handing him the stack of photographs.

"Ah," said Moberly, as he glanced through them. "I see."

"There was a list in the drawer too," said Bridget, handing it to him. "It's in code, as I told you, but a friend of Jo's figured it out. Each letter is really the one next to it in the alphabet. You'll see the actual names there too."

Moberly looked at the list, which seemed non-sensical. Then he looked at the names neatly written beside each item, in pencil.

"Not complicated, but still clever," he said. "I take it there are names here that you know."

"Yes, several," said Bridget. "But the ones that jumped out at us were Cecil Robson and Dante Gabriel Rossetti. They're both painters."

Moberly sighed. Quite a few of these ill-clad women were the age of his daughter Althea. Only a few were older. But he'd seen a lot of things in his time as constable. This wasn't particularly shocking.

"And you didn't know Mr. Pratchett took such photographs?" he asked.

"Oh, I knew," said Bridget, "even though I hadn't seen them. I was urging him to pay the young ladies more, like royalties for when their image was sold."

Moberly realized he'd underestimated Bridget. She was young, but sensible and pragmatic. Perhaps she only seemed flighty next to her more solid friend, Jo Harris. He could see why Pratchett, since he had no other family, would leave the business to her.

"I'll need to take the list with me, but you might want to keep the photographs somewhere other than the shop," he said as Bridget handed him the list and locked the box. "I confess I'm a little confused about how they were made. Are these the same as what you use the glass plates for?" he said, nodding toward the door to the back studio.

"Not exactly," explained Bridget. "These are tintypes. They're made using a thin sheet of iron, not a glass plate. They're very inexpensive to make."

"That must be why there are so many. What happens to the iron sheet when you're done?"

"It's right there, Constable. That is the image itself. The black backing on the card is what makes the various tones of dark and light."

"They're really quite remarkable," said Moberly, then cleared his throat to clarify. "I mean the likenesses. So clear and—I assume— true to life." Bridget smiled. But Moberly was still bothered by the fact that Bridget had been locked in the dark-room.

"I'd like to talk to the people in the area, perhaps in the nearby shops, to determine who might have seen your intruder. Will you be here in the studio for awhile?"

"I shall be here for an hour or two, going through the books."

"Then if I'm not too long, I'll return and let you know what I've found."

Moberly walked along the front of the shops on Theobalds Road. At the tobacconist's next door, the proprietor explained they kept the door to the alley closed at all times, and no one had seen anyone suspicious, but as it was almost two weeks ago, he couldn't be sure. The staff at the corset maker's were no help either. He had better luck at Mrs. Randolph's hat shop. Two girls who worked at the back of the shop claimed to have seen a small, spry man in a tweed cap walking down the passageway toward Pratchett's studio.

"We saw him right out here," the first girl said. She was a slip of a thing and looked like she didn't get enough to eat. Her blonde hair kept falling in her eyes, and she pushed it back. Moberly had to resist the impulse to run back to the studio and fetch her one of Bridget's sweet rolls. She was pointing out of the window. "He went by this way."

"You girls were both working here the afternoon of the 20th?"

The other girl, sturdier, with dark hair and a northern accent, nodded. "We're both here on Wednesdays," she said. "The light's better back here, and we do see everyone coming and going in the passageway. He was a small man, and spry. Moved quickly."

"So did you see this man pass both directions?"

"No," said the blonde girl. "We saw him pass us here and go toward the photography shop, but we didn't see him return."

Moberly wanted to take down a detailed description, but both girls were short-sighted and couldn't say more than that he was a small, spry man, with a dark coat and a tweed cap. Mrs. Randolph came back to show him out.

"Neither girl can see very far," he said to her. "Makes it hard to identify this man."

"It's the sewing," she said. "Most seamstresses and piece workers become very short-sighted at an early age. It's a trial to me, I can tell you."

He supposed it was. He could imagine it was also quite a trial for the girls.

"I'm afraid I cannot see the connection, Sir Charles."

Eastlake was pacing in front of his desk. Detective Inspector Harkness was standing on the carpet, holding his notebook and trying not to look irritated.

"It's me. The connection is me! Or my institution, at any rate," said Eastlake. His face was creased, and several of his hairs were poking out of his head, as if they were uncombed. "The photographer Pratchett was killed here at the Exhibition, and now the art critic Morelli has been attacked. Mr. Morelli is here at my invitation. I arranged for his rooms at the Westminster Palace Hotel."

"But Mr. Morelli was not attacked in the gallery," said Harkness reasonably, "He was attacked near his hotel." He did not mention that despite the fact that the hotel was fully within his jurisdiction, he thus far had very little information about the occurrence.

"They're both connected with this gallery!" Sir Charles tried to be patient. "You must see that the two are related."

"It is possible. I will investigate fully, Sir Charles. You may rely upon it." This was what Harkness always said to higher members of society. It typically reassured them. Sir Charles did not look reassured.

"See here, Inspector," said Sir Charles. "It's been well over a week since the body of Hugh Pratchett was found in my Exhibition. Haven't you any news at all? Any leads, as you people call them? The London Photographic Society wants to know what happened. It's quite shaken them up. No one expects this sort of thing. We can't just sit around waiting to hear."

"I understand, Sir Charles," Harkness looked down at the carpet, hating the feeling of humiliation that was creeping up on him. Sir Charles was speaking quietly, but insistently. His displeasure would do no good for Harkness's career in the force. Harkness was a respected man, but not at Sir Charles's level, and he knew that.

The blustery weather outside matched Harkness's mood. It was only a short walk from the National Gallery back to Scotland Yard, but he took the long way around the building. Moberly was waiting for him.

"Cup of tea, with sugar," Harkness barked at a new recruit as he stomped into his office. "Moberly, I've just been given a dressing down by Sir Charles Eastlake. He insists that the attack on Mr.

Morelli last night is related to the death of Hugh Pratchett." He hung his hat up with a tug that was not good for the hat, and sat down hard in his chair. "I was supposed to be in Leicester Square. Please tell me you have news?" He buried his head in his hands.

"Yes, sir," said Moberly. "I have a general description of the man who locked Bridget Williams in the dark-room."

Harkness raised his head slowly, his expression one of amazement.

"You have *what*?"

Moberly sat down and calmly took out his notebook. "A general description. A small, spry man, wearing a dark coat and a tweed cap. He was seen going down the passageway toward the photography studio at the time in question."

Harkness stared at Moberly. A career constable, he knew. Why had he been assigned to him? Not enough to do at Piccadilly?

"What the bloody hell difference does it make who she thinks might have closed her in the dark-room? What on earth does that have to do with Pratchett's murder, or anything else?"

He had raised his voice, which helped explain the timidity with which the new recruit entered with the tea. He put it on Harkness's desk without a word, then glanced over at Moberly, raising a brow. Moberly shook his head. He'd have his tea later, where it was quiet.

Harkness took a gulp of tea, and Moberly saw the tears form in his eyes. "Damn, too hot," growled Harkness. But he had calmed somewhat.

"Sir, may I have leave to be candid?"

Harkness thought for a moment. Moberly had been on the force a long time. Maybe his methods could be helpful. Goodness knows nothing else was at the moment.

"Yes, go on."

"The photography shop. Pratchett was not just taking photographs of pictures at the Royal Academy Exhibition and the National Gallery. He was also photographing women in various poses and states of undress."

Harkness looked up and nodded, his eyes meeting Moberly's in understanding.

"There were a few well-known men on the list to purchase those photographs," continued Moberly. "We need to talk to them, sir."

"How well known?"

"A couple of painters, two businessmen, a lawyer . . ."

"Then go and talk to them," said Harkness.

"And then there's the pictures that are missing. Whoever locked Miss Williams in the dark-room took some of the photographs, ones with paintings from the National Gallery. Why, sir? It's obvious the man locked her in so he could take his time finding the photographs. But why did he take certain ones and not others?"

"I'm following, Moberly." Harkness gingerly took a sip of tea. Not as hot now, thank goodness.

"So I spoke with people in the nearby shops, and we have this general description. It's not much, but it's something. He's a small, spry man."

"Yes, but a tweed cap? Every villain's got a tweed cap!"

"I know, sir. But I wonder whether he got everything he came for?"

"What do you mean?"

"The more questionable photographs were locked in a drawer. If he's coming back, we should have a man nearby, sir. Miss Williams is alone in the shop."

"Moberly, I understand you're trying to protect the young woman, but I have no men to spare."

"Yes, sir. I can volunteer, sir."

"I cannot spare you. We have to find out about Morelli. I dare say Sir Charles is right about the connection. Even if he isn't, we can't let the attack go without an investigation. You need to do that first. Now, in fact." Harkness stood, so Moberly did too.

"I want you to go to the hotel immediately, Constable. On your way out, find out about the constable who was on the beat last night. Did anyone see anything?"

"Yes, sir," said Moberly, putting on his hat. It was the old top-hat style. The helmet had been hard to get used to.

"And Moberly," said Harkness, "when you're done, you may go to the studio to make sure the young woman is all right."

On his way to the Westminster Palace Hotel, Constable Moberly stopped at the King Street Police Station to speak with Constable Thorne, who had taken Morelli's report. No, no one had clearly seen the man who attacked Mr. Morelli. Morelli had been accompanied by Dante Rossetti, the artist, who had tried to grab the man's leg and was kicked in the face for his trouble. The doctor had seen to Mr. Morelli at the hotel. Thorne had taken statements from a few witnesses, but all they could say was that the man seemed small and spry, and was wearing what looked like a tweed cap, although they couldn't be sure from that far away.

Given the urgency in Harkness's attitude, Moberly proceeded immediately to the hotel. He had never been there before, since Piccadilly was his usual station. It was a hive of activity. Professional men were going past on the busy street in rather large numbers, toward the back of the hotel. Then he remembered. The India Office was here now. They were waiting for their new government headquarters to be built and were occupying the entire back wing of the hotel. He'd been told they held 140 rooms. Remarkable.

The Ascending Lift was remarkable too. You stepped into a small room, and the room moved, taking you to the upper floors. A driver worked the machinery. Moberly stood in the little room, trying to look like he did this every day.

"Which floor, Constable?"

"Three, please."

Mr. Morelli was sitting in a chair in his hotel room, trying to take a little food.

"I am sorry to disturb you, Mr. Morelli," Moberly said. "I won't keep you long. Inspector Harkness of Scotland Yard sent me to make sure you were all right, and to ask just a few questions."

Morelli had a white bandage around his head, and a smaller one was wrapped across the palm of his hand. He gave a nod, winced, and instead gestured to a chair.

"Have a seat, Constable. Ask whatever you like." He picked up a piece of toasted bread and bit into the tip carefully.

"Thank you, sir. I have spoken with Constable Thorne, who was here last night, so I have his notes. I understand the man attacked you from behind?"

"Yes, that's right," said Morelli. "I'm afraid I didn't see him. Then he ran off. My friend Rossetti helped me."

"So I understand," said Moberly. "Very kind of him. We are trying to ascertain whether it was a random attack, or whether it was personal. Did the attacker say anything?"

Morelli began to shake his head, then thought better of it. "No, Constable."

"Was anything taken from about your person?"

"Nothing at all."

"Do you know of anyone in London who might wish you harm?"

Morelli sighed. "A man like me has enemies, inspector. I am active in the Risorgimento."

Moberly repeated, "The Risorgimento?"

"The effort to unify Italy. To some that makes me a hero, but to others a traitor."

"May I ask what you're doing in London, sir?"

"I am not a revolutionary, although I have marched with Garibaldi. No, my vocation is art critic and scholar. I have developed methods for determining the artists of unattributed paintings."

"Unattributed?" Moberly was writing in his notebook.

"Paintings where the artist is unknown, or where the wrong artist has previously been named."

"And this is how you know Sir Charles Eastlake?"

"Precisely. While I am in England, I am looking at works in his National Gallery."

"Sir, I don't know much about art. But is it possible that in your vocation as an art critic and scholar, you could offend or harm someone enough that they might want to hurt you?"

Morelli paused. He looked balefully at the piece of toast, took a sip of tea, and leaned back in the chair.

"That is a very interesting question, Constable. I hadn't thought of it before. But I would have to say yes. It is possible. A misattribution can change the value of a painting, even making it unsellable. I do not believe I have ever ruined anyone, but I suppose it could have happened at some point. Then, of course, there are my methods."

"Your methods, sir? Are they unusual?"

"They are scientific, in the sense that they are empirical and based on many years experience. I recognize patterns. Some disagree, and look only at brush strokes, or subjects. I compare internal elements of the work: hands, beards, drapery. How an artist paints these things can be unique."

Moberly was not at all sure he understood, but he could tell from the conviction in Morelli's voice that he was a strong personality with absolute certainty about his own method.

"I see. Is it possible this man followed you? Constable Thorne said Mr. Rossetti reported that you had been coming from"—he checked his notes—"the Hat and Tun in Clerkenwell?"

"Yes, the Hat and Tun. I was told the name is a joke of some kind, something about Hatton, or Hatton Gardens. I suppose we could have been followed. We stopped briefly in front of the new church, but we weren't looking to see if anyone was following us."

Moberly nodded, and took another note. Morelli adjusted his bandage a little.

"That's all I need for now, sir," said Moberly, rising. "I'm sorry to have disturbed you."

"I understand, Constable. I just need a little rest, I think."

After he left Morelli, Constable Moberly found a bench outside the hotel and took out his list of photography customers. It would take him days to get to them all. He decided to begin with Rossetti, since he had also been a witness to the attack. Cheyne Walk was out in Chelsea. Another cab. He hoped Harkness would defray the expense.

A large, blowsy, lovely woman opened the door at 16 Cheyne Walk. Her face became still when she saw Moberly's uniform.

"Can I help?" she asked, her curling tresses lifted by what had become a rather chilly breeze.

"I'd like to see Mr. Rossetti, please."

"Neither of them are here at the moment."

"Neither of them?"

"The Mr. Rossettis. Gabriel or William. Both are out. No idea when they'll be back."

"Can you tell me where Dante Rossetti is? It's important that I speak with him."

"Oh!" suddenly she seemed to realize. "Is this about Mr. Morelli?"

"Yes."

"The poor man. Yes, Gabriel's down by the river, at Cadogan Pier. Trying to catch the evening light." She pointed vaguely across Cheyne Walk.

Moberly found him sitting on the pier, sketching.

"Mr. Rossetti?"

Rossetti looked up, his wild wispy hair blowing across his face as he smiled at Moberly. He was wearing a coat covered with a peacock feather design. It glowed in the evening light. Moberly had never seen a garment this colorful on a man.

"Hello, Constable."

"Good afternoon," said Moberly. "I'd like to speak with you for a few minutes, if I may. I come on behalf of Inspector Harkness of Scotland Yard."

"Excellent!" said Rossetti, getting to his feet with a bit of stiffness and stretching his back. "I'm delighted my friend's plight will get the attention it deserves." Moberly wasn't sure what to say, and Rossetti frowned. "This is about Giovanni Morelli, isn't it?"

"Oh, yes, sir," said Moberly. "And I have some questions about what happened."

"Of course!" said Rossetti. "But all I can tell you is some blackguard jumped out at us and began pummeling Mr. Morelli."

"Pummeling, sir?"

"Beating him. As if he wanted to kill him. I tried to grab his leg." Rossetti lifted the hair from his forehead. Near the hairline was a crescent-shaped mark, like from the heel of a shoe. "Got this for trying!" Moberly looked at his eager face and assumed he got into scrapes as a younger man. Not without some enjoyment, apparently.

"And then you helped him to the hotel?"

"Yes, me and a constable." Rossetti suddenly looked worried. "Is he all right?"

"Yes, sir. I've just seen him. Bit of a headache, I think."

"I can imagine!"

"And you have no idea who might have done this?"

"None, Constable. But whoever it was, I'd like a chance to thrash him."

The dining table at the boarding house buzzed with conversation, the occasion to celebrate Jo's new position at *The Illustrated London News*. That afternoon, Mrs. Bagley had sent Esther to buy some bottles of claret. After dinner was eaten, she passed the bottles around, and everyone poured herself a glass.

"Ready?" asked Mrs. Bagley.

Almost all the women raised their glasses and called out, "To Mr. Gladstone!"

There was hearty laughter around the table. Esther looked confused. It had been humiliating enough to go by herself to buy the wine. She'd had to cross Holborn to go to Hatton Garden, where Mrs. Bagley said to find H. B. Fearon, Wine and Spirit Merchant. She hadn't known exactly what to ask for. But the man had been very kind, inquired about the occasion, and sold her three bottles for the three shillings she'd been given.

"Why Mr. Gladstone?" she asked.

"The duties!" said Bridget. Esther still looked confused.

Jo explained, "Gladstone did away with the high duties on wine like this. Claret from France. That's how we can afford to drink it. And we can buy it by the bottle, not the case, and from a shop."

"To you, Jo," said Esther, raising her class. "And your post at *The Illustrated London News!*"

"Hurrah!" said all, as they drank.

"And to Bridget inheriting a business!" said Jo.

They all drank again.

"So did they ever find who killed poor Mr. Pratchett?" asked Mrs. Bagley.

"Not yet," Bridget said. "We have a nice constable helping us now. Reminds me of my tad. Sorry, my father. And," she said, "we found the pictures."

"What pictures?" asked Esther.

"The ones Mr. Pratchett took of women."

Eyes opened wide around the table.

"Can we see them?" Annie blurted out.

"Why yes, if you wish," said Bridget uncertainly. "Constable Moberly told me not to keep them in the shop. I think he was afraid someone would break in to get them. I brought them home, along with a list of the models. But this must stay within these walls. We want to protect the women." She rose with a questioning look around the table. Everyone nodded.

As she went up the stairs, she heard Mrs. Bagley say, "Now, ladies, don't you go telling anyone we've been looking at such pictures. I won't have it said that my boarding house is disreputable." She hiccupped her wine and lowered her voice to a whisper. "And I do think it's not legal."

Bridget came down, opened the tin box, and passed the photographs around. The joviality quieted and the women became serious.

"Do you suppose they wanted to pose like this?" asked Annie.

"I don't know. This one isn't showing her face," said Mabel. "Perhaps she's ashamed."

It was very quiet as the photographs were examined.

Then Jo said, looking at the one with the woman wrapped around the pillar, "They are well-posed, though. Pratchett had a good eye for what was lovely."

"They could have been worse," said Esther. "I've seen ones where women were showing a good deal more of their bodies, very brazenly. These women look kind of shy."

"Maybe that's why the men liked them," said Bridget. "They look like ordinary women, not actresses or prostitutes. They're women a lonely man might actually be able to know."

"I think you're right," said Jo, peering more closely. "I'm not seeing any rouge or artificial enhancements to their skin or hair."

"Oh!" said Bridget suddenly, dropping the photograph she was holding.

Everyone looked up.

Bridget paused. "I might know this woman," she said.

"Who is it?" asked Annie, leaning over to see.

Bridget frowned. "I can't remember her name," she said slowly. "I'll need to think about it."

More of the pictures were passed around.

"But you say you're going to visit these women? Get their stories?" asked Annie.

"We're certainly going to try," said Bridget.

"And do it as discreetly as we possibly can," said Jo.

After the celebration was over, Annie and Mrs. Bagley cleared up, while the women who had to rise early went up to bed.

Jo was just coming back from the bathroom when she saw Bridget waiting in the hall. Bridget pointed to Jo's room and raised her eyebrow in question. Jo nodded.

Once they were both inside, Jo closed the door.

"What is it?" she said.

"This woman in the picture," said Bridget. She handed Jo the photograph of the older woman, the one facing away from the camera with long hair hanging down her back. "I know who it is." She opened up the list of initials.

"Who?" said Jo. "You didn't do a very good job pretending you didn't remember."

"I didn't think I should say in front of everyone. I think it's Lady Millicent!" She pointed to the initials "M.S." with the address "Grosvenor Square."

"Lady Millicent? That rude woman who came into the photography studio demanding her picture?"

Bridget nodded. "I've never seen her like this, obviously, but the hair, and something about the way she has her head turned."

"You could be wrong," said Jo.

"I could be," said Bridget. "But I don't think I am. Should we do anything?"

"I'm not sure," said Jo. "It seems premature to tell Constable Moberly."

"Or a violation somehow," said Bridget.

"Of her privacy?"

"Well, yes. Plus, it might be illegal."

"I don't think posing is illegal," said Jo. "Selling the picture might be."

Bridget sighed. "Obviously I'm not going to do that. Besides, Constable Moberly has the list of buyers."

Jo sat down on the bed. Bridget sat beside her. Both women stared at the floor. A full minute passed.

"Perhaps," said Jo, "we should confront her."

Bridget looked horrified. "Why would we do that?"

"Maybe she knows something. About the pictures. Whether anyone might be angry about them. Whether her husband knows about them."

"Husband?" Bridget looked curious. "Does she have a husband?"

Jo shook her head. "I have no idea. Perhaps we should find out. And we should discover whether she is well-off or needs the money."

"How do we do that?" asked Bridget.

"We'll just go talk to her," said Jo with more confidence than she felt.

It had been a quiet evening at the house in Craven Street. A very good dinner, pork roast and greens, had been served as always in the dining room. The children had been taken up to bed by Nurse. Even Muggles was curled up on her rug in front of the fire, asleep. Detective Inspector Harkness had leaned back in his wing chair, his head gently touching the antimacassar, his freshly-lit pipe in his mouth when the bell rang at the front door.

No, he thought. I've done with my day. There shall be no disturbances.

"Excuse me, sir," said Polly. She looked sleepy too. "Constable Moberly is here. Says he needs to speak with you, sir." She gave a lazy curtsy and left to go upstairs, hoping for a cold bath and bed. I'd never marry a policeman, she thought to herself. The hours would be too awful.

Harkness shook his head with a low growl, making Muggles wake up and look warily at him. She may have been a mere terrier lounging on a rug, but she knew her master's moods.

Constable Moberly entered the study.

"I'm sorry to disturb you at home, sir," he said, standing in the doorway.

"Come in, come in," Harkness said, waving a hand. "Sit and tell me why you've come."

Moberly sat as carefully as possible on the settee and took out his notebook. He reported on the day's work, and what had been said when he spoke with Mr. Morelli and Mr. Rossetti.

"It's the same man, sir," said Moberly. "I'm sure of it. The man who broke into the photography shop and the man who attacked Mr. Morelli are one and the same."

"Then it's possible that this small, spry man with the tweed cap is also the murderer of Mr. Pratchett," said Harkness.

"Yes, sir."

"Good work, Moberly," Harkness sighed. "Now we need only to find a small, spry man with a tweed cap from among the entire population of London. Can't be too many."

"He may come again for Morelli, sir. I expected there might be an attack on Miss Williams, but I think he's after something else."

"Morelli's Italian. Could be one of those Garibaldi sorts. You said he thought it was a political attack."

"He said it could be anyone, because of his politics. But that doesn't make sense if this same man also killed Mr. Pratchett. I can find nothing political about Mr. Pratchett, unless one of the girls he photographed is connected to someone famous."

"That may be it!" said Harkness. But the idea didn't make him happy. If there was an M.P., or God forbid a member of the royal family involved, it would not be good for his career. "Stay with Morelli, then. But perhaps not in uniform."

Moberly looked perplexed. "Not in uniform?"

"Look, I just don't have enough men. I should use a detective, but I can't spare one unless this does turn out to be connected to someone important. The Leicester Square case isn't solved yet," Harkness ran his hands over his eyes. He really was tired.

"You want me in plain clothes, sir?"

"Yes, I'm sorry. I know it's more dangerous for you. But do you think this killer will show himself if a constable in uniform is guarding Morelli?"

Moberly knew that was true. But he'd never performed in his capacity as policeman in plain clothes. He never thought he'd have to, and he certainly wasn't looking for promotion. Of course, if he were promoted first, he might retire with a better pension.

"I'll do it, sir," he said.

Samson had come to the Slaughters full of hope on Thursday morning, wishing to see Prudence. But he found Hannah there in the kitchen as before. Since he'd arrived early, Tommy was still upstairs, dressing for their journey to the Grant Museum. Ellie had ushered him into the kitchen and put the pot of tea in front of him.

"I'm sorry I can't visit this morning, Samson," Ellie had told him, "but I have to get Jo's design for the abolitionist posters to the Reform Club. Have a good morning doing the lessons." She had then hurriedly put on her coat and gone out. Samson noticed she didn't bother to say *Women's* Reform Club. He rather liked that she didn't. The club was the club and did far more good than any gentlemen's club he'd ever heard of. They offered free talks on subjects of moral concern, including the care of prisoners, the health of prostitutes, and the abolition of slavery. They used their money to sponsor efforts to make the world better. Samson had never been in a gentlemen's club, but he had heard they mostly sat around reading, playing billiards, and smoking. It didn't sound very reforming to him.

He laid out his books, then poured a cup of tea and took a sip. It had been very cold outside, but was pleasant in the kitchen, and there was a fresh-baked loaf of bread on the sideboard. Hannah was on her hands and knees, cleaning out the still-warm oven. She had her hair up under a cap that had seen better days, but her boots were clean and her square face was placid as she used a wire brush to dislodge the baked-on food. She glanced up at him.

"So, you're the young master who's teaching Tommy the science," she said. Her voice was deep and pleasant.

"I am," he said. "I'm studying to be a biologist."

"What's a bi-ologist, then?" she asked, turning her attention back to the oven. "Tommy told me bi-ology is the study of life."

"I study forms of life. Plants and animals, mostly."

Hannah didn't reply, and Samson glanced at the newspaper Ellie had left on the table.

"Looks like they haven't found out who killed the photographer yet," he said, looking over the articles.

"That was the one at the Exhibition?" Hannah asked.

"Yes, a Mr. Hugh Pratchett. Member of the London Photographic Society."

"Oh, them," said Hannah, obviously unimpressed.

"You don't like photography?" asked Samson.

Hannah leaned back on her heels, wire brush in hand. "I like some of them pictures." She stopped and looked at Samson, as if considering whether he were trustworthy. "Been in some," she said.

A bit of pride was evident in her tone, Samson noted. He thought it couldn't possibly result from being photographed as Prudence had been. Must have been on holiday or something. Did women like Hannah ever get a holiday? he wondered. They worked so awfully hard. "You've been photographed before? Like a family picture?"

"No, not family. I been photographed by massa"—she stopped as if she had used a forbidden word—"by the lawyer, Arthur Munby. He doesn't like the Photographic Society. Says they don't do enough pictures of women like me."

Samson thought about that for a moment. "You mean women who do the harder labors of life?"

"Yeah, and women what look like me. Big, strong women who don't mind the dirty work. Mr. Munby likes to photograph us. As a study, he says. Of our"—she searched for the word—"culture."

"You mean like an anthropologist?"

Hannah shrugged, leaned forward and scrubbed some more. She had said "massa," like people who parodied the speech of American slaves. If Munby was her master, then she was his servant. Many people let their servants work elsewhere, so this wouldn't be unusual. But Hannah had obviously let the word slip as something she shouldn't have said. Samson was curious, but he didn't want to be rude.

"Your master is very lucky to have such a hard-working servant," he said. He looked over, and saw beneath the grime that she was blushing, pleased.

"He knows it, too," she said, with a small smile. "I do the boots, and the scrubbing in the scullery, and the mold in the corners. And I'm strong enough to carry him, for all his book learning."

Now Samson was shocked. "You've—lifted your Mr. Munby?"

"I have done, to show him I could. I'm very strong. Handy to be able to do that, 'specially if tending a person what's ill."

Samson thought that was true. "Have you thought of being a nurse?" Miss Nightingale certainly wasn't an Amazon, but it seemed like such strength would be good for hospital work.

"I s'pose I could. But I like to work on my own. And that way I have time to pose for Mr. Munby's photographs." She stopped scrubbing and leaned toward him, lowering her voice. "Once he had me covered all over with coal dust. That was all that was on me, just the coal dust and a cloth. Looked a sight, but he was very happy with the picture. Said I was noble."

Samson had no idea what to say to that. Perhaps he had been wrong about the kind of photographs Munby took. Were they taking advantage of women like Pratchett's photographs, just in a different way?

He said, "Apparently Mr. Pratchett took pictures of women too, but not to make them look noble."

Hannah nodded. "I've seen pictures like that, at the shop near my lodgings. Skinny young things in their underclothes. Men buy them and take them home." She thought for a moment, leaning back on her heels again. "Maybe it makes the men think they own them, to take home their picture. But you don't own people. That's why I work on my own."

She was quite right, of course. He was thinking about Prudence again. Men didn't own her because they had her picture. He didn't want to own her either, he thought. He wanted to help her, and have her help him, in life. He wanted a partner. But surely not now. Now he had to earn some money for his keep and take his examinations.

"I'm ready!" said Tommy, skidding into the kitchen.

8

The Rossetti garden party was more of a family tea. Jo sat under the tree in the garden at 16 Cheyne Walk, her sketchbook on her lap.

"Isn't my house wonderful?" Rossetti was lying on the grass beside her, holding an apple up to the sky. His brother William was strolling around, looking down morosely at his shoes. The rest of the family was still inside.

"It is," said Jo as she tried to sketch William. "Why is he so unhappy?"

"A woman, probably. He broods a lot on Ford Madox Brown's daughter, Lucy. Or maybe it's because he's just read *Leaves of Grass* again, by that American Walt Whitman. It makes him thoughtful."

Jo kept sketching.

"Or it could be because he's the only one of us with actual employment, at the Excise Office, instead of just writing and reviewing. We've done everything we can to make him a ne'er-do-well like the rest of us. Did I tell you he took Ruskin's drawing class at the Working Men's College a few years ago?"

Jo shook her head.

"I thought he was good, and he even writes some poetry. But he insists on keeping that damn position. Probably just wants to make sure we all don't starve." He took a bite of the apple.

"Tea!" Christina called from across the garden.

The chatter was continual at the table, but everyone seemed to be engaged in something different. William had a notebook out and was writing, Christina was reading a letter, and Rossetti was talking to his mother in Italian. Maria had gone back inside to get out of the sun.

"What are you reading?" Rossetti asked his sister.

Christina looked up and sighed. "It's another invitation from that painter Cecil Robson." She rolled her eyes at Jo.

"What does he want this time?" asked her brother.

"To take me to the Royal Academy Exhibition." Her heart-shaped face showed annoyance. Jo thought the expression was similar to the one her brother had painted in the annunciation picture.

Rossetti said to Jo, "Cecil Robson fancies himself a painter. He's technically good, but there's no heart."

"Ugh." Christina dramatically put her head down on the table.

"And my sister is all about heart."

Christina's voice was muffled. "I'll have to tell him I'm just not interested."

"You will, unless you want to go with him," her brother teased. "Or go just to be in the same space where a dead body has been!"

"Has there been any progress on that murder?" William inquired of nobody in particular.

"My friend Bridget worked for the victim," said Jo. "I think there's more to it than just a murder."

"I do too," said Rossetti. "When Morelli was attacked—I'm sorry, Mother," he acknowledged Frances' distress, "—I started to wonder. A small, spry man. Similar to the words the *Times* used about the man they saw running from the National Gallery the day the photographer was killed."

"There are small, spry men all over London," said the woman serving the tea. She was large, with a fascinating face. Round and a bit puffy, with wide-set eyes and a jaw so forceful it might have belonged to a man. Her wavy red hair was tied at the back with a ribbon. Jo wondered whether she'd be offended if she started sketching her.

The woman looked up, saw Jo looking at her, and smiled. It was not a particularly pleasant smile. Surely that color of hair came from henna, thought Jo uncharitably.

"Ah, Fanny," said Rossetti, following Jo's gaze. "Come over here, my darling one." He moved his chair back from the table and patted his thigh.

Fanny smoothed her dress and came around the table, keeping her eyes on Jo. Sitting in Rossetti's lap, she wrapped her arm around his neck.

"Fanny, meet Jo Harris. She's an artist for the magazines. Jo, this is Fanny Cornforth, my . . . housekeeper."

Fanny glared at her, and Jo struggled not to laugh. Housekeeper indeed.

"Nice to meet you," Jo said politely. "You two look beautiful together. Would it be all right if I made a sketch?" she shifted her sketchbook and pencil.

Fanny seemed mollified a bit.

"Of course!" said Rossetti. "Doesn't my girl have an incredible face? I've drawn her many times. Fascinating chin." He drew his finger tenderly along her jawline.

Frances, Rossetti's mother, asked, "Miss Harris, have you been to the Exhibition?"

"Yes, I've been twice already. But it's so hard to see everything."

Christina lit up. "Maybe you can go with Cecil Robson."

"No, thank you," said Jo. "I met him once. That's enough." Christina nodded as if that confirmed her feelings.

Out of the corner of her eye as she drew, Jo could see Fanny sizing her up, a look of increasing satisfaction on her face. Ah, thought Jo. She has guessed my predilections. Well at least it will keep her from being jealous of me and her man. She noticed Rossetti's hand was stroking Fanny's leg.

William glanced over with a look of displeasure.

"Perhaps Fanny could fetch us some more biscuits?" he said in a level voice.

Jo woke with the sun on Friday morning, determined to combine her day's work with interviews of at least one of the women in the photographs. Now that Bridget had more time during the day, she would visit the models furthest from Shoe Lane and Holborn: an M. F. in Spitalfields, and a P.I I. in Gouge Street. If they weren't home, she'd also try the B.N. in Kensington. She would use some of the money from the shop for cabs.

Jo would try to visit the one nearest her assignment in Camden. Her professional responsibility was to meet with the Dalziel Brothers about the engravings of her work on the Thames bridges. Only two had been published in *Once a Week*, and the others were wanted for a feature on engineering. Mrs. Ingram had spoken with her the previous day, explaining that getting to know the engravers would help ensure that they would be faithful to her work. But Jo knew this wasn't the case. Knowing the engravers was important to teach her how to cater to their particular style and skills.

Woodpeckers, as they were called on the street, could enhance or destroy an artist's drawings when they appeared in the press. But the Dalziel Brothers had an excellent reputation. They worked not only for *The Illustrated London News*, but for *Good Words* and *Punch*. They had also created book illustrations drawn by Holman Hunt and Millais. Rossetti had worked with them too a few years before, and he warned Jo.

"One might think that their role is to just copy what you draw, but they are more in the business of training you to draw like an engraver," he had grumbled.

Jo thought he was being too sensitive. Engraving couldn't be easy, making reversed wood images for printing.

At almost three miles away, it was too far to walk to Camden High Street and be able to visit anyone afterwards, so she took a cab. This will get expensive, she thought, as the cab cut through Bloomsbury on its way northwest. She didn't want to waste Bridget's money, so she resolved to pay the cab fare back home on her own.

She arrived at Camden Press in the High Street before nine, and asked for George Dalziel, as she had been told. Anne Ingram had also told her to be sure to pronounce it properly: Dee-ehl, rather than Dal-zeel. The clerk at the desk was young, but tired; he looked as if he had been awake for hours.

"I'm sorry, miss, but Mr. George isn't here at the moment. May I ask what this is regarding?"

"I'm Jo Harris, an illustrator for *The Illustrated London News*. Mrs. Ingram sent me."

"Yes, miss," said the clerk. "Please have a seat, and I'll be back in a moment." He went off behind the desk, down a hallway that turned to the left, but returned a moment later, before Jo had sat down.

"Miss Dalziel will see you now," he said, pointing down the hallway. "Third door on the left."

How curious. There were several "Brothers Dalziel," as they often styled themselves, so who was Miss Dalziel?

The office door was open. A lovely stout woman, her dark hair wrapped around her head, stood from behind the desk and reached her hand across to Jo.

"Good morning, Miss Harris," she said with a firm smile. "I'm Margaret Dalziel. Do sit down."

"Good morning, Miss Dalziel." Jo sat on the wooden chair. "Mrs. Ingram sent me, to look over the engravings of my Thames bridge pictures, and to learn how best to work with your engravers."

"Ah, yes, Anne mentioned you might be coming. Two of the lads downstairs, Jimmy and Frank, are working on your drawings. They told me they are quite suitable for engraving. Would you like to meet them?"

Jo agreed and spent the next hour with the engravers, asking questions, discussing shading, and learning how to improve her work. She also discovered that Margaret Dalziel was the sister of the more famous brothers, but that she did fine engravings in her own right, and had been doing so for years. Since the credit was always to the Dalziel Brothers, rather than individual members of the family, she was considered one of them.

Jo quite lost track of time, and it was after eleven by the time she emerged to find Camden Street and the model known only as "A.C."

The house in Camden Street was a Georgian row house, with an arched doorway and windows getting smaller as one ascended the three floors. A.C. was not, Jo mused, badly in need of money. Or was she? Appearances could be deceptive.

Jo and Bridget had not discussed how to ask after women whose names they didn't know. Jo looked around for a plate with a name, but this was clearly just a residence. Her knock was answered by a young woman who looked more like a maid-of-all-work than a parlor-maid.

"I'm sorry to disturb you," Jo said, glancing at her list, "but I'm afraid my notes have smudged. I'm here to see a woman with the initials A.C.?"

The maid's eyes narrowed. "And who might you be then?"

"I'm Jo Harris, from *The Illustrated London News*." She decided not to mention that she was only an artist.

The maid brightened considerably. "You've come to interview Miss Alice?" she asked with interest.

Jo thought quickly. "I have indeed. Is she available?"

"Wait here, please. I'll see if she's at home." She hurried toward the back of the house.

Jo closed the door behind her and stood in the small foyer. It was tiled in black and white, and the noonday sun came through the fanlight at the top of the door. There was a golden umbrella stand by the door that somehow managed to look cheap, and a vase of fading flowers on a table at the foot of the stairs. On the wall was a small framed poster announcing "Alice Carville as Lady Macbeth."

The woman who came out to her was in her mid-forties, with rich blonde hair and large blue eyes. Her wrapper was elegant, light blue and trimmed in lace, but it was clear she hadn't been expecting visitors. Her smile was friendly, and one eyebrow was arched in curiosity.

"Miss Harris. What an unexpected pleasure. How nice to meet you." She extended a plump pale hand to Jo.

"I apologize, Miss Carville, for calling upon you so early. I was around the corner at the Dalziel Brothers, and I suddenly recalled that you live here."

"Oh, yes, have done for years," Alice said breezily. "Do come in?" She gestured to the front parlor.

The room was papered in a design featuring pink flowers on a yellow ground. The settee and chair were upholstered in what must have been white and gold a number of years ago, but had since faded in the sun. Jo noticed that the carpet, though an elegant Persian blue, was a bit threadbare, but tried not to make her observation obvious. She sat on the settee and took her sketchbook from her bag.

"Patience said you had come to ask for an interview?" Alice said, touching her hair.

"I am an illustrator, rather than a reporter," Jo said, taking out her sketchbook. "Would it be possible for me to sketch you as we talk? I promise not to take up too much of your time."

She could tell by the expression on Alice's face that she had made the right choice to focus on drawing her. She looked pleased and sat up a bit straighter.

"Oh! Yes, of course. For *The Illustrated London News*, I hear?"

"That's one of the journals I work for, yes."

"And why did you come to me?" asked Alice, turning her best side toward Jo and smoothing her bodice. "I haven't been on the stage in almost four years."

"Well, you are still known, of course," said Jo, beginning to sketch the rounded profile, the sharp eyebrows, the generous mouth. She had never heard of Alice Carville and tried to be as vague as possible when she spoke. "But many wonder what artistic endeavors have been occupying you recently?"

"Well," Alice said, trying to move her mouth as little as possible, "I have been corresponding with a French company that may be staging a revival of *The Rivals*, which as you know I starred in a few years ago."

"Yes?" said Jo noncommittally, frowning as she drew so Miss Carville could see she was concentrating.

"And I have been working on a play of my own."

"Oh?"

"Yes, it's about a woman from a lower-class family who is led astray by a photographer."

Jo stopped with her pencil in the air.

"Oh! My goodness, Miss Carville. It's just occurred to me that I've seen you most recently in a photograph." She pretended to be embarrassed. "Although perhaps I should not say where I saw the photograph."

There was a pause.

"At *The Illustrated London News*?" Alice said stiffly.

"No, no, my goodness," said Jo, and kept sketching. "It was a lovely picture, just somewhat . . . familiar. Not for public view, certainly."

"How did you come by this picture?"

"It was in a batch with others of beautiful women. For the appreciation of men, I fancy. Not something I would share." She hoped she sounded trustworthy. "And not something I'd mention, except to you."

"I see," said Miss Carville, and Jo could see her shoulders relax a bit. She is deciding whether we are both women of the world, Jo thought.

"It is so easy for women to want to be photographed, don't you think?" Jo said airily, continuing her drawing. "It is a way of showing one's beauty forever, like a drawing,"

"That's true," said Alice cautiously. "You are likely too young, however, to understand that it might also be a way to suspend time."

Jo nodded. She was sketching rapidly now, wanting to show Miss Carville her good looks in a portrait. She felt sorry for her, a woman whose glories may have been in the past, but who retained a loveliness she wanted to shine through her picture.

"The photograph I saw was in a selection taken by Hugh Pratchett, if I recall correctly. Did he photograph many beautiful women, do you suppose?"

Alice's eyes narrowed. "Precisely why are you here, Miss Harris?"

"To draw you," said Jo, cautiously.

"Miss Harris, you come into my home uninvited, and now you talk about photographs and Hugh Pratchett. Pratchett was killed, as I'm sure you know. Are you somehow connected to the case?"

Jo lay down the sketchbook in her lap at an angle where Alice could see the sketch if she chose.

"Yes, I have a friend who worked for him. That's how I saw the photograph, and how I found you."

Alice nodded. Jo could see her vacillate between throwing her out or continuing the conversation.

"And what is your interest, exactly?" she asked coldly.

"I have two interests, as it happens," said Jo. "One is in finding out whether any of these women were forced to pose."

"I was not," said Alice firmly.

"And the other is to discover whether anyone who did pose hated Pratchett enough to hire someone to kill him."

Alice stared at Jo, then a chuckle started deep in her throat.

"My dear," she said with assurance, "I wanted the pictures taken. I wanted men to buy them and think me beautiful again. And if I did want to kill someone, I'm ashamed to say that I wouldn't have the money to pay someone to do it. I'd have to do it myself."

⁂

"I will no longer require your services," said the gentleman. The ripples of the Thames could be heard lapping against the warehouse. "You have brought me worthless pictures, killed a man unnecessarily, and botched an attack. I have no more use for you."

Will Carney felt his face go red. He had tried in good faith to do what he was told. But surely he had stolen the right photographs.

"Whatcha mean worthless pictures?" he demanded.

"They can make more," the gentleman said. "It's a kind of photograph where they can print more from the plate."

Will looked up, surprised and hurt. "Well, I wasn't to know that, was I? You told me to steal the photographs. And I did."

"You did," growled the gentleman. "And I paid you for them. But I will not pay the full amount for Morelli. He's back walking around. I wanted him disabled."

"Look, I don't know what this is all about. But I'm a good fixer and I won't have it on the street that I'm not. Killing the old man was an accident, but I couldn't let them find me trying to steal the painting. And I did damage Morelli. It's not my fault he's hearty."

This speech made Will a bit breathless. He didn't usually say so many words together. But, more than money, his reputation was at stake. There was silence for a bit. He could hear one of the piers creaking in the river.

"All right," said the gentleman. "I'll pay you, and I won't talk you down on the street. But only if you disable Morelli before he can get back to the National Gallery. And I mean disable permanently."

"Yes, sir." Will couldn't hide the tone of relief in his voice.

"He's at the Dulwich Gallery today. You can choose your time, but it must be before Monday morning."

Will nodded and turned to leave.

"And Mr. Carney?"

"Yes, sir?"

"We won't be meeting again."

Will was fine with that. Jobs like this weren't worth it.

Bridget planned to ask about her first quarry, an "M.F.," at the carts selling second-hand clothes. The woman's address was number 92 Whitechapel High Street, but she didn't want to just ring the bell and ask for someone she didn't know. Esther had seen her list of addresses and knew the neighborhood. She'd recommended going up Commercial Street to Wentworth Street first. Wentworth, also known at that end as Petticoat Lane, had many street merchants. Bridget could say she was collecting something for M.F. and see if anyone volunteered the name.

It had been a difficult morning. The first two Eastern Route omnibuses that had come through Fleet Street had been completely full, with people crowded on the top and no room inside. Bridget had finally been able to board one around half past ten. Then a cart had overturned at St Paul's Churchyard, blocking the road for half an hour until it was sorted out. She'd alighted at Whitechapel and gone up the street to Wentworth. The area was filled with people selling and shopping in a loud, seething mass. Not only were there stalls on the pavements and in the gutters, but some were right in the middle of the road. She discovered this as she tried to avoid a gutter stall and tripped on the legs of a trestle table with jars of honey and jam. Nothing was broken, thank goodness. No one noticed amid the hubbub.

Despite her concern, finding M. F. proved to be easy. The first stall she stopped at sold cotton lace. The proprietor was wearing a white apron and a cap trimmed with the lace she sold. The woman gave Bridget a big smile and asked if she could help, and Bridget decided not to bother pretending.

"Yes, please," shouted Bridget across the piles of lace, "I'm looking for a woman with the initials M. F.? She lives in Whitechapel High Street."

"A young woman?" the seller asked. Bridget nodded. "That would be Miriam Frankel, then. But she won't be at home." She pointed down the stalls. "Go that way, on the left. The stall with the trinkets and clocks."

Bridget thanked her and began to slowly make her way through the shoppers. Many were bargaining with the sellers, and it was easy to tell by the manner with which the vendors greeted each other that most were from the neighborhood. She heard many of them speaking in a language Esther had told her was Yiddish, a mix of German and Hebrew and other languages. But she also saw men shopping in formal coats and hats, bargaining in English. These must be buyers from West End shops, thought Bridget, looking for things they could sell at higher prices on the other side of London. At one point she almost bumped into two well-dressed ladies, their arms full of parcels. This was a place to buy things cheaply, without anyone in society knowing. Smart women bought undergarments, petticoats, and lace here rather than in West End shops.

A man bumped into her, apologizing with a mumbled *"antshuldig."* She felt a pang of recognition, and realized she was homesick for Wales. Of all things, she thought, in this noisy and gray part of London, to be missing home. It was the double language, the mix of English and a tongue that was native to the people who lived here. A culture of its own, British and yet not British, where the streets smelled and sounded different. It was the way the people greeted each other, people who saw each other every day, and knew not only names but families and histories. As she passed through, she saw mothers scolding children, old friends embracing, loud and vehement arguing. So many other places in London people now walked with a look of determination, moving onward on their own business, speaking only to the person they were with. One heard the noises of conversation in public places like the omnibus, but only of pairs or groups of three together, not speaking to the other groups. Here the conversation seemed to include everyone.

The stall had trestle tables under a canvas awning, protecting the small clocks, cut-glass dishes, miniature picture frames, and silver-plated snuff boxes. Bridget recognized Miriam immediately from the photograph: heart-shaped face, bow mouth, large brown eyes, curly dark hair. She was standing next to a young man wearing a tweed cap. He was probably her husband.

"Hello," Bridget said, leaning over the trestle. "My name is Bridget Williams. I'm wondering could I speak with you for a moment, where it's quieter?"

Miriam frowned, but nodded to her husband and came out from behind the table.

"It's a little quieter over here," she said, pointing to the front of a shop showing paintings in the window. She stepped under the awning and Bridget joined her. "Have you bought something from me before?" asked Miriam.

"No. I apologize for bothering you," said Bridget. Now that she'd found her, she wasn't sure how to begin. "I've come because I was employed by Hugh Pratchett as his assistant."

Miriam blanched at the name, and Bridget glanced back, glad to see that her young man was busy at the stall showing a wooden clock to an older man with a beard.

"He died, didn't he?" said Miriam in a hushed voice.

"Yes, he was killed. I'm trying to discover why. I found your photograph in a locked drawer."

Miriam's large brown eyes glanced back at the stall then looked into Bridget's with a plea. "You mustn't tell Jacob," she said.

"I won't," Bridget promised. Miriam's eyes started to glisten with tears.

"I did it so we would have the money to get married," she said, and lowered her eyes to stare at her boots.

"You're recently married?" Miriam would not have been married when the photographs were taken, yet she was still M.F.

"Yes. We're cousins, but the family wanted to make sure we could manage on our own."

"It's all right," said Bridget. "I won't tell your husband. But I need to ask a few questions. Is that all right?"

Miriam nodded.

"Did Mr. Pratchett force you to have the pictures taken?" Miriam shook her head.

"Did he say anything about who was buying them from him? Or mention any particular customer?" Miriam shook her head again.

"Did anyone contact you about the picture after you had it taken?" Another shake.

"Did you pose for more than the one photograph?"

Miriam nodded. "I posed for several. He said it was needed because each one makes only a single print."

Bridget wasn't sure what other questions she should ask. Then something occurred to her.

"You live a long way from Pratchett's studio," she said. "How did you find out about him, that he could take this kind of photograph of you?"

Miriam thought a moment. "Jacob's landlady told me," she said. "She said another woman had told her she could make money that way if she needed to. It was someone who used to live in the house."

"Is it all right if I go talk to her?" Bridget asked, excited. Finally, a clue. "May I tell her I have your permission to ask?"

Miriam looked down at her boots again. Bridget noticed the boots were worn, but of good quality. Whatever money this woman had earned, she had not squandered it.

"Yes. She told me she wouldn't tell anyone." She reached down and took a pot metal pin off her apron. "Her name is Mrs. Gretz. Give her this, and she'll know it's me that sent you."

When Bridget knocked on the door next to the shop at 92 Whitechapel High Street, the woman who opened it did not look happy. Bridget heard a child's shriek from inside. "Yes?" she asked, glancing back and saying, "sha sha sha" to the child.

"I'm sorry to bother you. Are you Mrs. Gretz?"

"Yeah, I'm her."

"I've been speaking with Miriam Frankel in Wentworth Street." She held out the pin. "May I speak with you for a moment?"

Mrs. Gretz took the pin with a raised eyebrow.

"You may, but not for too long, mind." She stepped back to let Bridget into the narrow hall. There was a strong smell of frying onions. A little girl of about five, with ringlets of dirty blonde hair down to her shoulders, looked up at her with red eyes. "Upstairs, then to the right," said Mrs. Gretz, picking up the child and brushing her hair back.

The room was cleaner than Bridget expected, and she sat down near the fireplace. Mrs. Gretz sat on the faded couch, lifting the girl up to sit in her lap. The child put a thumb in her mouth and turned her face into the woman's chest, sniffing.

"Don't mind her," said Mrs. Gretz. "She doesn't want her hair washed, and she knows she must. It's Friday," she said, as if that explained everything.

"Of course," said Bridget with what she hoped was sympathy. "I need to ask about a recommendation you gave to Miriam." She glanced at the child, unsure how to continue in her presence. "About having a photograph done by a Mr. Pratchett."

Mrs. Gretz nodded slowly. "What about it?" There was a thundering sound on the stairs, and two small boys skidded into the room, one tow-headed and slender, the other dark and chubby. They caught sight of Bridget and ran back down the stairs.

Mrs. Gretz shoved the girl next to her on the sofa, stood, and hollered after them. "Get in the kitchen, you two! Help Margie finish up the cooking!" She sat down again, and the child crawled back in her lap. "You was saying?"

"Well," Bridget said, "I worked for Hugh Pratchett before he—passed. Apparently Miriam sought him out based on your information about him." Keep it general, Bridget thought.

"Yes," Mrs. Gretz said. "She needed some money. That husband of hers, Jacob. Sweet, sweet man but not a brain in his head." Her head tilted as if to imply Bridget would know the type.

"How did you know about Mr. Pratchett? To send Miriam to him for that—type of photograph?"

"Say, what's your interest in this?" said Mrs. Gretz, narrowing her eyes. "Are you one of them reformers? You ain't dressed like one of them reformers," she said, taking in Bridget's plain blue work dress.

"Mr. Pratchett's passing left some questions," said Bridget. "The police aren't being very helpful."

Mrs. Gretz nodded. Unhelpful policemen were something she understood.

Bridget continued. "I am trying to discover who knew about what he was doing. It appears as though there might be more than one person involved in his—departure."

Mrs. Gretz smiled wryly. "Don't concern yourself about your words in front of this one," she said, squeezing the child to her. "She's heard everything, she has, living here."

Bridget smiled back and waited.

"Let me think. It was a woman who lived here, Ruthie her name was. Said she'd heard about Pratchett from a young man at the university. Some arty type. Not sure I can remember his name . . ."

She looked up at the peeling plaster on the ceiling. "Perry? Parker? Something like that. Short surname, that's all I remember."

"Is Ruthie still living here?"

"Oh no, dear, she died. Smallpox." She smiled at the child. "Not this one. I had her vaccinated. Not like some round here."

The smell was changing to burnt onions.

Bridget rose to go. "Thank you for your help, Mrs. Gretz. I do appreciate it."

"Glad to do it, if Miriam wanted it. She's such a help to me here."

Bridget opened the door and was just about to step out into the street, when Mrs. Gretz suddenly said, "Percy! That's it. His name was Percy. Percy Fry."

Constable Moberly, in plain clothes, accompanied Giovanni Morelli to the Dulwich Picture Gallery that Saturday. Although his head was still sore, Morelli declared himself much improved and wished to get back to work.

"But today I look for pleasure, Constable Moberly, *il piacere*," said Morelli as they traveled in a cab. He winced as they hit a bump. "Do you enjoy art?"

Moberly thought for a moment. He enjoyed beauty, especially landscapes that reminded him of the countryside. He'd come to the city from Garsdale when he was a much younger man, and he missed Yorkshire, the green hills, the silence, the weather you could see coming. He liked paintings with trees, meadows, grass, and quiet light. What he didn't like were Bible story paintings. He felt they were just excuses to show crime and violence, while claiming to be portraying something spiritual.

The day was blustery and cold, and Moberly missed his wool uniform with its blessedly high collar. Morelli shivered and adjusted his scarf. "We will go inside directly," he said. "The gallery will be warm."

"When we get inside, sir, I want to have a word with the guards."

"Why?" asked Morelli.

"I want to ask them to keep watch on you, to be alert to anything unusual."

"You think that man would attack me here?" he waved his hand at the imposing building.

"It's possible, sir. Please, just wait near the cloakroom while I speak with one of them and ask to see the Curator."

"Mr. Denning sees no one, not even me. And I've never seen more than two guards here. I'm sure I'll be quite all right."

"Indeed, sir."

"I'll wait by the cloakroom." Morelli said, shaking his head.

Moberly had just finished talking to the two guards when he saw Jo Harris enter the building. He came up to her, keeping an eye on Morelli.

"You come here to work, Miss Harris?" he asked her.

"I do," said Jo with some pride, "I am assigned to sketch the portrait of Ozias Linley, for *The Illustrated London News*. They're doing a story on the Linley Bequest to the gallery, about 25 years ago."

Moberly knew nothing of Linley or bequests, but he knew *The Illustrated London News*.

"Well done, Miss Harris," he said. "How is your friend, Miss Williams?"

Jo couldn't help but notice the fatherly tone. "Bridget is doing well, Constable. She's considering opening a bakery."

"Ah," said Moberly, looking around.

Jo smiled. "But why are you here, Constable Moberly?"

"Guard duty," he said, nodding toward Morelli.

She saw the bandage peeking out from below the brim of Morelli's hat. "Oh, is that poor Mr. Morelli? Do you think he'll be attacked again?"

"I think it quite likely, miss. I think all this is tied together: the art, the photographer, and the attack on Morelli. So you stay back from him, miss. Just in case."

"Thank you, Constable." Usually, Jo would have ignored the advice, and stayed closer than she should just to see what happened. But the portrait of Linley was in another room. She was an employed artist now, not a piece worker with time to waste. She bid him good day.

Morelli and Moberly began perambulating. Moberly felt somewhat naked wearing his daily clothes. He'd replaced his truncheon with a blackthorn walking stick, but he was painfully aware that he was untrained in stick fighting and would be at a disadvantage against a gentleman who had leisure time to indulge in hobbies of self-defense. Luckily, he thought, there was no sign that this small, spry man was a gentleman. Since it behooved him to be cautious, he had spent the previous night practicing a few moves from a book Constable Brennan had given him. It was written by someone named Larribeau, and it was in French. But the drawings in the back were useful. They showed two men, fencing with canes, the paths of the moves mapped with dotted lines. Moberly hoped it wouldn't come to that.

Morelli glanced over at Moberly with a twinkle in his eyes and whispered, "If you are trying a disguise, you should use your walking stick to help you walk." He was ignored.

Morelli could never resist an audience, however, and this one couldn't get away. They looked together at several paintings, with Morelli talking expansively about each one, but Moberly wasn't paying attention to the art.

"Ah," said Morelli, as they approached *Madonna and Child with St John*. "This is supposed to be a Carracci. Isn't it lovely? The Madonna's rounded arms, the babies' rounded legs. Her face is rounded, her hair, the children's hair, everything. Even her shoulder. So beautiful. But"—he held his palms up— "a copy. Over a century after the original, and on copper."

He peered more closely as he continued. "You can see it isn't a Carracci. Look at the ear on St. John."

"I have heard of Carracci," said Moberly, scanning the room. "Did a lot, didn't he?"

"Sí. But there is more than one Carracci," said Morelli. "This is a copy of an Annibale Carracci. He worked with his brother Agostino and his cousin Ludovico. There are several paintings by Ludovico at the National Gallery."

Moberly nodded absently. Morelli was still looking at the painting.

"I think," he said, "that I would like to offer to buy this painting. To add to my collection."

"You're a collector, too?" Moberly asked.

"I am everything. Art critic, intellectual, Senator, collector. I even trained as a doctor and have taught anatomy. Come, let us find the mysterious Mr. Denning. I want to buy this painting." He began to move toward the stairs.

"I don't think that's a good idea, Mr. Morelli. Perhaps another day."

Morelli looked at Constable Moberly and felt sorry for him. Poor man, not in his uniform and having to protect him. Protect him, he who had manned the barricades in Milan in '48.

"*Bene, bene,*" said Morelli. "Not today. Could we step outside, do you think? I would like to smoke my pipe for a bit. There is a nice garden, with perhaps some shelter from the cold."

Moberly nodded. They collected their coats and walked out through the front door, turning right into the gallery garden. Later, the constable would report that he first saw the man out of the corner of his eye, waiting around the corner of the building. The man had stopped like he'd dropped something, looking back to see whether one of the guards was nearby. Morelli stopped too, and the man jumped out at him. He was holding a shillelagh above his head to strike Morelli. Moberly raised his stick and hit the man just before he could, and the small, spry man crumpled to the ground. Morelli himself had only just turned, his arm over his head for protection.

Moberly took out his whistle and blew it, and one of the guards came running out the door.

"He's the one," said Moberly to the guard, handing over the handcuffs he pulled from his pocket. "Are you all right, Mr. Morelli?"

Morelli had gone completely white. He swallowed slowly. "Yes, Constable, I am all right. *Grazie.*" At least at the barricades in Milan, you knew where the enemy was.

Jo was unable to visit any of the remaining photography models, but she knew Bridget had planned to talk to the last three: a P.S. in Salisbury Court, an M.D. in Hanging Sword Alley, and a B.T. in Camden Street. Jo put her apron over her clothes when she arrived at the boarding house that evening, marveling at how well the brown duck sleeves at the studio protected her dress. Bank clerks and others in the ink trade wore such things, of course, and Jo was proud to have something like a uniform when she worked at the offices of the magazine. But when she came downstairs, it was just Bridget and Mrs. Bagley at the table.

"Where is everybody?" asked Jo.

Mrs. Bagley shrugged. "They're still at work. Saturday is heavy for everyone. Bridget made cold supper, so we can keep it for them. But you must be hungry," she said, handing Jo a plate. "I must be off to the market to do the shopping." Most working people were paid Saturday night, so the markets with the cheapest goods were open Saturday evenings. Mrs. Bagley wanted the best deal on everything. Jo sat down with Bridget.

"I'm sorry I wasn't able to visit any more of the models. I did send a note to Tommy Jones, and P.H. is definitely Prudence Henderson, because Tommy says she lives in Gough Street."

"Gough Street? Near Coldbath Fields prison?"

"I assume so. I suppose we can talk with her later."

"That's fine," said Bridget. "I was able to discover the last three, and two are fairly near here."

"Oh, good." Jo took a bit of cold ham and some pickle. "What have you found?"

Bridget had her notes spread out on the table.

"Patricia Samuels is the young wife of a bank clerk who doesn't make much money. She was horrified at the idea that her husband might find out, but I reassured her. Maureen Douglas is a Scots woman who cleans houses near Fleet Street, and Beatrice

Thompson works at a tobacco shop in Camden. All of them posed for the money."

"Did you find out where they discovered that Pratchett took such pictures?" Jo tore a slice of bread off the loaf. Goodness, Bridget made good bread.

"Mrs. Samuels said she heard through a woman she met in the market, but she didn't know her name. Mrs. Douglas heard about it through a friend who also cleans houses, and Miss Thompson overheard it from one of her customers."

"Not much help there."

"No, it isn't."

Jo sighed, discouraged. "I'm not seeing signs of some sort of pornography ring, even if some of the photographs did end up on Holywell Street."

"Neither am I. No one has mentioned being contacted or harassed by anyone."

"I have not yet spoken to Rossetti about the fact that he's on the list of customers," admitted Jo.

"You have a soft spot for that man, Jo," said Bridget, "and that's a fact."

"It's true. But we have not yet visited the model we know to be Lady Millicent. And we must pursue our other line of inquiry."

Bridget raised a brow.

"The paintings. The gallery. We must go back and take a look."

"But tomorrow's Sunday. Both the National Gallery and the Royal Academy Exhibition are closed."

Jo just smiled.

9

Bridget had brought the key from the tin box, and they were able to enter the National Gallery through the side door. It was a sunny afternoon, and the galleries were well-lit through the skylights. The varnish on the paintings seemed to glow, and the gilt frames looked even more gold than usual.

"I'm glad no one has asked for the key back yet," Jo said quietly. The hush in the gallery was palpable, but she was listening for guards.

"Me too," said Bridget, "but I feel like we shouldn't be in here."

"Don't be silly," said Jo, "You own the shop now. You're just trying to finish the job given to Mr. Pratchett." Her satchel clunked against her thigh. She had offered to carry three photographic plates in her bag. That was all that would fit.

"Then why didn't we just ask Sir Charles if it was all right to be here?" said Bridget, shifting the heavy camera to the other shoulder.

"Because, as I read in a book on Mary of Modena, it is easier to ask forgiveness once a deed is done, than to ask for permission doing it."

Bridget looked perplexed.

"Because he might have said no," said Jo. "You aren't a member of the Photographic Society. He didn't hire you. This way, we can say that we thought it was all right, to finish up Pratchett's work. Then we apologize."

"Where should I put the camera?"

"Let's lean it here, next to the vestibule. Then we can look on either side. With our notebooks, we shouldn't look too suspicious."

First, they walked down the galleries of the Exhibition, Jo leading the way. When they got to the closet where Pratchett had been found, she opened the door.

"He was here," she told Bridget. "He fell out when someone opened the door." Now there were only brooms and a ladder, some wire, and tools. Bridget shivered.

"All right," said Bridget, "He was here on Sunday, a fortnight ago. I was with him. When I left, he was way over there." She pointed back toward the room nearest the vestibule. "He was walking with the list, checking what we'd photographed already and what we still needed to do. He told me he'd see me Monday. I went out through the Exhibition." She pointed toward the far door.

The women went through the archway into the vestibule.

"Would he have gone into the National Gallery wing?" asked Jo.

"Could have done," said Bridget. "In fact, I'm sure he did. We'd finished most of the Exhibition pictures. He wanted to see how high up the remaining gallery paintings were."

They crossed into the National Gallery wing and began to wander down the center.

"Do you know which paintings?" Jo asked.

Bridget bit her lip. "I don't remember them all. Mr. Pratchett had the list."

"The police must have it now, then. Do you remember any?"

Bridget squeezed her eyes shut, a trick she used for remembering things. "Yes, I remember one had a couple, a man and a woman, holding hands, with a mirror in between them and a brown dog at their feet. I think it's in the next room."

"*The Arnolfini Portrait*. Van Eyck," said Jo. They walked over and stood in front of it.

"What are we looking for?" said Bridget.

"I'm not sure," said Jo. The painting was hung fairly low. Jo walked up and looked at the frame, then down at the ground, then stepped back to where Bridget was. "What else?"

"There was one with a lovely white sailing ship being tugged by an ugly steamboat."

"The Fighting Temeraire. Turner. One of my favorites." She knew where it was. Again she looked at the frame, the picture, and the carpet. "What else?"

"One of a half-naked woman getting unwanted attention from two men," said Bridget.

"Carracci," said Jo. *"Susannah and the Elders."*

"That's a Bible story, isn't it?"

"It is." She knew where this was also, in the next room. She looked at the painting and the frame. Then she looked at the carpet. "What's this, do you think?"

Bridget came over to look. "Paint?"

"In here? This isn't the Exhibition. No painters are in here touching this up. This work is from the early seventeenth century."

They looked around. Nothing of that color was painted nearby.

"Is it brown?" asked Bridget.

"Yes. It looks like it doesn't belong."

The women looked at each other. "Blood?" asked Bridget.

"It's possible," said Jo. "The police must have not seen it here."

"Why would they come in here?" asked Bridget. "The body was way back there, in the Exhibition."

"I'm going to see if I can collect some," said Jo. She took out a hairpin and a handkerchief. Carefully scraping the carpet with the hairpin, she collected quite a few flakes.

"Is that enough?" she asked Bridget.

"For what?"

"For a microscope." Bridget shrugged. Big lenses she knew, not small lenses.

Once they were outside, the door safely relocked, they carried the camera out into Trafalgar Square. "Might as well," said Bridget. "We've got the plates." She set up the camera, looking up at the angle of the light.

"If Mr. Pratchett were killed in front of the Carracci, why was he found in a closet halfway across the Exhibition?" asked Jo. The day was getting warm, and it was nice to stand here in the square, despite the traffic. St Martin-in-the-Fields glowed white and lovely on their left, and they could see the Elizabeth Tower peeking over the rooftops of Whitehall.

"The only place to hide him?"

"No, there was an identical closet in the National Gallery wing. Didn't you see it?"

"Maybe he was dragged?" Bridget had been reading penny dreadfuls again, thought Jo. But in this case that might not be a bad thing.

"If he were dragged, it would be impossible to tell. On Monday, both wings were full of people trampling the carpet. I was one of them," said Jo.

"Maybe he caught the murderer doing something with the painting?"

"Like what? Trying to damage it? Or steal it?"

Bridget shrugged, waiting for the right moment. Then she removed the lens cap for what seemed to Jo like a split-second, then replaced it. "That should be about right."

"Do you want another plate?" asked Jo, reaching into her bag.

"No, I need to save them in case I really do want to finish Pratchett's commission." She folded up the camera legs, then checked her pocket for coins so they could get a cab back to Theobalds Road.

"Excellent job, Constable Moberly," said Detective Inspector Harkness, the relief barely concealed on his face. "I will discover the trial dates for Mr. Carney and will let you know when you'll need to testify."

"Yes, sir," said Moberly.

"I regret to tell you, however, that you've been called back to Piccadilly now that the Pratchett case is solved. I shall miss your good sense, to be honest." Harkness did not often give words of appreciation, but he was feeling particularly generous.

"Thank you, sir. I would like to inform Miss Williams and Miss Harris that the villain is apprehended, sir. I think they might sleep better at night."

"Of course." Having used his allotment of goodwill for one day, Harkness waved him off and returned to the papers on his desk.

Moberly stepped out of Scotland Yard and crossed over toward Whitehall. The day had dawned bright and the light breeze was warm, and he decided a walk to Theobalds Road would be a fine idea. Walking through Trafalgar Square, he thought about the lions that were promised but weren't there yet. Artists were interesting people, he thought. Heads in the clouds, never ready to get down to business. Except that Miss Harris, though. She seemed to have good sense.

He passed the Friends Meeting House and, as always, thought of his sister. She had joined the Quakers after her husband Jemmy had died in India. The Sepoy Mutiny had taken his life when the rebels attacked unexpectedly in Meerut. Jemmy had only been a junior officer then, in the East India Company. Gertrude's response had at first seemed like mourning for her lost husband, but gradually she developed views against war and violence and joined the Quakers. She had been much happier after that.

The heavy traffic on Long Acre had Moberly regretting he hadn't taken a cab, although he knew he would have just been stuck sitting in it instead of walking. He began taking side streets and arrived at the boarding house by eleven.

Mrs. Bagley told him that both Miss Harris and Miss Williams had already left for work, so he continued on to Theobalds Road. Miss Williams was the one he'd been concerned about. She answered his knock on the covered window of the photography studio and let him in with a wary smile.

"Constable Moberly," she said. "How nice to see you." She did look pleased, but he sensed reticence.

"Thank you, miss." The morning light was coming in dimly through the fabric covering the windows. He noticed the crates on the floor in the shop. "Are you packing?"

"Yes," said Bridget. "I've decided not to keep this as a photography shop. I want to open a bakery." She looked a little hesitant, but determined. Moberly had seen that look before, on his own daughter.

"A bakery? What about the ovens?"

"There is room under the shop. If I can get enough money for these cameras and devices, I can put in ovens. I don't need anything large. I will specialize in pastry and cakes."

Moberly nodded, thinking about the kind of shops available in the road. "That should do well here." He took a seat by the counter. "I've come to tell you we've captured the man who locked you in the dark-room, killed Mr. Pratchett, and attacked Mr. Morelli."

"Oh!" exclaimed Bridget. "That's wonderful. Who is he?"

"A canny dodger named Will Carney. Lives near the docks. We caught him trying to attack Morelli again at the Dulwich Picture Gallery."

"Why did he do it?"

"Do what, miss?"

"All these crimes?"

"We don't know. That's for the barristers and court to determine. But we have the right man, based on all the descriptions. You may need to testify, but I'm not sure yet. So may the girls down at the hat shop."

"I didn't see anything, as you know, but I can tell the story to the judge," said Bridget. She paused, picking up a stereoscope and placing it in the crate. "At any rate, I'm glad it's all over." She still looked uncomfortable.

"I am too, miss. So I'll be back at Piccadilly Station now if you need anything." He rose to leave, but she clearly wasn't ready for him to go.

"I must admit I'm perplexed, Constable. What would this man hope to achieve with what he was doing? Why did he steal the photographs? And attack an art expert?"

Moberly shook his head and held up his hands. "The criminal mind," he said, "is often beyond me. We usually don't know why criminals do things, why they steal or kill. Some people are just touched in the head. They don't know why themselves."

"Did this man—Carney, did you say?—seem touched in the head?"

"I can't say he did, miss. Seemed like an ordinary criminal to me. A bit cannier than most, even."

"Then he must have had a reason."

Moberly nodded. "I agree, but there's no use worrying about it now, is there?"

Bridget looked at the floor for a moment, biting her lip. Then she took a quick breath. "We found something, Constable."

He rose an eyebrow. "Who found something?"

"Jo and I. We, well, we—" she stopped. She'd done something she shouldn't, but it might be important.

"What have you found, miss? Something I'd need to report?"

"I hope not," she said. She glanced toward the door, took out her handkerchief and twisted it between her fingers. "Oh, I was so wishing Jo would be with me when we saw you again. We were going to come by Scotland Yard this afternoon to find you. You see—"

Moberly used his most soothing voice. "It's all right, Miss Williams. What did you find?"

"Something. Near one of the paintings in the National Gallery. It could just be paint. But it could be blood, so we might have more to think about. About Pratchett's murder." She looked at him, her eyes clear, almost defiant.

Moberly felt pity for her. The case was over, and he was sure she'd be safe now, that Carney would go away for a long time. She was worrying herself over something she found in the gallery, likely when she wasn't supposed to be there. Surely it would have nothing to do with the case; after all, the body was found in the Royal Academy Exhibition, not the National Gallery. It was her friend Jo, he thought. That artistic, insightful mind. He admired it, but such minds could stir up trouble in impressionable young women. His impulse was to protect Bridget.

"It will be all right, miss," he said kindly. "If there's anything to be learned, it will come up in court. There's no need for you and Miss Harris to take your time uncovering puzzles that aren't even there. This man was seen by enough people that I'm sure he'll be going to prison for a long, long time."

Bridget stared at him. He saw her eyes narrow, as if she were deciding something. Then she smiled, that sweet smile that lit up her face.

"I'm sure you're right, Constable." She walked to the door and opened it for him. "Do say hello to Mrs. Randolph for me."

Jo left *The Illustrated London News* studio just before lunch time, the handkerchief with the blood (or was it paint?) safely in her bag. She had sent a note to the Slaughters' house the previous evening, asking Tommy and Samson to meet her if they could and she'd buy them a coffee at George's Coffee House in the Strand. Sure enough, they were waiting for her there.

Dinner the previous night at the boarding house had been lively. Monday night was mutton night, and the meaty smell filled the kitchen. Bridget had prepared Yorkshire puddings with gravy, and fresh spring peas were served alongside. Bridget told the women what Constable Moberly had told her: a man named Carney had been caught, and he was surely the man who had locked her in, had killed Mr. Pratchett, and had attacked Mr. Morelli.

"I don't understand," said Esther. "Why did this man Carney do all this?"

"That's what I asked Constable Moberly," said Bridget. "He said we cannot know the criminal mind, and it will all come out in court."

There was much scoffing and shaking of heads.

"I thought you said he was a good man, this constable," said Mrs. Bagley.

"He is," said Jo, "but he's a policeman. The man who did the crimes has been found, so the case is closed."

"Well, isn't it?" said Annie. The other women groaned.

"No, it isn't. We need answers!" said Esther. She turned to Jo. "Did you ask him about the photographs of the women?"

"No," said Bridget. "He was so sure the case was over. I didn't see any point. They won't be investigating any further."

There was silence at the table, just the sounds of water pouring into glasses and knives cutting mutton.

"However," said Jo. "Bridget and I did find something yesterday at the National Gallery."

"The gallery's closed on Sunday," explained Bridget, "but I still have a key. So we didn't reveal ourselves, but we went to look near all the paintings we still needed to photograph. Mr. Pratchett was taking a survey of all the ones we needed when I left him that Sunday he was killed."

"And," said Jo, "we found something in front of one of the paintings. Carracci's *Susannah and the Elders.*"

"What's that a picture of?" asked Annie.

"It's the story from the Bible," Jo said. "It's a tale attached to the Book of Daniel. A young woman named Susannah is bathing and watched by two lustful men. They waylay her on her way home, telling her they'll ruin her reputation by saying she was meeting a man, unless she has carnal relations with them."

"With both of them?" Annie asked, her eyes widening.

"Yes," said Jo. "She refuses and is arrested, but when the two men are questioned separately they differ in their reports of what kind of tree she was under when meeting this man. The false accusers are put to death. It's been the subject of a great many paintings."

Heads turned toward Esther, but she shook her head. "Don't ask me," she said, waving her hand. "It isn't a story with which I'm familiar. David spied on Bathsheba while she was bathing, but that turned out differently."

"I assume it's a popular subject in art so men can draw a naked woman with two men slavering over her," grumbled Annie. There was general agreement around the table.

"I assume the men are drawn as horrid creatures?" asked Esther.

"Yes, they are usually unattractive," said Jo. "Not exactly drooling, but certainly portrayed as unpleasantly lecherous."

"That's so the viewer can feel virtuous ogling her instead," said Esther in a sardonic tone. Jo had to admit she had a point. The paintings of Susanna and the Elders had always annoyed her.

"What did you find near the painting?" asked Mrs. Bagley.

"A substance on the carpet," said Bridget. "Could be paint or some kind of brown varnish. But it could be blood. Jo has a friend who studies science. We're going to see whether he can tell by putting the flakes under a microscope."

So Jo had sent the note to Southwark the next morning, and now she, Tommy, and Samson were at George's Coffee House.

"May I really order coffee?" asked Tommy, looking around at the smartly dressed working people. They were able to sit down and talk, not just order from a cart on the street.

"Yes," said Jo. "It's my treat. I need a favor of you two." She explained her concerns about the arrest of Mr. Carney being the end of the case for the police, and the substance she and Bridget had found in the National Gallery.

"So, I wanted to ask if you have access to a microscope, and could tell us whether this is blood," she said, taking out the handkerchief.

Tommy and Samson were just peering at the brown specks when the coffee arrived at the table, along with three biscuits.

"I do have a friend who will let me in to the laboratory at the Royal School of Mines," Samson said. "If we don't interrupt any classes, we can go there."

Jo was delighted and happily paid for their coffees, giving Samson the handkerchief. Tommy and Samson set off for Jermyn Street to use the microscope.

Lady Millicent Stroud's house in Grosvenor Square was enormous. Jo and Bridget stood outside for a moment, just looking up at it, before they knocked at the door. The day had been sunny and very bright, and when the butler opened the door, they were unable to see much inside.

"May I help you?" he asked. He was not a tall man, and his graying hair was pomaded back over his ears. His accent was Welsh, which made Bridget smile.

"Yes, please," said Jo, proffering her card. "We would like to see Lady Millicent, if she is at home." It was the correct time for calling, she knew. Bridget had thought they should go to the back door and talk to the servants, saying that Bridget had come to collect the money for the photographs. But Jo insisted they come to the front door as equals and see Lady Millicent directly.

"But we're not equals," Bridget had protested. "She's titled."

Jo had shrugged. "We all make our living our own way," she'd said.

The butler peered at the card, glanced at their attire, then said, "Lady Millicent is with a caller. May I ask you to wait in here, please?" He motioned to the front parlor.

The room was extravagantly decorated. The carpet was a rich burgundy color, and the chintz settee covered in a diamond gold pattern. There was a handsome spinet against the wall, and above it a portrait of an expansive man in his forties.

"Perhaps that is Lord Stroud?" Bridget whispered to Jo. Jo shrugged again.

A round table with marquetry, polished to a shine, displayed a stereoscope with a stack of viewing cards, a box of small ivory carvings, and several small photographs in frames.

The door to the hall had been left open, and they saw a small woman in a large crinoline pass by on her way to the front door. This must have been Lady Millicent's caller. They heard a tea tray rattle down the hall, and then the butler appeared at the door of the parlor.

"You may go up now," he said, gesturing to the staircase. "The withdrawing room is to the left, at the top of the stairs."

That was odd, thought Jo. Usually women at home met their callers on the ground floor. As she admired the paintings hung along the staircase as they ascended, it occurred to Jo that this is what Lady Millicent wanted. This way visitors would get a look at the vast hall and sweeping staircase covered in oriental carpet with fashionable brass stair rods holding it in place. Jo had to admit the place was impressive, if a bit tawdry.

Lady Millicent Stroud was sitting on a chair facing the settee, her back to the fireplace.

"Miss Harris," she said, rising and extending her hand. "How are things at the Women's Reform Club? I'm afraid I have not attended lately." She turned toward Bridget, and her eyes opened in surprise.

"You're the young woman from the photography shop," she said in a tone that said she wasn't at all pleased.

"Lady Millicent," said Jo. "This is my friend Bridget Williams. And it is about photography that we have come."

Lady Millicent drew back a bit. One did not come with a topic during calling hours. One came to sit and look at the furnishings out of the corner of one's eye, exchanging meaningless pleasantries before descending into polite but vicious gossip. She motioned to the settee, then took the taller chair nearby for herself.

Jo looked at Lady Millicent. She had only met her a few times at the Club and had never seen her in her own home. Her face was most expressive, and she could see hardship in the lines of her mouth below the haughtiness. An interesting subject. Perhaps there was a way to establish common ground.

"I have brought your bill for the photograph," said Bridget, reaching into her reticule. "Mr. Pratchett left the shop to me, and . . ." Jo gently stopped her with a hand on her wrist.

"No need for that now," she said. "Lady Millicent, we fear that you may be deeply concerned in a serious business."

Lady Millicent's expression became wary. "Me? Whatever do you mean?"

"We are interested in the events surrounding the murder of Mr. Hugh Pratchett."

"Events surrounding?" Lady Millicent's eyes grew wide, but then she shook her head. "Have you not heard? They caught the criminal, the one who killed him and attacked that art critic. I read it in the paper this morning."

"Yes, but there remain some very disturbing factors in the case," said Jo. She searched Lady Millicent's face, seeking a way to establish a connection between them. "Factors related to the treatment of women."

"I am very concerned about the treatment of women, as you know." Lady Millicent sat up straighter. "Which women are we talking about?"

"Women who are taken advantage of by men," said Jo. "Men who want to gratify their base instincts, even if only with a photograph."

There was a silence. Jo handed over the photograph of the older woman with hair down her back, her thighs exposed.

Lady Millicent looked at the picture, her face expressionless. Jo could see wheels turning as she decided what to do. Then her eyes crinkled, and she started to laugh, a charming tinkling sound.

"I do look rather fetching, don't I?" She laughed again, and little tears began in the corners of her eyes. There was a sound at the door of the room. The butler had arrived, looking concerned.

"Is everything all right, madam?" he asked.

Lady Millicent hiccupped. "Yes, Stromond. Just a small amusement. Would you bring us some tea, please?"

For a split second Stromond looked confused. Lady Millicent did not serve tea to two callers in a row. She also did not serve tea to women dressed like this. And he'd never heard her laugh. He went to fetch the tea trolley.

Lady Millicent wiped her eyes and handed the photograph back to Jo.

"I'm not paying for that one," she said to Bridget with a chuckle. Bridget blushed.

"Very well, Miss Harris. Obviously, I was not the only one who posed for such pictures. May I assume from your concern that the others were in less advantageous circumstances?"

"We believe so," said Jo. She had not expected Lady Millicent's reaction and was unsure how to proceed.

"And that all this has something to do with Pratchett's death?"

"Yes," said Jo. "Whoever this man Carney is, his actions don't make sense. Why kill Mr. Pratchett and then attack Mr. Morelli? Why lock Bridget in the dark-room?"

Lady Millicent looked perplexed, her brow knitting. "What do you mean?"

Bridget spoke. "I was locked in the dark-room at the photography shop a few days before Mr. Pratchett was killed," she said. "The girls at Mrs. Randolph's shop described this same Mr. Carney, seen leaving the shop."

Lady Millicent stood and walked to the window. Her bearing, Jo realized, wasn't merely haughty. It was regal. This was a strong woman, not just one who pushed people around. Her taste may be execrable, thought Jo, looking around at the gilt on every frame, but she has an inner strength.

"I assume the police have been of little help since they believe they have apprehended the culprit," Lady Millicent mused. "Do we know who was buying the boudoir photographs? Was it anyone important?"

"We did have a list of names from the orders," said Bridget. "They were locked in a drawer. The police have the list, but I remember some of the names."

Stromond arrived with the tea trolley and rolled it to near the settee.

"Stromond, please bring me pen and paper, then see that we're not disturbed." She turned to Bridget. "And while we take tea, let me have that bill."

"We can't just wait for Lady Millicent to write letters to people," said Bridget, tripping on a pavement stone as they made their way back to the boarding house. It was over two miles, but Jo had been trying hard to save her money, and as yet, Bridget had few funds to spend on luxuries.

"I know, but we must be patient," said Jo. "There shouldn't be any more killings with Carney caught, I have to work, and you need to start your business."

They walked down Brook Street and across Hanover Square, Jo turning left because she knew Bridget would want to take Oxford Street despite the traffic. They were already too late for Bridget to make dinner, so she'd want to look in the shop windows along the way. Perhaps, Jo thought, it will give her ideas for her business.

"Oh yes, I've changed plans about the business," said Bridget. Jo was unsure whether Bridget's determined frown was from commercial considerations or from having to walk so far. "I've decided I don't want it to be just a bakery. I want a baking area and oven downstairs, but a tea house on the ground level."

"A tea house?"

"A tea house," said Bridget, "where I can serve my cakes and pastries and watch people eat and enjoy them. And, here's the important thing: a lavatory at the back."

Jo understood immediately. It had been a topic of conversation at the Women's Reform Club the year before, the lack of conveniences for women in London. They had heard a talk given by the Ladies Sanitary Association at the Club, a Mrs. Morris. Those who remembered the Great Exhibition in 1851, she had told them, remember the lavatories. Families could come to the Exhibition and stay as long as they liked because toilets and wash basins were available for a penny. Even after the Exhibition was over, George Jennings, who designed the conveniences, kept the facilities open because they were so popular.

But since then, the speaker had told them, little had happened. Despite the advice of medical doctors and specialists in hygiene, and even the influence of Florence Nightingale on cleanliness, only men had access to toilets in public. Pubs and taverns, where respectable women were rarely seen alone, might have conveniences, but they were for men only. The discussion after the talk had been lively. Many women reported curtailing shopping, able to stay out for only a few hours before returning to their homes to relieve themselves. The wealthier women admitted to calling more often at the homes of friends who made their bathrooms available. Women who were employed found life difficult, forced to leave the offices and shops where they worked to find a quiet corner in a back alley. Jo, who traveled the city daily, kept in the back of her mind a map of such places. She also knew which coffee houses had facilities.

"There is already running water to the dark-room," continued Bridget. "It would be a simple matter to install one or two toilets, with enough space around them for women to be comfortable. I'll even provide a basket of cotton wool and rags for women who need them."

She was stopping every few shops in Oxford Street, looking in the windows, until Jo finally had to warn her that it was dark and they needed to get back. When they returned, there was a note waiting for them from Lady Millicent.

I will be hosting a tea on Friday afternoon, it said. Please come.

She had thoughtfully enclosed a note for the cabbie saying she would pay upon their arrival.

After a cold supper, Jo and Bridget prepared for bed. Jo put the finishing touches to her sketch of the Dulwich Picture Gallery painting in the glow of the lamps. Although she was allotted only one lamp in the room, she had two additional small oil lamps that she used for night work. She was just about to put out her last lamp when Bridget tapped quietly at the door. She came in and sat on the bed.

"Jo," she said quietly, "I know how you must feel about Rossetti being on that list. Do you think you should talk to him?"

Jo sat in the semi-darkness and thought about Rossetti. "I feel strange about it, because although he has a reputation with women, I don't think he'd like it if some of those women posed because they had no other choice," she said.

"I mean personally, Jo. Do you find it disturbing that he wanted such intimate pictures?"

Jo looked carefully at Bridget. They had never talked about Jo's proclivities directly; Jo just assumed she knew. But Bridget was not a worldly person. She took life as it came, and her lively imagination was defined by the visual and the culinary.

"No, I don't find it disturbing," said Jo. "I am not intimate with Dante Rossetti." Bridget's face fell, and Jo saw that she'd been imagining a romance with the painter. "Besides, he loves all that is beautiful. And fragile. And female." She smiled at Bridget. "So I'm not even surprised."

After Bridget had left, Jo thought about the photographs. There were at least eight different women, most of them young. If they had sad stories, as she suspected some might, it would be interesting to draw their portraits, to see if she could show their challenges on their faces even as she showed their beauty.

Rossetti was lying in bed with Fanny at 16 Cheyne Walk. It was late in the morning, yet neither had bothered getting up for breakfast. They could hear the rattling of breakfast dishes downstairs.

"Christina and Mother must be up," said Rossetti.

"Mmmm," said Fanny. It was much too cozy under the feather comforter to rise now.

"You're supposed to be the housekeeper," he said, tickling her shoulder with his fingers.

"I am the housekeeper," mumbled Fanny. "I just don't keep house until noon."

Rossetti sat up in bed, bunched the pillows behind his back, and reached for his pipe.

"I keep thinking," he said.

"'Bout what?"

"Morelli. They have Will Carney, and he'll go on trial. They say he killed that photographer, Pratchett. And Jo says it's the same man that locked Miss Williams in the dark-room."

"Oh. Jo." Fanny rolled over away from him.

"But it doesn't make sense. What do the three of them have in common?"

"The three of who?" said Fanny into her pillow.

"Miss Williams, Pratchett, and Morelli."

He thought about it as he smoked, and he could hear Fanny snoring again. Miss Williams lived in the same boarding house as Jo. Photography assistant and fantastic cook. Pratchett, Miss Williams' boss, photographer, took pictures at the National Gallery and the Royal Academy Exhibition, where his body was found. Morelli. Art critic and Italian senator, supporter of the Risorgimento. What did they have in common?

Photography? No, Morelli didn't like photography. Said it took away the beauty, belittled the work of the true artists. So, pictures. Images. Visual representations. Art. But was photography an art? He wasn't sure. Perhaps that was the thread: photography as art, or not. But you don't kill people over that. And from what he'd heard, Will Carney was hardly a connoisseur of fine art. Lived near the docks, not that this mattered. But he'd heard about how he'd been identified. A tan tweed cap with a dark gray coat? Clearly, he knew nothing of design.

Surely Jo had the same questions. Perhaps talking to the women in the photographs had uncovered something? Rossetti tapped out his pipe, carefully got himself out of bed so as not to wake Fanny, and dressed. Something subtle? No, he wasn't a secret spy. He was Rossetti! Gold striped trousers, blue waistcoat, burgundy neckcloth. Cane, hat, clean shoes. He crept downstairs and went out the back door before the family knew he was awake.

Where would Jo be at noon on a Wednesday? The *Illustrated London News*. Either there, or they'd know where she was. He did not envy Jo, having a regular position. Even though she could come and go, she was still tied to someone else's timetable, someone else's demands. While Rossetti admitted he was willing to do that for a short time (the disastrous Oxford Union frescoes came to mind), he couldn't manage it every day. As it was, he could barely manage a commission. And there was that half-finished portrait of Annie Miller. And the just-started Aurelia, which Fanny was posing for. And the Beata, of his poor dead Lizzie. The Adoration watercolor for the triptych wasn't finished either.

He bought a hot pie from the stand on the corner before hailing a cab for Holborn. He was still brushing the crumbs off when he entered the office of *The Illustrated London News* and asked for Jo. She was upstairs in the studio.

Rossetti was pleased with the studio, its northern light and broad tables for the artists. Jo was working in the corner, near the front window. She had before her three thick pieces of paper, with drawings of men in hats. They looked, he thought, peering over her shoulder, like they had no personality at all. That couldn't be Jo's depiction, he thought. These must be colorless men.

"Who are they?" Rossetti tended to omit the preliminaries and hadn't bothered to say hello or good morning. She'd known he was there, however, since his entrance had, as usual, disturbed the room. She heard a flutter of coat tails as the other artists rose in respect. He didn't even seem to see them.

"Bank owners," she said, not looking up. "They're part of a meeting we need a picture of."

"They look amazingly dull."

"They are." He watched her sketch for a few more minutes.

"Are you here for a reason?" she asked. "Or just visiting?"

"Oh, for a reason," he said. "May I speak with you here?" He looked around the room. The three men turned away and busied themselves as if giving them privacy.

"Of course," she said. "But you mustn't stay long. You're distracting everyone." She looked at him out of the corner of her eye and saw him smile and preen a bit.

"I was thinking about Morelli. And Pratchett. And Miss Williams."

"And Will Carney?"

"Yes. He doesn't seem that intelligent. Why would he go after those three people? He wasn't trying to steal. Morelli had money on him, and it wasn't taken. Pratchett and Miss Williams have nothing valuable other than the photography equipment, and that wasn't stolen either."

"It may have had something to do with the boudoir photographs," she said, quietly.

"What boudoir photographs?"

"The ones you ordered."

She turned and looked him in the face. At first Rossetti looked confused. Then his eyes widened. "We should talk," he said under his breath.

"We are talking," she said under hers.

"Outside," he said.

"Oh, the Strand is so much quieter than here."

"Walk with me to Temple. I can buy you lunch, and we can talk."

Jo looked around the room at the three men trying to focus on their work, and failing. She put her pencil down. "All right," she said, "but I need to be back in an hour."

Rossetti walked quickly, but Jo, with her long legs, had no trouble keeping up. He bought her a pie from the cart near Temple Bar, then they walked down Middle Temple Lane and through the inns to the round, imposing Temple Church.

"Did you know," Rossetti said as they sat on the bench outside and she bit into her pie, "that the Knights Templar founded this?"

Jo looked at him. Even in his increasing portliness, he was handsome and vibrant with the sun reflecting off the yellow stone onto his animated face. She could capture his appearance in a sketch, she thought, but not his life force.

"About the photographs," she said. The pie was not very good. Steak and kidney. Bridget could make better.

"Yes," he said. He paused looking up at the church walls, pale gold and rounded like a castle tower. "I wanted some photographs of a woman I know, a model who agreed to have pictures taken. She is very young and isn't able to spare the time to sit for me."

"You mean if her family found out, you'd be in trouble," said Jo.

He looked at her and smiled, his eyes twinkling with humor. "Well, yes," he said. "I thought if I had her photograph, I could work from that. I've never painted from a photograph before."

Jo had to know. "Is her name Prudence?"

Rossetti shook his head. "No. Her name is Elizabeth. Just like my darling Lizzie." He leaned forward with his elbows on his knees.

Jo thought back to the pictures. This would be E.J., the one with the long wavy hair, lighter in shade than the others. They hadn't visited her yet in Charles Street in Hatton Garden. But it didn't matter. She could tell from the expression on his face that Rossetti was trying to reclaim something of his dead wife. It was pitiful, and very human.

"So what were you thinking about Mr. Morelli, Mr. Pratchett, and Bridget?" She realized that the pie was dry, and she had nothing to drink. Rossetti pulled a bottle out of his coat pocket. Jo looked skeptical.

"It's fizzy lemonade," Rossetti said. "Supposed to help with my indigestion."

Jo was aghast. "You're not supposed to carry those around. It might explode!"

Rossetti shrugged, then held the bottle out from his body as he pulled out the cork. It popped loudly in the quiet courtyard. He handed her the bottle. She took a sip and gave it back.

"Thank you," she said. He lifted the bottle to her in tribute and took a sip himself.

"Does it help?" she asked.

"I'm not sure. It's interesting. I think I prefer beer." She laughed.

"So," he said, "I've been thinking on the Will Carney problem. He's rather dim, but there must be some connection among the three people. I can't think what. Miss Williams is your partner in this investigation, so I thought you might have some ideas."

Jo took the bottle from him and had another sip. It tickled her throat.

"Bridget and I went to see Lady Millicent Stroud," she said. "She was in one of the boudoir pictures. Have you met her?"

Rossetti shook his head.

"She's a large, wealthy, formidable woman, but very shrewd, I think. She's writing to the men who ordered the photographs. You might receive a letter yourself. Perhaps a connection among the men might help us link together the rest."

"No, no. It must have something to do with art."

"You don't think boudoir pictures are art?"

"Not the point."

"All right, try this. Bridget and I found a substance in front of one of the paintings in the National Gallery. We think it's blood. If it is, that tells us Pratchett was in a completely different part of the building when he was killed. And that might tell us more.”

“Now that is interesting. Send me a note when you know. We’ll need to take a closer look at that part of the gallery.”

They walked back to the newspaper office more slowly than they’d left.

“Do you like working here?” he asked, looking up at the building with all its signage.

“I do,” she said. “It’s good to have steady work.”

Rossetti didn’t think so, but said nothing.

10

Lady Millicent's afternoon tea was carefully, if quickly, planned. She had invited a mix of people who would make possible the best gossip and the best opportunity to observe. Every man on the indecent photographs list, or at least as many as Bridget and Jo could remember, were sent invitations. Several members of the art community, including Sir Charles Eastlake, Giovanni Morelli, and James Robson, were asked. Her house in Grosvenor Square was thrown open for the afternoon, but everyone knew to arrive at a quarter past four and stay only until six.

Since the invitations were sent on Tuesday and the party was on Friday, Lady Millicent had added an inducement. Two of the paintings she had recently bought for her private collection would be on display. She had set up the withdrawing room with chairs and two settees, but instead of service, the sandwiches and sweets were on the sideboard next to two urns, one for coffee and one for tea. She wanted to be sure that people circulated and talked to each other, rather than sitting at a table. She also enjoyed the awkwardness of her guests balancing tea cups on their knees. It kept them off guard. The pictures were displayed on easels just outside the drawing room door.

Although she had offered to lend Jo and Bridget some suitable attire, both had declined and had simply arrived in their cleanest dresses and boots. Rossetti was there, laughing with Morelli and observing all the females in the room as he conversed. And since it was a casual tea rather than a formal meal, others not directly invited had felt comfortable coming along.

Percy Fry was one of these, accompanying Cecil Robson, who had wanted to look at the paintings. Jo didn't notice them as she took Bridget aside in the hall.

"I have the note from Samson and Tommy," she said, taking it from her reticule. "It says there was blood."

"Whose blood?" asked Bridget.

"We don't know, but it is blood. There's no reason for blood to be on the carpet in front of the Carracci. It's possible Mr. Pratchett was killed there, or at least attacked."

"What does that mean?"

"That he was in the gallery in front of the painting and was assaulted in the National Gallery."

Mr. Morelli had come out into the hall, nodded to them, and began looking at one of the paintings. Bridget decided to leave the artists to it and returned to the drawing room. The first painting was a small work, a woman holding a baby, and it looked very old. The gilt frame was engraved *Joos van Cleve, Virgin and Child*. Morelli stepped closer, took a glass out of his coat pocket, and peered at the lower part of the painting.

"Is something wrong, Mr. Morelli?" Jo asked him.

"No, no," Morelli said slowly. "But I do not think this is the picture our hostess believes it is."

"What do you mean?"

"It is not Joos van Cleve. It's a follower of Joos van Cleve, if that. Look at the hands. He has tried for that awkward bend at the knuckles, but he failed. Her left hand looks entirely different from her right."

Jo knew nothing of Joos van Cleve, but Morelli was fascinating. The turn of his head, the way one shoulder lowered as he approached the painting. He held the glass to his eye gently, as someone might hold a favorite handkerchief.

Morelli looked over at Jo, noting her interest, then moved to the other painting. It was much larger and showed a Venetian canal at sunset. The stone of the buildings glowed in the golden light, the canal shining with blue water.

"Ah, a Canaletto." He turned to Jo and winked. "*Di norma*, I would complain that an Italian painting has been purchased by an English collector. But in this case, Canaletto was painting for the foreign market. And he spent three years working here."

He stepped back to take it all in, then again went forward with his glass. "That's odd," he said.

"Another problem?" asked Jo, sketching his posture in her mind, and the way his dark hair flopped over his brow when he moved.

"Well, yes, but this is more serious. I don't believe this is a Canaletto, nor any of his imitators. I think this was painted more recently, although I cannot be sure."

"What do you think, Mr. Morelli?" said Lady Millicent in her rich, loud voice. "Did I make good purchases?"

"*Certemente*, Madam, depending on what you want."

She looked at him doubtfully. He bowed slightly and explained, "You want beautiful pictures to show in your home, *sì*? These are beautiful pictures."

Lady Millicent smiled. "I know they are beautiful," she said. "I was hoping they are also valuable."

Jo saw Mr. Morelli's face change expression, to one of discomfort.

"Perhaps I could come call upon you tomorrow? We could talk about these in more detail."

Lady Millicent nodded. "I am not usually in on Saturday, but I will be sure I am. I'd much appreciate your opinion, Mr. Morelli." She sailed off into the drawing room. Morelli nodded to Jo and followed.

Across the room, Percy Fry was talking to Cecil. "Did you see the paintings?"

Cecil was pushing a bit of sandwich around on his plate, frowning and not listening. He kept stealing glances toward the hall, then around the room as if he were looking for someone.

"Cecil!" said Percy.

"What?"

"The paintings?"

"Oh. Yes."

"What's the matter with you today? Your nerves have been on edge since we arrived."

"Sorry."

Cecil caught site of Bridget across the room. "Excuse me, Percy. Be back in a moment."

He found Bridget next to the serving table, admiring the spread of food.

"Miss Williams?"

She looked up and smiled at his open face. "Mr. Robson. How nice to see you."

"Are you enjoying the afternoon?" He glanced back at the door.

"Very much, thank you. I was just admiring the way the food is arranged. I wonder whether I could do something similar at my new tea room."

"Your tea room?"

"Yes, poor Mr. Pratchett left me the photography shop, but I will be creating a tea room instead. With my own bakery."

"My goodness, Miss Williams, what an excellent idea!" He seemed a bit nervous, she thought. Perhaps he wasn't accustomed to parties like this. She certainly wasn't.

"I'll want to decorate it, of course. Do you do that sort of thing, or are you strictly an easel painter?"

He smiled in a conspiratorial way. "Just oils, I'm afraid. And the occasional watercolor. But if you need something in a frame, I might just be your man." He took a slice of cake on a plate. "Say," he said, "did you ever discover who locked you in the dark-room?"

"Yes, haven't you heard? They arrested a man named Will Carney."

"Oh! Yes, for killing Mr. Pratchett and attacking the art critic. Mr. Morelli."

"Carney is also the person who locked me in the dark-room. He was seen."

Cecil nodded with raised eyebrows and took a bite of cake. "Well, I am very pleased that you won't be worried by him any more. Seems he was a very dangerous man. I hope he's put away for a long time, or that he's transported to Australia. I wonder whether they'll hang him?"

Bridget lowered her voice. "Hardly a subject to discuss with a young woman," she chided him, making sure he could see she wasn't serious.

Percy sidled up to Cecil. "Why, Cecil, who is this?" He turned to Bridget. "I'm afraid we haven't been properly introduced. I'm Percy Fry, artist and a student of life." He bowed over her hand when she held it out to him.

Bridget froze inside. Percy Fry. This was the person Mrs. Gretz had mentioned, the one who had recommended Mr. Pratchett's studio to Miriam Frankel as a way to earn money by posing. What on earth could she say to him?

"Good afternoon, Mr. Fry. I'm Bridget Williams." Cecil looked distinctly annoyed. Bridget knew that there was no possibility of questioning Percy. She could not think of any way to bring up any subject that would be helpful. But at least now she knew he was a friend of Cecil Robson, and it was obvious Cecil enjoyed her company.

"He's an actual student, of art," said Cecil, and grumbled, "at the University of London."

If this was supposed to make Bridget think less of Percy, it didn't work. University was quite above anything she had experienced.

"That sounds fascinating," she said politely. "What do you think of Lady Millicent's acquisitions?"

"Interesting in their own way," said Percy. He was tall and very attractive, Bridget noticed, with a careless manner that made you want to get his attention. "But not my style at all. Are you an artist too, Miss Williams?"

"No, just a friend of one," she said, catching sight of Jo giving her an eyebrow from across the room.

"Oh, there's Jo. We need to be going soon. It was nice to see you, Mr. Robson. Mr. Fry."

"And you, Miss Williams," said Cecil, stepping in front of Percy to shake her hand again. "I hope I have the pleasure again soon."

Jo was waiting impatiently at the side of the room. "Have you overheard anything? I haven't. Except that it looks as though Lady Millicent might have bought some suspect paintings."

"No. I did meet Percy Fry, but I couldn't think of what to ask him," said Bridget. "Should we ask Rossetti about returning to the National Gallery to look again? Maybe he could help us."

Jo smiled at Bridget's eager face. Of course they had to return for another look, now that they knew what they were dealing with. They set off to find Rossetti.

"Mr. Morelli, I believe you've met my friend Miss Harris? And this is Miss Williams," Rossetti said, as Morelli reached out to shake hands. They were standing in the vestibule of the National Gallery.

"*Piacere di conoscerti.* Very nice to meet you," he said to Bridget, who blushed as he bent over her hand. "And my friend from the hall at Lady Millicent's party," he said to Jo, with a wink.

Rossetti, wearing a burgundy brocade vest with a flat lace stock, said, "I discovered Mr. Morelli was coming here today and decided we should all meet. And, of course, take a look at what you may have discovered. I have explained to Mr. Morelli that there might be a clue here to a mystery."

"A mystery that has already been solved," said Morelli, holding out his hands with the palms up, "since the man has been arrested. But no matter! If my friend Rossetti says there's a mystery"—he clapped Rossetti on the back—"then there's a mystery."

The quartet walked down the gallery, stopping to look at a few paintings on their way to the Carracci. The space was crowded as usual for a Saturday, the men's tall hats blocking the view for those who were shorter, like Bridget. The first room was quite noisy. A woman in a strict black dress pulled a young boy by the hand, mumbling something about "*those* sorts of pictures," while two soldiers clattered by with their swords. It's a wonder their plumes don't touch the ceiling, thought Bridget. The carpet failed to muffle the sound of competing crinolines, creaking boots, and continual conversation. These will be my customers, thought Bridget. Someday, they'll come to me for tea and cake.

They moved on through to the third gallery room. The Carracci was hanging as before. *Susannah and the Elders*, the poor pale woman pulling away from the ogling men. There were fewer people looking at this one.

"Welcome back, Mr. Morelli." Smith had suddenly appeared by their side. "Sir Charles will be so pleased to know you've returned. Mr. Rossetti." He nodded to Rossetti, somehow, Jo noted, without looking at him. Was Rossetti not a welcome visitor? Jo looked inquiringly at Smith. "Good afternoon, Miss Harris," said Smith in a somewhat lower tone.

"I'm Miss Williams," piped up Bridget. "You must work for Sir Charles Eastlake."

"Yes, miss, I do." He looked at the Carracci. "I could go and fetch my catalog if you have any questions about this painting?" he asked Morelli.

"Actually," said Rossetti, "we're interested in why Mr. Pratchett would have been standing here."

"Mr. Pratchett?" Smith knitted his brow and lowered his voice. "You mean the unfortunate gentleman who died in the Exhibition?"

"Yes," said Rossetti.

"And we're interested in this," said Bridget in an undertone, pointing at the brown area on the carpet.

Smith looked startled, then peered down at the carpet, trying desperately to look as though he was not doing so. "Oh dear. I must have that cleaned tomorrow."

"I'd advise against it," said Rossetti. "Have you no idea what it's doing there?"

"None," said Smith. His supercilious manner is starting to crack, thought Jo. He doesn't know what that stain is, but he's worried.

"And have you any idea why this painting would be of particular interest to Mr. Pratchett?" Rossetti asked.

Smith shook his head, a bit confused now. "No, although I do know it was on the photography list. Sir Charles wanted it photographed. But it's very odd . . ."

"What's odd?" asked Jo.

"It was crooked," said Smith.

"What do you mean?" asked Bridget.

Smith looked down at the floor, as if trying to remember. "It was that morning, before Mr. Pratchett was discovered in the cupboard in the Exhibition." His voice was low, but he looked over furtively at Jo and Bridget. He thinks we might faint, thought Jo. Ridiculous.

"I came in here and this painting was crooked. I straightened it, of course, before the gallery opened. Thought nothing of it. But now" —he glanced at the stain—"now I wonder. Why would it have been crooked?"

Morelli had said nothing, but took his glass out of his coat pocket and approached the painting. It was hung too high to examine anything but the bottom few inches.

"Would it be possible to take this down so I could look at it more closely?" He asked Smith.

"Yes, it would, Mr. Morelli," Smith swallowed. "Would you care to enjoy the gallery while I send a note to Sir Charles to approve the removal? It shouldn't take more than half an hour." Smith was somewhat relieved. He did not like the idea of Morelli perusing the painting *in situ*, in front of all these people. It would be best to have it removed and examined in Sir Charles' office.

"Pru, please come back to the Slaughters to work," said Samson. "I'm so unhappy knowing you're not earning the money you need for your mother."

They were sitting on the steps of the National Gallery, but Prudence's coat was thin and she was sorry she'd come. After five letters from Samson, explaining and pleading, however, she had decided to talk with him.

"I'm not sure," said Prudence. "Look, Samson, could we go inside? It's very cold out here."

Samson jumped up immediately. "Yes, of course."

The vestibule wasn't much warmer despite the many people in it, so they turned left into the gallery rooms. They walked through, saying nothing, Samson with his hands in his pockets. He walked slightly ahead of her so as to encourage people to move around them.

As they entered the next room, Prudence said, "You were going to bring me here. To show me paintings," she said.

Samson stopped and turned toward her. They were in the middle of the room. First a woman bumped into him, then her husband went around them, glaring. Samson looked into Pru's face and saw there the possibility of forgiveness, and, if he wasn't imagining it, a bit of hope. He held out his arm, and she put hers through it.

"Now here," said Samson, going up to *The Arnolfini Portrait*, "is a masterpiece, and one of my favorites. Jan van Eyck."

Prudence waited until the tall man in front of her had moved on, then let go of Samson's arm and stepped closer.

"They are rich, aren't they?"

"They are. The painting is full of images of wealth. The chandelier" —he pointed—"the oranges, even the dog. And they're wearing fur even though it looks like it's summer."

"Are they married already? Because she looks like she's"—Pru lowered her voice—"expecting."

"Probably. There are things in the room that symbolize faithfulness and fertility, like the dog and the cherry tree outside."

"Her hair is done up, like a married woman," said Pru.

"True, but this is from the 15th century," said Samson.

"The 15th century? You mean the 1400s? How's it so bright and clean then?"

"It's taken care of. And I'm sure it's been retouched a bit."

Pru nodded.

"May I show you my *new* favorite?" asked Samson.

Prudence laughed. "Of course!"

He guided her into the next room, past a trio of children being shepherded by a governess, two men in hats who looked like they'd be more comfortable in a bank, and an art student carrying a pad and an easel.

The large painting showed a scene of people watching a science experiment. It was night, inside someone's house, but you could only see the people and the experiment by candlelight. A bird was being asphyxiated in a glass bubble, while a man lectured, adults looked askance, and two little girls were watching. One child was horrified and hid her face in her hands. *An Experiment on a Bird in the Air-Pump*, the sign said.

"It's by Joseph Wright," Samson said. "He painted it in 1768, as science was really getting started. A man named Edward Terrell gave it to the National Gallery just two weeks ago. Isn't it amazing?"

Amazing it was. Prudence stared and stared. "What is that man doing to the bird?" she asked.

"They are learning about the qualities of a vacuum by placing a living being inside the air pump, pumping out the air, and showing that without air living creatures die."

"But we know that, don't we? Through drownings, and people being trapped underground."

"Yes, but here the exact amount of air can be measured," he said. "And it's not just a tribute to science. The children are upset, but even the adults don't really understand. And the demonstrator looks a little crazy, like he got up in his dressing gown to show wealthy people what he does. It's about time, and knowledge, as well as science."

"I'm not sure I understand," said Prudence. "Will he give the bird some air and save him, do you think?"

Samson looked at her troubled face. She was so kind, was Prudence, caring for her ailing mother and now wanting an imaginary bird to survive. "Oh, I'm sure of it," said Samson. "He's only trying to show what's possible. Look, there's a boy at the window waiting to put the saved bird outside in the air."

Other visitors had found the new painting too and were beginning to crowd them. Samson guided Prudence to a quiet corner.

"I would like to see more," she said, "but I must get back home to my mother."

"May I accompany you?" asked Samson, almost afraid to ask. Prudence thought for a moment, then looked into Samson's face. She began to speak but was pushed heavily from behind by a woman in black bombazine hurrying to keep up with a small boy.

"Sorry," she said, and hesitated. Then she nodded, but her face was uncertain. "Yes, you may. But you probably shouldn't come inside. She's been very poorly."

"May I treat you to a cab?" he asked. "We shouldn't walk if your mum needs you home."

"Now you listen to me, Samson Light," said Prudence, frowning. "You don't have money for a cab."

Samson thought a moment. "You walked here?" He wasn't sure exactly where Pru lived, but it must be well over a mile. She nodded.

"A cab is cheaper than the omnibus because there are two of us," he said. "Please allow me. The traffic isn't bad since it's Saturday. Where do you live?"

She paused. "Near Guilford Street," she said, not looking at him.

"Good," he said, stepping over to hail a cab. "I can walk home from there."

❧❦❧

The cab bounced up St. Martin's Lane, then Long Acre. After some time traveling up Greys Inn Road, Prudence had decided she needed to speak to Samson.

"About my house," she said. "It's . . . um . . . not in Guilford Street. It's on the other side, right near . . ." She stopped and looked down at her hands.

Samson reached out and took her hand. She looked near tears.

"Near the Middlesex House of Corrections," she said quietly.

"You live near Coldbath Fields?" That was the prison for male convicts. It was reputed to be horrible. Men were forced to pick oakum till their fingers bled, walk tread-wheels to raise water, and endure long periods of silence for supposed contemplation. "Why?" he asked gently.

Samson could see tears in the corners of her eyes. "My father," she said, and turned her head away.

He drew a quiet breath, put his other hand also over hers, and said, "It's all right."

The building of flats in Gough Street was next to the church and had seen better days. He paid the cabbie, and they walked up the steps. Prudence turned as if to say goodbye, but Samson shook his head.

"I don't want to intrude," he said. "But I would like to meet her. In case I can help."

Pru looked skeptical.

"Even just by being a new face," Samson said. In his mind, he saw a future with Pru in it, as his wife and helpmate. If he could, someday he would want to care for her mother too. He knew the expression on his face must show both kindness and determination.

"We're on the second floor," said Pru, and he followed.

The stairwell was dirty and smelled stale, and the floorboards on the landing were worn unevenly. But when she opened the door to the flat, he noticed the room was spotless. Prudence sat in a chair by the door and took off her boots, then stood and motioned for Samson to do the same. "To keep the floor clean," she explained, "and to be quiet for her."

She walked towards the window, and he saw that a bed had been pulled into this room. Pru's mother was in bed with many pillows behind her so she could see out. The day was cold, but the window was open a few inches, and the air was fresh. There were blankets both on her and nearby on a chair. Prudence moved the blankets and sat down on the chair next to the bed.

"Hello, Mother," she said in calm but cheery voice. "I've brought a visitor to see you."

The woman inhaled as if awakening, and Samson heard the rattle in her chest. He approached the bed slowly, seeing her struggle to sit up more fully. Prudence moved some of the pillows to help.

"Hello, Mrs. Henderson. My name is Samson. I'm a friend of your Prudence."

She was not a tall woman, and her slight form, he thought, used to be larger. Her hair was gray and plaited, and she wore her nightdress. A handkerchief was in her hand. She smiled at him and he saw the twinkle in her violet eyes.

"A friend of my Pru?" she said, and took another breath. "I'm very pleased to meet you."

"I'll get you some tea, Mother," said Prudence. "But do you need the chamber pot first?"

"No thank you, dear," she said, not at all disturbed to be discussing such matters in front of Samson. "I managed. You've only been gone a little while. And don't worry—I washed my hands." Prudence reached out and squeezed her hand, and then went into the kitchen.

"She's such a gem, my Prudence," said Mrs. Henderson. "I don't know what I would do without her, and that's a fact."

Samson smiled at her. "Do I hear a bit of Scottish brogue in your voice, Mrs. Henderson?"

"Aye, you do," said Mrs. Henderson with some pride. "And my husband too. Borders Lowland people, both of us." She took another breath.

"Are you cold?" he asked. "Would you like me to close the window?"

"No, no," she said, "I'm warm enough in these blankets, and Pru likes it open. Says it's more healthful." She lowered her voice. "She's been reading Miss Nightingale's book. Everything clean and lots of fresh air." She winked.

"Pru has told me about you," she said confidentially. "Said you two had a bit of a tiff. I hope that's over now?"

"Yes, it is. I was in the wrong, and she forgave me."

"Well, that's Pru all over," said Mrs. Henderson. "She can be tough sometimes, but she forgives even if she doesn't forget." Another breath. "She says you are going to school? To be a doctor?"

"Yes. I'm studying for the exams in animal physiology. It will take a long time to be a doctor."

"Too late for me, I daresay!" She started to laugh but held her handkerchief to her mouth when it turned into a cough. Samson listened, a concerned expression on his face.

She caught her breath, then sighed. "Do you study herbs and things in school? My mam used to make me a potion for coughs when I was a child, but I don't know all that was in it."

Samson saw a bottle on the table. "Is that what the doctor gave you?"

Mrs. Henderson shook her head. "Not the doctor. The apothecary down the road, and it does help a little. Makes things hurt less."

Samson took up the bottle, opened it, and sniffed. Laudanum, he thought. And some honey.

"Have you tried a bronchitis kettle, Mrs. Henderson?"

She shook her head. "What does it do?"

"Just makes steam, like a tea kettle. But you can put things in the steam that might help," he said.

Pru came in with the tea plus two cups and a mug on a tray, setting it on a low table in the middle of the room next to the small settee.

"What are you telling her, Samson? Some kind of kettle?"

"Just an idea," said Samson. "I've seen one that a medical student was using. I'll see if I can find one for you to try."

"Thank you," said Mrs. Henderson. Prudence put a towel on Mrs. Henderson's lap. Then she went to the table, poured tea, added sugar, and handed the mug carefully to her mother.

"Easier to handle than a cup and saucer," explained Pru as she returned to the table and Samson joined her. They all sipped in silence for a while, watching the color of the light turn to golden in the afternoon. On days like this, the gray and smoky sky allowed the sun's amber glow to warm all the buildings.

When they were finished with their tea, Samson rose and approached the bed. "I'll be going now, Mrs. Henderson," he said. "I have no wish to tire you. But I would like to come again?"

She held out her hand to him. "You are always welcome, Samson." She gave a weak smile. "So long as Pru says so."

Pru watched as Samson put on his boots.

"Thank you, Samson. You are good."

"Happy to meet her. And thank you for showing me your home."

She opened the door for him.

"I'll be back at the Slaughters' on Monday," she said. Then she took his hand in the same way as the woman in *The Arnolfini Portrait*, her right in his left. "Goodbye."

He smiled the whole walk back to Bloomsbury.

"Don't be ridiculous," said Lady Millicent. "Of course these are valuable pictures!"

"What makes you so sure?" asked Bridget, and was answered with stunned silence.

She and Jo had called on Lady Millicent to see what, if anything, had been discovered at the tea party. From their perch on the settee, Bridget and Jo had shared the information about the bloodstain in front of the Carracci painting, and the interviews they'd made of the women in the photographs, including the possible procurement by Percy Fry. Then the three women spent half an hour exchanging useless information: Mr. Morelli ate too many of the sandwiches to be polite, Dante Rossetti's waistcoat was the most wonderful brocade, and since the M.P. Mr. Wood of the City had died in office, the big question was whether the man who succeeded him, George Goschen, could ever truly be considered a Liberal. And then Jo had decided she must raise the issue of the two paintings.

"I must tell you that Mr. Morelli confided in me," said Jo, "that both of your paintings had something doubtful about them."

"Which doesn't mean he's right," Bridget added as she saw Lady Millicent bristle.

"Which doesn't mean he's right," agreed Jo. "But if there's something to it, we thought we might ask from whom you bought them?"

"Cecil Robson, of course," said Lady Millicent. "As a painter himself, he has the most exquisite taste. And when he comes upon something special, he contacts me."

"We had no idea he sells paintings," said Bridget.

"He doesn't 'sell paintings.'" Lady Millicent sat up even more stiffly, and looked down her nose at Bridget from her slightly higher chair. "Cecil Robson obtains particular works for highly selective clientele."

Jo and Bridget had spent much time on Saturday trying to work out what, if anything, might be important from the party and what connected all three assaults. They had decided that since the main theme was clearly images, they would pursue any line of inquiry related to visual arts.

"I'm sure Mr. Morelli did not want to embarrass you. In fact, I'm sure he still doesn't. He is not in London to attest to the provenance of paintings in private collections. But according to Rossetti, he can tell if a painting is" —she took a deep breath as Lady Millicent stared coldly at her, but it was best to get this out now, she thought, in private— "a forgery."

Lady Millicent looked as if she would explode. Her lips turned down at the corners, and her mouth opened, causing her eyes to close into slits. Then she paused, forcing herself to take a breath "If these are forgeries," she said slowly, "I could be disgraced."

"But if we find the forger, and some connection to the attacks, you will be lauded," said Jo.

"True. Then all that will be lost is money. Significantly less important than reputation." She stood with a determined air and pulled the bell for Stromond. "I shall invite Morelli back here to examine the pictures and tell me the truth," said Lady Millicent. "Thank you for coming. Stromond will see you out."

Jo and Bridget walked together as far as High Holborn, then Bridget went to the shop on Theobalds Road to finish the packing up of photography equipment, while Jo went to meet Joseph Bazalgette.

Her assignment, the first to use her skills in drawing underground constructions, was to draw Bazalgette's new sewer. Sunday, he had written in answer to her note, was the only possible day for this. He was far too busy during the week and she'd have a better view with the workmen gone.

She arrived at Regent Circle, the northern one on Oxford Street, to meet Bazalgette and found him standing near an iron cover near the pavement. He was easy to find, with his w-shaped mustaches and his balding head, eyes twinkling over an enthusiastic smile. He was waiting for her, holding a roll of papers in one hand and doffing his hat with the other.

"Miss Harris. Pleased to meet you!" Then he glanced down at her dress, and frowned.

"For some reason, your skirts had not occurred to me," he said, abashed. "Most of my sewer guests are men. The passages are quite narrow."

Jo smiled in a way she hoped was confident and reassuring. "Although I realize it is not polite to discuss such matters, I do not wear a crinoline. If you are not offended, I can tuck my skirt into my . . ." She shrugged rather than saying the word "drawers."

He smiled and tilted his head in approval, then motioned for her to follow him to the edge of the circus and the curved wall of Nash's building. Taking the rolls from under his arm, he pulled out the topmost one and splayed it open against the wall. Jo helpfully reached up to pin down the other end.

"Here is my plan," said Bazalgette. "There are three sewer lines north of the river, and three in the south. They all go east-west."

"To intersect the rivers that drain into the Thames?" Jo asked.

Bazalgette beamed. "Precisely! It is an intercepting system. We are here—" He pointed to the Main Middle Level line on the drawing. "It will drain in this direction, to connect here—" He pointed to the right on the map, downriver. "Most of these are buried deeper the closer they get to the river. Right here where we stand it's about thirty feet down."

"So it runs on gravity?" asked Jo.

"Yes!" said Bazalgette. "That and the subterranean rivers are what make it work. The subterranean rivers flush through the system."

"This drawing is excellent," she said.

"Thank you. I firmly believe that drawings can help persuade people. In fact, I have just been allotted millions of pounds to complete the system. Communicating with images, that's important. People need to *see* their investment, see the future!"

"I understand," said Jo. "Perhaps I could see them all?"

"Once we return," he said. "Peter! Where is that boy?" A young boy in a soft cap and knickerbockers appeared from around the corner of the building, carrying an oil lamp.

"Sorry, Mr. Bazalgette."

Bazalgette handed him the papers and took the lamp. "Now stay here until I return." The boy nodded.

"Are you ready to go below?" he asked Jo.

"Yes, indeed."

The hole into the street was surrounded by a grill to prevent carts and foot traffic getting dangerously close. Bazalgette moved aside the grill, lit the lamp, and gestured toward the hole. "There are stairs," he said, "but as I mentioned, it's quite narrow. I'll go ahead with the lamp."

Looking around briefly to situate herself and swinging her bag toward the front of her body, Jo began descending the steps behind him. The steps themselves, the tall sides, the arched ceiling overhead were all brick. Gradually the height shrank, until she had to bend to continue. She reached down over the front of her skirt and began tucking the top section in to her drawers so it still draped but was bunched at her hips. At the bottom of the steps, the brick sloped away into a tunnel. Continuing ever downward, she followed Bazalgette, who occasionally turned back with the lamp to make sure she was all right.

"As you saw on my map," he said quietly, his voice echoing against the brick, "this line will connect with the Main High Level Sewer at the end, and there will be two branch lines also. One will be just below us here near Piccadilly, and the other at Aldwych. What do you think?"

"It's fascinating," Jo said. "The water and sewage will run along the floor here?"

"Storm water will run here," he said, stopping at a teardrop-shaped opening into another part of the sewer and pointing ahead, "then sewage from here. All helped by gravity to the big pumping station, then further toward the ocean. The subterranean rivers will be kept clear, except when there is a lot of rain. We're still working on that problem."

"Why the teardrop shape?" asked Jo, peeking into the channel.

"Makes the water keep going," answered Bazalgette. "Would you like to return to the steps where there's some light so you can sketch?"

"It's tempting to go on, but yes, I should." He motioned for her to turn back and handed her the lamp.

"Now where it's just piping," said Bazalgette from behind her, "I'm using Portland cement. That's one of the reasons our costs have increased, but I'm using it for all the longer lengths."

"Portland cement is new, isn't it?"

"Fairly new, yes. And it sets wet and fast. It will keep these sewers going for decades, maybe even a century."

They came to the steps. Jo asked, "Shall I turn and sit here, or would you like to go ahead of me?"

"I'll stay below you, but I'll hold the lamp," he said, taking it from her. She turned toward him and sat on the step. Light filtered in from the hole above. She was very glad she had brought the smaller sketchbook, as there was barely room to hold her elbows out in the passageway. She began to sketch the tunnel. Bazalgette watched in silence for several minutes, then nodded.

"You're quite good," he said. "A good touch with light. Shading is so important. I spend a lot of time on shading for my technical drawings. Makes for better engravings for printing, too. It's been so helpful to me that *The Illustrated London News* has taken an interest."

"The public is interested," said Jo. "More than interested. They are fascinated by the idea that such an enormous problem can be solved with engineering."

"When I was a child," he said, "this was a city of one million people. Now it's well over three million. It's been the finest city in the world since the Napoleonic Wars. I want to keep it that way, even when it has six million or more."

Jo nodded, hurrying in her drawing.

"Imagine, no more cesspits in people's basements. No more toxic miasma coming up into homes and streets, making people sick. No more 'Great Stinks' for the *Times* to write about. Pure water in, waste out far away."

He leaned over her and said softly, "I won't be able to get the money for it, but you know what my goal is? Have pipes all the way out *beyond* the Thames, into the North Sea. It's the only body of water big enough for me."

Jo smiled at him. He was a force to be reckoned with, this man, with his mustachioed smile and his vast dreams. Unlike most people, he was fulfilling them, through a mixture of engineering genius, charm, and a knowledge of how to involve people in his ideas.

"You're an artist," she said, closing her book and putting it back in her bag, "with your palette of bricks and cement and drawings and underground worlds. You're an artist of sewage." He laughed delightedly, the sound echoing into the depths of the city.

"Who was it, then, Mr. Carney?"

"I don't know. Some gent. Met me in a warehouse."

"A warehouse? Where?"

"Limehouse Docks."

"And he was a gentleman. Can you describe him?"

"No, he never let me see his face."

"How did he find you, Will?"

"Heard that I sometimes help gentlemen with their troubles."

"What sort of troubles? Killing people?"

"No! Never! Convincing men to pay their debts. Getting back property what's been taken. Paying women to not make a fuss about things."

"And he paid you to steal some photographs?"

"Yeah, from that shop in Theobalds Road. But then he found out something, about how the pictures were made. Wanted me to steal the picture from the National Gallery. Couldn't do it. And that photographer, he attacked me in the gallery. I was defending meself."

"Then why did you hide the body instead of calling the police?"

"Don' like police."

"We don't like you much either. But we don't think you'll be around much longer. You're going to hang, Will. The judge will put on his cap and you're going down."

"I was hired!"

"And after you killed Pratchett, there was more this gentleman told you to do?"

"Yeah. He tells me to attack that Eye-talian gent. So I do, but then he tells me he's done with me."

"And you have no idea who he was?"

"No. I never saw him. I don't know his accent except he was posh. And he paid well."

"And no idea why he wanted you to do all these things?"

"No. He just paid. Didn't spend time talking about it!"

"Mr. Carney, why should we believe you? How do we know you didn't just steal pictures to sell them, kill Hugh Pratchett because he was in your way, and attack Mr. Morelli to steal his money or his watch?"

"But I didn't, I tell you. This gent wants me to take the fall, for all of it."

11

Jo turned and looked in the glass she'd borrowed from Mrs. Bagley. Bridget had tucked and sewn until Lady Millicent's dress fit Jo well enough. The maroon color was flattering, she had to admit. And the black trim. The bonnet was also attractive, back off the face and with a modest black plume at the back. The girls at Mrs. Randolph's had been more than happy to help when Bridget had explained what they were doing.

"You'll need to learn to walk," said Bridget, jumping up from the bed to tuck an errant hair under Jo's bonnet.

"Whatever do you mean?"

"You're . . . just . . . not accustomed to a crinoline."

"That is not what you were going to say," Jo said, narrowing her eyes.

Bridget lowered hers. "You walk like a man."

Jo's eyes narrowed further, but then she laughed. "You're right. I'll keep my feet closer together. These boots pinch, which should help. Will that do?"

Bridget nodded. "And you received a reply to your note?"

"I did," said Jo, taking it from her reticule, also borrowed from Mrs. Randolph's shop, and reading. "Dear Mrs. Moorpark, I'd be delighted to have you call upon me at my atelier in Portobello Road on Monday after ten. I have a number of paintings that might interest you. Your servant, Cecil Robson."

"So you'll be pretending you're a wealthy woman wanting to buy a painting. Are you sure it will work?"

"Of course it will work," said Jo with confidence. She had only met Cecil Robson once, outside the Exhibition, and his eyes had been on Bridget anyway. No one would know her dressed like a member of the upper class. She was old enough to have come into her own money. And at least her direct gaze, considered inappropriate for a woman of her station, wouldn't be questioned as a wealthy woman.

"What exactly will you look for?"

"Anything that seems unusual to me. It's more difficult to forge something very old, so I'll feign an interest in late Renaissance and the eighteenth century."

Jo had thought about this since Lady Millicent's tea party. If Lady Millicent's paintings were forged, and they had come from Cecil Robson, he was either dealing in forgeries or creating them. She had tried not to consider her personal reaction to his particular brand of charm. She didn't like him, and she knew it. One should never judge people like that. His appearance was perfectly respectable, and she didn't think he could kill anyone.

At the same time, what she was doing could be dangerous. What if he were the one who had killed Mr. Pratchett?

Jo's cab arrived at Cecil's atelier in Portobello Road just after eleven. She stepped down from the cab carefully, so as not to soil her borrowed boots or lift her skirt unnecessarily. She turned as gracefully as she could and paid the cabbie. He tipped his hat to her.

The atelier was quite elegant, even from the outside. Anyone peeking in the windows would have seen easels with paintings. While it was a workroom rather than a shop, Lady Millicent had said this was where Cecil Robson showed and sold paintings. Unsure whether to carry her umbrella and reticule in the same hand, she decided to try. It made it easier to manage the skirt on the steps.

Cecil opened the door.

"Good morning, Mrs. Moorpark. I'm Cecil Robson," he said with a small bow. No sign of recognition in his eyes, just a touch of admiration and the open friendliness of a sales clerk. Jo had to stop herself from smiling in triumph, and she swept past him into the front room.

"Good morning, Mr. Robson. Thank you for seeing me with so little notice. I am only in town for a few days." Lady Millicent had felt that, given Jo's bearing and inexperience, she should pretend to be from one of the northern cities. If she had to name one, Bridget had suggested Carlisle.

Jo looked around at the work displayed in the room.

"What sort of piece might you be looking for?" inquired Cecil graciously.

"Something colorful," said Jo carelessly.

"For decorating a particular room, or for a more formal showing?" asked Cecil.

"More formal, I think," said Jo, "My friend Millie said you might have something from the Renaissance, or the eighteenth century perhaps?"

"Ah yes, I understand you're a good friend of Lady Millicent Stroud," said Cecil.

"Indeed," said Jo, trailing a white glove on the frame of a modern artwork showing people in a park, with a factory in the distance. It looked rather fuzzy, she thought. Almost as if one had glanced quickly at the scene, then merely painted an impression. "You sold her two excellent pieces. I would like something similar."

"A woman of good taste, I see," Cecil fawned. "Do you like this one?" he asked, gesturing to the fuzzy painting.

"No, it is not to my taste." She sniffed for emphasis.

Cecil responded by sidling over to an Italian landscape. "Perhaps this might interest you. It's a Carracci."

Jo strove to keep her face looking only mildly interested. "Oh?" she said.

"Yes, a very famous painter. The picture will only increase in value. And, as you can see, it is quite a beautiful landscape."

Jo began to cough, taking a lace handkerchief out of her reticule to cover her mouth. "I'm so sorry," she said, and coughed again. "Might I have a glass of water, please?"

"Yes, of course," said Cecil. "There's a little kitchen at the back. It will only take me a moment."

As soon as he had left the room, Jo quickly took her pen-knife from her bag. Leaning in to the corner of the painting, she scraped off a small piece of varnish and a flake of red paint, wrapping them quickly in her handkerchief as Cecil returned.

"Thank you," she said weakly, taking the glass of water and drinking several gulps. She took a breath. Cecil had a practiced look of concern on his face, as if he were ready to fetch her a chair if necessary. "I'm much better now."

She handed back the water glass.

"This Carr-acci," she said. "How much might you be asking for it?"

"Well, normally I would sell it for three hundred and fifty pounds." Jo tried to look shocked. "But as you're a friend of Lady Millicent's, I could certainly manage three hundred."

Jo nodded, looking at the picture as if considering.

"I will take the afternoon to decide," she said airily, looking around the room. "I don't see anything else that really attracts me."

"Of course. When you decide, simply send me a note to my house in Brunswick Square, as you did yesterday. I could have this painting delivered to you as early as tomorrow if you let me know where you're staying?"

Jo thought quickly. "The Westminster Palace Hotel."

"I know it well," said Cecil as he moved to open the door for her. "What do you think of the hydraulic lifts?"

"Quite . . . uplifting," said Jo. She saw no response in his eyes. "Good day, Mr. Robson."

Morelli and Rossetti were waiting for her in the coffee room. Despite what she had told Cecil, Jo had never been to the Westminster Palace Hotel. She was glad she was dressed properly. The coffee room was on the east side of the building, but even so she saw numerous clerks walking around the corner to the western side to reach the India House offices.

At first she had been confused because the doorman had pointed her the opposite direction when she asked for the coffee room. The passage had led to a separate ladies' coffee room, which was quite small. She could see women meeting each other through the glass and had realized there must be another coffee room. She'd been a few minutes late.

"*Buon giorno*, Miss Harris," said Mr. Morelli, rising as she came to the table and greeting her with a slight bow. "How very nice to see you." Rossetti grinned at her with a twinkle in his eye and remained seated. Both already had ordered cups of coffee.

Morelli gestured for the waiter. "May I order you some coffee?" he asked Jo.

"Yes, please," said Jo. "With milk, if I may," she said to the young man who came over to attend them. Morelli blinked several times but said nothing.

"So," Rossetti said, "you have some samples for us? Obtained with the subterfuge of a borrowed dress?" He tried not to laugh. Jo looked quite elegant, he thought, then dismissed the idea of painting her in Lady Millicent's gown. He was rather startled to realize that he did not like her looking so bourgeois.

Jo took out the handkerchief. "I had very little time with Mr. Robson out of the room," she said. "Is this enough for you to tell anything?" She moved aside Morelli's coffee and opened the cloth in front of him.

Without looking away from the samples, Morelli reached for his eye-glass. Lifting it to his eye, he peered at the flakes. He took up his fork and separated the two. "No, no," he mumbled, and moved the varnish flake to one side, examining the paint fragment.

Then he looked up at Jo with a smug expression, handing the glass to Rossetti, who leaned over to look.

"The painting you took these from cannot be a Carracci," he said, his eyes creasing and his generous mouth curving into a smile.

"Why?"

"Because neither the varnish nor the paint was used in the sixteenth century. This is tinted varnish, used to make paintings look older than they are by using bitumen. And the paint . . ." He looked at Rossetti.

"The paint is the new ultramarine. It's a recent man-made paint. Darker, less azure, and far less expensive than aquamarine made from lapis lazuli," said Rossetti. He looked up at her. "My Lord, Jo," he said. "You've done it. You've caught a forger."

Jo took a breath. All right, she thought. The Carracci was a forgery. So was the one Lady Millicent had bought from Cecil. She felt relieved, but also nervous. She had missed a day of work, and she sensed more than saw that today's light was fading. Her drawings of the sewers needed to be delivered to Mr. Sterne, the picture editor, by ten the next morning. She couldn't do anything about the forgery until tomorrow afternoon, and even then, she wasn't sure what might be the best approach.

"I'll tell Bridget tonight," she said, "and we'll visit Cecil Robson tomorrow afternoon."

Rossetti's eyes widened. "You mustn't do that," he said, concerned. "He could be dangerous. He'll recognize you and will know he was tricked."

"I'll keep the dress and go to his house as Mrs. Moorpark again." She thought for a moment. "I won't be able to take Bridget with me. She doesn't have the right clothes. But I'll be all right." Even as she said it, she wasn't sure. People can act strangely, especially when their livelihood or reputation is at stake. Would he even tell the truth? Would he brush off her suppositions? Or would he behave like a cornered animal?

"You should not go alone," said Morelli. "If Cecil is himself the forger, he may harm you. In fact, he may attack even if he is only the dealer."

Jo frowned. "He may have been desperate enough to hire Will Carney to protect himself. That doesn't mean he'd commit violence personally," she reasoned. They stopped to think, sipping their coffee.

"I'll go with you," said Rossetti. "He knows me. We will accuse him together and see what he says."

Rossetti arrived at *The Illustrated London News* just before lunch to see if Jo might be finished with her work. He knew she'd have to go back to the boarding house to change into Lady Millicent's dress, then to Brunswick Square, but he had nothing better to do, and he decided to accompany her.

Waiting downstairs this time, he shifted from one foot to another on the pavement. He had much to report and was getting impatient. His conscience pricked at him a bit because it was more fun to engage Jo's mystery than it was to work on the three (was it four?) things he should be working on at his own home. He did love his house at Cheyne Walk, and Fanny, and his family, but having a reason to run all over London was exciting. He hadn't had this much fun away from home since he was—well, younger.

The day was gray and it had begun to drizzle, but he had his cloak and his pipe. He took up a position under the awning at the corner and had a smoke, watching the light change. Contrast always faded when the clouds came in. Edges that had been sharp and distinct (pre-Raphaelite, he thought) softened and dissolved. His friend James could paint this kind of light, he thought. In *The Thames in Ice* (who bought that? Dr. Haden?) the sky dissolved into gray clouds of nothingness. James had painted it in only three hours, which Rossetti had found preposterous. Actually, he'd been unwilling to admit his admiration for the task. It took him weeks, months, to finish a piece, and sometimes he'd paint it over. His *Beata* was just sitting there on the easel, looking like Lizzie but not seeming truly begun. He'd even reworked several of his paintings from years ago. He envied his friend's satisfaction in his own work, his certainty that a piece was complete.

And now James was Rossetti's neighbor and was painting sketchy interiors, like the portrait of his business manager, Joanna, last year in Paris, standing still in a white dress with her copper hair flowing down. *Symphony in White*, he called it. Refused by the Royal Academy, the huge painting, with the subject's vague and unfinished bedroom look, had shocked society. Rossetti smiled to himself. He'd see more of James Whistler and Miss Hiffernan when this adventure was over. She seemed to have some potential as a medium, and Rossetti wanted very much to know whether Lizzie was happy on the other side. A séance would be just the thing.

Jo came out of the door as he was musing, and he jumped up and emptied his pipe into the gutter.

"Where to? Home?" he said. "You need to change your clothing."

"Where did you come from?" Jo asked, startled. "I thought you were meeting me at Robson's house."

"Decided to come along and watch the transformation."

"As if you would be allowed in my room while I changed," Jo laughed. "Mrs. Bagley would call a constable."

It was less than a mile to Shoe Lane, but instead of turning right, Rossetti steered Jo across the street past St. Mary's church.

"Where are we going?" she said.

"Holywell Street," he answered, and her eyes widened as she walked along beside him.

The row of publishing houses, many of dubious distinction, were clustered behind the Strand. The narrow lane featured bookshops and printers, some with extensive collections of pornography.

"May I ask why?"

"The letter," said Rossetti, taking it from his pocket and handing it to her. A sprinkling of rain had started, and Jo handed him the umbrella to open as she read the letter. It was from Lady Millicent Stroud, addressed to Rossetti, and it asked him about the photographs taken by Mr. Pratchett.

"It occurs to me," said Rossetti, "that if other photographs were sold, they would be sold here."

Jo knew she had been avoiding the questionable photographs and felt badly. Lady Millicent had no husband at the moment, but what if the women in the pictures hadn't all been poor and in need of money? What if some were the wives of important men in society? She could easily picture such a man hunting down Pratchett and killing him. And she'd forgotten all about Prudence, who had been in one of the pictures. *Guilt won't help,* she thought. *I can struggle to do my job and be a good friend to Bridget and, to be honest, do the police force's work for them, but I'm not perfect.*

"The police still have our list, but they aren't doing anything about it," said Jo. "I haven't been able to do anything either. I'm afraid I'm not much of a detective. And you said this was about art, not boudoir photographs."

"Pffft," said Rossetti. "We just need more information. Pratchett had a ring, you might say, a licentious photography ring. People's emotions get involved with something like that."

"Now you think this might be more important than the forgery?" The rain had stopped and Rossetti closed the umbrella.

"Possibly," he conceded. "Forgeries are about money. Pornography is about people."

"I'm not sure about that," Jo argued. "Forgeries can also be about reputation. And pornography can most definitely be about money."

They were in Holywell Street now, and it annoyed Jo that Rossetti seemed to know where he was going. He turned into a shop with the name *Albert's* on the sign above the door and walked through the room to the back counter. A boy looked up from sorting stereoscope pictures. "Yes, sir?" he said. He glanced at Jo to see whether he should use Rossetti's name, making it rather obvious that he knew who he was. Jo rolled her eyes and waited.

"I'd like to speak with Angus, please." The boy nodded and went to the back. Angus appeared in a few seconds. He was a small man, blinking through spectacles. Not at all what one would expect, thought Jo.

"Mr. Rossetti," said Angus in a questioning tone, nodding.

"Angus, I've come about some photographs. Not the kind you usually carry. These were photographed by a Mr. Pratchett."

"Hugh Pratchett?" Angus looked concerned and removed his spectacles, unhooking them one ear at a time. "I heard what happened. Horrible. Simply horrible. Member of the Society, you know."

"I do. Did you ever sell any photographs for him?" Angus shook his head. "Or have you ever seen them? Boudoir photographs? Not very explicit. Scantily clad girls—"

"And a few older women," Jo inserted.

"—and a few older women, barely dressed but not obscene. Just . . . cheeky."

Angus shook his head. "Nothing like that came through here. Or elsewhere on the street, I dare say. We had a few like that from Paris, though. Looked like tourist pictures. The Eiffel Tower, Notre Dame. You had to look closely to see the ladies were in their underthings."

"These were more like portraits," said Jo. "Many had a pedestal column and an aspidistra."

"A what?"

"A potted plant."

Angus shook his head again. "I'm sorry, but no. And if they were selling on this street, I'd know about it."

Bridget was not downstairs when they arrived at Shoe Lane, so Jo left Rossetti in the parlor for Mrs. Bagley to wonder about and went upstairs. Bridget's door was closed. Jo listened and thought she heard crying. She knocked on the door, then opened it.

Bridget was sitting on her bed, her handkerchief wet and a photograph in her lap.

"What's the matter?" Jo said in a kindly tone, sitting next to her.

"It's—Mr. Pratchett," said Bridget. "I think it just occurred to me that he's really dead."

Jo looked at the photograph. It was of Bridget when she'd first begun working at the studio, almost two years before. She was wearing her straw hat and a summer dress.

"I've aged quite a lot since then," sniffed Bridget.

"You were all of twenty-four," said Jo.

"He was very kind to me, you know. Even if he had some odd ideas. It was my first good job. And he trusted me." The tears were running slowly down her cheek. Jo took up Bridget's handkerchief and tried to dry them.

"I know," said Jo quietly. "All we can do is try to find out why he was killed. I don't think Mr. Carney did it alone."

Bridget bristled at the name of the man who'd locked her in, who could have killed her too.

"And poor Mr. Pratchett had no family. He left the shop to me." The tears were coming faster now.

Jo put her arms around Bridget. She was unsure what to do and wished one of the other women were around. But there was no one else upstairs. They were all at work except Mrs. Bagley, who was in the kitchen.

"He knew you are a good person," said Jo. "And we'll find out why he died. I promise." She took out her own dry handkerchief and handed it to Bridget, who blew her nose and wiped her eyes.

"All right," said Bridget, sniffing. She stood up and took a deep breath. "I'll help you dress."

Jo came downstairs in the maroon gown. Mrs. Bagley was just taking an empty plate from Rossetti, whom she'd plied with one of Bridget's sweet rolls.

"There you are," said Mrs. Bagley. "Don't you look nice." She glanced at Rossetti, who was rising to dust the crumbs off his waistcoat, then at Jo. Not possible, she thought.

Bridget came downstairs, nodded to Rossetti, and went off to the kitchen.

"Take a cab," called Mrs. Bagley as Jo and Rossetti left for Brunswick Square. "You'll muss the gown if you walk!"

Brunswick Square was white and elegant in the afternoon. The clouds were clearing and a glimmer of sunshine made the square sparkle. It hadn't occurred to Jo to be concerned with what Rossetti was wearing. His clothes were outlandish, but expensive. Today he was wearing a waistcoat of rich purple with a dash of—oh goodness, was that lace?—at this throat. She reached over and dusted a crumb from between the folds. They rang the bell, and a parlor-maid opened the door.

"Good afternoon," said Rossetti. "Mrs. Moorpark and I are here to see Mr. Cecil Robson." He handed her a card. Jo wondered where he got cards.

"Yes, sir," said the parlor-maid, stepping back so they could enter. She looked about eighteen and was pert and pretty as parlor-maids were supposed to be. Not worth drawing, thought Jo. Nothing behind the eyes.

"Please wait in the parlor," she said. "I'll see if Mr. Cecil is at home."

The parlor was flooded with light from the square. Two pale and perfect landscapes hung on either side of a small fireplace. Tables throughout the room displayed wax flowers under glass, gilt-framed photographs, and a small curled-up rabbit that looked like it was made of stone.

"Netsuke," said Rossetti. "Looks expensive."

"From Japan, aren't they?" asked Jo.

Cecil entered from the hall. "Ah, I see you're admiring my father's netsuke. It's a Kokusai, as he's always telling me." He shook Rossetti's hand, then turned to Jo with an obsequious smile. "Mrs. Moorpark. Won't you sit down?" He waved for both of them to sit on the settee, but Jo was distracted by a large cylindrical object on its own small table.

"Oh my," she said to Cecil, "is this a zoetrope?"

Surprised at her enthusiasm, he joined her at the table. "It is indeed," he said proudly. "Would you like to view something?"

Jo didn't answer but bent her knees so she could see the sides of the slotted cylinder. Cecil spun it, and she saw flashing through the slots a couple dancing together. They were silhouettes, and it looked like they were moving smoothly through the dance.

She rose and smiled at Cecil, then remembered that she was Mrs. Moorpark, come to expose Cecil as a forger and possible murderer. Rossetti spoke from the settee.

"Mr. Robson, we need to ask some questions."

"About the Carracci? I'll tell you what I can."

Jo joined Rossetti on the settee, smoothing the maroon dress as she sat, and Cecil took his place in the chair.

"Three hundred pounds is a great deal of money," said Jo. "My friend Mr. Rossetti would like assurance that it is authentic."

Cecil frowned. "I bought it myself, eight years ago, when I was in Italy with my father. I have the document of sale at the studio if you would like to see it."

"I have reason to believe," said Rossetti in an offhand tone, "that it is a forgery. The varnish, the paints—I would like them evaluated by an expert."

Cecil said, "But the documents—"

"Could be forged as well. I have a friend in Gray's Inn who would be happy to look at them for me." Rossetti flicked some fictitious lint from his trousers.

Cecil paled, his hands on his knees. "If the Carracci doesn't please you," he said slowly, "I'm sure I can find you another painting that is suitable." Sweat began to bead on his forehead.

Rossetti spoke casually. "It may interest you to know that Mrs. Moorpark took two chips from your painting when you showed it to her on Monday in your studio. We have taken them to an expert: Giovanni Morelli."

There was a long silence as Cecil stared at Rossetti.

"You'll ruin me," whispered Cecil. Then, "How much do you want?"

Jo had not expected this response. Denial, yes. Wounded pride, certainly. But an offer of money to not reveal his crime? Rossetti, however, was prepared.

"We will think on it," said Rossetti, rising and tugging his waistcoat over his broad stomach. "We will be in touch in a few days. I do hope nothing happens to the painting in the meantime."

Jo rose too but said nothing. At Rossetti's gesture, she walked to the front door. Cecil followed meekly to open it for them.

Lady Millicent was waiting for Jo and Rossetti in the morning room. While Jo spent little time in society, she was familiar enough with its habits to know that this was an honor. The morning room, on the ground floor, was in essence the office of the woman of the house. It was furnished with useful items rather than decorative pieces. Only the most familiar callers would be met there rather than in the first-floor drawing room. Stromond showed them in and closed the door behind them.

"Ah, the famous Dante Gabriel Rossetti," said Lady Millicent. She rose from an enormous desk in front of the window and held up a lens to her eye as she looked at him, an affectation Jo could not recall seeing her use before. "It's a wonder we have never had a chance to talk until now, given our mutual interest in art."

Lady Millicent was dressed in a splendid jewel blue day gown suitable for receiving visitors. Jo immediately regretted having changed back into her own clothes. In her plain gray dress, Jo could not help feeling like a mourning dove perched in a tree near an exotic tropical parrot. Rossetti bowed over Lady Millicent's proffered hand.

"A pleasure to meet another art lover, Lady Millicent. Do you paint? Or do you prefer drawing?"

Lady Millicent's feathers ruffled, but just for a second.

"Neither, Mr. Rossetti. Although I am aware that you do both."

"I do," he said, walking past the end of the huge rosewood desk toward the window. "But it is a shame that you do not. The light in here is quite perfect."

Lady Millicent gave a small smile. "But it never lasts," she said.

"Like youth?" asked Rossetti. Lady Millicent's smile was sad.

"Exactly."

Rossetti turned from the window with a look of sympathy. He did not want to regret the wilds of his youth, and he suspected Lady Millicent didn't either. He had hurt a number of people with his arrogance and his desperation to be a great artist, and he had to admit that some of his work had been poor, not just uninspired. The murals in the Oxford Union haunted him, fading as they were. He had known nothing about preparing a wall for a fresco, and had gone at it with only confidence and an extravagant Arthurian legend. Then he had fallen in love with one of the models, Jane Burden. She married William Morris, but he was fascinated by her and it meant he neglected poor Lizzie. So many regrets. It had been only six years ago but felt like a lifetime.

"Lady Millicent," Jo was saying, "we have cornered Cecil Robson with evidence of his forgeries. I thank you again for the loan of the maroon dress. But," here she glanced at Rossetti, "we are far from convinced that he would be able to commit murder."

Lady Millicent nodded in agreement. "I felt that too," she said. "He's so smooth and conniving, but there seems to be no drive underneath, no ambition."

"I'm afraid we are at a loss," said Jo. "Have your letters to the men buying the photographs uncovered anything?"

"Nothing of use, I'm sorry to say." She looked up, cognizant that Rossetti himself had been one of those men. "Two of the gentlemen told me politely to mind my own business, two denied they had agreed to purchase such photographs, one helpfully offered his opinion about poor women needing to support themselves however they can, and several indicated that they did not appreciate the tone of my letter. I could continue to press a few more, I suppose—"

Stromond opened the door. "Excuse me, madam. Would you like me to bring some tea?"

Lady Millicent raised an inquiring eyebrow at her guests.

"No, thank you," said Jo, rising. "I must return to work." She glanced meaningfully at Rossetti.

"Yes, and I have several paintings that need my attention," he said.

Lady Millicent rose to accompany them. Stromond, surprised, stepped back from the doorway to the morning room into the hall.

"Whatever will happen to poor Mr. Morelli?" Lady Millicent asked. "Do you think the miscreant will come for him again? Or for Miss Williams?"

"It's not likely," said Jo. "Will Carney was the perpetrator of all three attacks. Whoever he was working for is clearly too cowardly to do anything himself." They reached the front door, and she opened it. "Or herself." She looked back and saw Rossetti's eyes widen. They had not discussed the possibility of the villain being a woman.

Outside, the late morning sun had appeared, and the Mayfair air was blessedly warm. They began walking along Grosvenor Street. It was almost two miles to *The Illustrated London News* offices, but the sun was shining and Jo couldn't bear the idea of the omnibus.

"You think it might be a woman?" Rossetti asked, changing his pace to keep up with her.

"Well, it makes sense," she said. "We have been unable to establish a connection to any of the men other than Cecil Robson. And who better to hire a man to do the dirty work than a woman?"

They walked a block in silence.

"Have they persuaded Will Carney to talk?" asked Rossetti.

"I don't know. There has been nothing in the papers. But there wouldn't be until the trial starts."

"He'd know whether the person was a man or a woman, wouldn't he?"

Jo thought a moment, not slowing her pace. "Not necessarily. A meeting in a dark alley, an exchange conducted only in letters. He may not have known his employer at all. Even if they met, a voice is easily disguised."

Rossetti had trouble imagining a meeting without people seeing each other.

"Consider," Jo said, "a note, carried into the rookeries near the docks, by a boy messenger. Our killer had heard of Will Carney, perhaps through a friend. Maybe he was known for this sort of work. The note could say let's meet in a dark alley behind a pub, near the docks, on Carney's ground."

Rossetti was picturing this, the unsavory smells and sights of the docklands, fish and sweat and sewage. A pub in which he might have been comfortable in his youth, but was no more, full of strong people who worked on the ships, sailors looking for trouble, criminals exchanging wares.

Jo continued. "Perhaps she was dressed like a man, in trousers and a heavy coat, hair cut short or tucked up in a hat. Or under a cap. A low voice, or a loud whisper so the voice can't be identified. Why even let Will Carney know who you are? The transaction could be done by messenger or envelope."

"You're a little too good at this," said Rossetti. "How do I know *you* didn't hire him?"

Jo laughed suddenly, startling a maid who was walking toward Grosvenor Square with her market basket.

"Aside from having no reason to want Hugh Pratchett dead, or my own friend locked in a dark-room, or poor Mr. Morelli struck on the head, I simply haven't the money to pay anyone."

"True," said Rossetti.

The shop on Theobalds Road was almost empty now, and Bridget was scraping the walls for the new paper. She'd already cleaned the window displays thoroughly, replacing rotten wood and doing a bit of painting. The cake trays and display towers were still in a crate, waiting their turn. The oven below was half-finished; the workers would return tomorrow.

Bridget had begun to like the shop in the quiet of the evening. She had been afraid at first, because the space missed Mr. Pratchett. It seemed to need his presence, with all the equipment. But now that the cameras and that horrid pillar were gone, and the floors properly tiled, it was her space. She'd had more lamps installed, especially in the back room for baking in the small hours. There were new locks on the back door, and the locksmith was coming again tomorrow to work on the new front door. The new door was leaning against the wall near the counter, waiting.

The drawers that had held papers and photos now contained a new order booklet and large drawings of cake designs. Another drawer held menu samples she was working on; Jo had been helping her draw curlicues in the evenings.

Her arms were tired from the scraping, and the evening light was dim in the front of the shop, so she went to the back to work on the bins. Three large bins stood near the back door. The first two were for flour and sugar, but she hadn't decided yet about the third. They were second-hand, and all three stuck a bit when you opened and closed them. Bridget picked up the wooden plane from the big table and resumed her work on the first bin, reducing the height of the hinged drawer. She didn't hear the front door open on the old hinges. She had oiled them just a few days before because the creaking annoyed her.

"So, you are here, Miss Williams," said a low voice.

Bridget gasped and looked up, dropping the plane into one of the deep bins. It was James Robson, his leonine head glowing amber in the lamplight.

"Mr. Robson," said Bridget. "You gave me a start. What are you doing here?"

"Looking for you," he said. "May I?" He motioned to one of the stools at the big table, and not waiting for an answer, sat with one foot still on the floor.

Bridget looked at him, her heart still pounding. Impeccably dressed, the famous art critic could surely have no reason to be here. He'd never been to the shop, to her knowledge. She didn't know him, and barely knew his son. He leaned on his cane, then sighed. Bridget noticed the lion's head on the cane. How suitable, she thought. And the expression in his eyes. Like a hunter.

"You've ruined my plans, Miss Williams. Everything was going well until you and your Mr. Pratchett began taking photographs."

"Of the women?" asked Bridget. She was beginning to become frightened. What did he want?

Robson shook his head. "No, not of the women," he said, disgust in his voice. "Photographs of women are for degraded men, men who are no more than animals. The photographs of the paintings, Miss Williams." His voice was slow and patient.

"What was wrong with the photographs?"

"They were of the Carracci. I couldn't let those photographs be seen, you see."

"Whyever not?" She realized somehow Robson had arranged for the theft of the photographs. Had he hired Will Carney?

"The forgery, Miss Williams. The Carracci is a forgery, like the one you discovered at Lady Millicent Stroud's. You and your friends."

Something about the expression in his eyes made Bridget think that he was threatening her. Why would anyone care this much about a photograph of a forged painting?

"The photographs were stolen from here," she said, swallowing.

"Yes, but you still have the plates. I know that you could make more prints. I want those plates now."

Bridget's eyes widened. She would have been happy to give them to him, but they were gone. "They aren't here, Mr. Robson. They went to the junk man to be scraped and reused."

"So they will be destroyed?"

"Yes, if they aren't destroyed already. No one will see them."

Robson thought a moment and looked down at his hands resting on the lion cane.

"That is fortunate. But now you know why they are valuable." He leaned his cane against the table and began to pull his gray silk scarf from around his neck.

Bridget became very aware that although she was fairly close to the back door, he could easily stop her if she tried to reach it.

"I don't understand," she whispered. "Why would you care that the paintings are forged? Did you pay a lot for them?"

"You are not a very intelligent young woman, are you?" he said. "It is no doubt due to your lack of education. The Welsh seem to care so little for the finer distinctions of learning, of art, and light, and truth." His voice was pitying. "My son painted those pictures."

"Cecil?" Her voice came out like a squeak.

Robson nodded, a bit of pride in the tilt of his head. "He is a very good painter. His mother said he could be one if he liked." He was rising from the stool and moving toward her.

"It's the disgrace, you see. I must protect him. He is my son. But it would also disgrace me. No one would listen to my ideas anymore if they knew what he had done, indeed what I have helped him do. Our family pride. It's very important to me."

Bridget was already backed up against the set of bins. She reached behind her, hoping for a weapon. But the plane was at the bottom of the bin, and nothing else was nearby.

"It's a shame. But somehow, you'll all have to go. Pratchett was an accident, of course. I was too careless in hiring my help."

"You hired Will Carney?" Bridget thought to keep him talking, if only so she could think what to do.

Robson didn't answer. He seemed to be just talking to himself. "I tried to incapacitate Morelli, and I failed. But I can probably discredit him instead. I have important friends. Your friend Miss Harris is another matter. I have discovered that she goes around the back of the newspaper office, into the alley, to do her business. I shall deal with her too."

He stretched the scarf between his hands and stopped, looking into her eyes but not seeing her.

"And that will be a shame, because your friend Miss Harris has a head like a Grecian statue. She fooled my son, my poor dim-witted boy, and discovered his talents."

Robson raised the scarf toward Bridget's throat. She readied her knee to kick him between the legs but then there was a loud crunching thud. A look of utter confusion and dismay took a second to cross his face, then he crumpled to the floor in front of her.

Constable Moberly stood there with his truncheon in his hand.

<h1 style="text-align:center">12</h1>

Detective Inspector Cuthbert Slaughter was sitting in the chair at his study, adjusting the items on his desk, awaiting Samson and Prudence. It was a somewhat formal occasion, a meeting requested by Samson, who had explained that he wanted to marry Prudence. Since Prudence had no father or male relatives available, he wanted Slaughter's counsel and advice. Cuthbert had been honored, but unsure whether he could be helpful.

"But dear," Ellie had told him, "you have known Prudence for years."

"And she seems quite delightful. But although she cleans the house and helps you in many ways, I don't really know her, not like a relative would. I don't even know where she lives."

It had been a quiet evening, and they were chatting in the study while Tommy studied in the kitchen. Ellie fetched her husband a glass of brandy, and he was smoking his pipe.

"She lives, Samson told me, near Coldbath Fields. Her father died there, a prisoner."

Cuthbert's eyebrows raised. "A prisoner?"

"Yes. We don't know what his crime was. Prudence doesn't speak of it. She lives with her mother, who is ailing with cough."

"I didn't know that," he said, puffing thoughtfully. "Poor girl."

"And Samson has no family in the city. His father was an apothecary and died a few years ago, and his mother lives with a friend in a cottage near Birmingham."

"What sort of advice do you think they need?" he asked. "I have certainly never counseled a couple before."

"True, but you always give good advice, Cubby," she said.

"I suppose I should ask about his prospects. Perhaps also about where they intend to live, that sort of thing."

"That would be a good idea," she said. "I get the feeling Samson wants a way to reassure Prudence, since he's still only a student."

The fact that they were meeting in the evening added to the strangeness. Prudence had worked that morning here in the house, then had gone home to give her mother dinner and change her clothes. Samson had spent the morning in the kitchen with Tommy, working on something about Galen and blood vessels, then joined Prudence for the journey back to the house. Tommy had spent the afternoon at Borough Market, carrying baskets for women doing their shopping and earning sixpence. Ellie had come home from the Women's Reform Club to make dinner, and Slaughter himself had been late, having been investigating a case involving a stolen horse and carriage in Lambeth.

Dinner was pleasant, if a bit awkward. Prudence had never sat at the kitchen table as a guest of the Slaughters instead of as a servant having a quick cup of tea. The Slaughters and Tommy tried to make her feel at home anyway.

The study was small, so Samson gave Prudence a chair and remained standing behind it. Tommy sat on the carpet next to the desk. He knew he hadn't been invited to the talk, but he had no intention of leaving.

Inspector Slaughter cleared his throat.

"Well. Samson. Prudence. I understand you two want to be married."

"We do, sir," said Samson, putting a hand on Prudence's shoulder.

"I know you both, of course," said Cuthbert, "and you have asked me to act as surrogate for Prudence's father, which I am happy to do. So, young man, I have a few questions for you."

He lit his pipe and watched Samson's face, which had a look of readiness. This is what he wants, Cuthbert mused. A chance to show himself.

"You are currently studying for the first Bachelor of Science examination, is that right?"

"It is, sir. I will take the examination in July, then the second Bachelor's Examination next year, while I work at a hospital."

"Have you already arranged for such a position at a hospital?"

"Yes, one of my professors has spoken to an administrator at St Bartholomew's, and there will be a place for me later in the summer."

"Excellent. So how would the two of you live for the next three years, before you have a position as a doctor?"

Prudence spoke. "I will keep working here, if I may?"

Ellie had just come in and interjected, "Of course you may," and took her chair.

"And Samson, you will continue to tutor Tommy, I hope?"

"Yes sir, if Tommy is amenable."

"I'm amenable!" said a voice from the carpet.

Slaughter studied the young couple for a moment. Prudence looked so capable, her eyes bright and intelligent. Samson looked determined, with a quiet wisdom beyond his years. But they both looked so young.

"Are there any difficulties with religion?" Cuthbert remembered Ellie saying that Samson was of the Hebrew faith, but he had not thought to inquire about Prudence.

"We don't practice any particular creed, sir," explained Samson, "but Mrs. Henderson would be very happy if we were married in the Church, so we will be." Prudence glanced up at him and smiled.

"And where will you both live?"

"Well, we did have to think about that quite a bit, sir. My boarding house only allows single men, even though it is close to my lectures and University College. At first it might be best for me to live with Prudence and her mother. I could help care for her. We may look for better lodgings later, if we have the money."

Cuthbert nodded. These two seemed to have a plan. He was not sure what else to ask. He had never been a father himself, but he was guardian to Tommy, for whom he would some day have this same conversation, he was sure.

"Can I answer any questions for you?" he said instead. "I'm happy to offer advice, but you both seem to have things well in hand."

"We do," said Prudence. "Samson was worried because he wants to be sure I won't think myself foolish later, marrying a student with no paying work. But you should see, sir, how he cares for my mother. He's so good with her. He even brought an inhaler with creosote to help ease her cough."

He'll make a good physician, if that's what he decides to be, thought Cuthbert. And I already know he's a good teacher.

"Excellent. And I assume you both are quite frugal with money."

"We are, sir," said Samson. "No worries on that score. Prudence knows how to stretch a shilling at the market and still feed her mother well."

There was a silence as the older couple watched the younger couple smile at each other.

"I think this calls for a celebration," said Ellie. "Shall I bring in some sherry?"

Tommy jumped up to fetch it.

Monday night dinner was late at Mrs. Bagley's boarding house in Shoe Lane. As the women came home from work, they were immediately distracted by their dinner guest.

Bridget had insisted that Constable Moberly come for dinner, that she wanted to make him the very best meal she could. He had escorted her home the night before, after another officer had brought the wagon to take James Robson to the station. By then she had missed dinner but hadn't been hungry anyway. Her stomach had not been happy with how close she had been to being killed. Moberly had done everything he could to reassure her.

"I still can't believe it," said Bridget as he accompanied her back to Shoe Lane in a cab. "How did you know to be at the shop?"

"I've been keeping an eye on you, and your shop, for some time," said Moberly. "Even after we arrested Will Carney. Mind you, Inspector Harkness was not in favor."

"Then why did you do it?"

Moberly shifted in his seat. "You remind me a bit of my daughter," he said quietly. "Determined, smart, canny. I wanted to make sure nothing happened to you."

"Well, you certainly did that. I'll be forever in your debt. You saved my life."

"All in a day's work, Miss Bridget." Now that it was over, Moberly felt rather tired. He wouldn't miss this sort of excitement when he left the force. "Or an evening's work, in this case. I walked the beat on Piccadilly this morning."

"I'm so sorry," she said. "It must have been exhausting for you to work your shift at the station in the day, then look out for me afterwards."

"It was my pleasure." Moberly smiled at her, and she smiled back.

"Do you think Mr. Robson is criminally insane?" Bridget asked him. "Why would he want to kill me?"

"Powerful men are a different sort, I think," said Moberly. "They are both too sure of themselves and not sure enough. Always afraid of losing what they have. And in this case, of course, he was trying to protect his son."

"Because Cecil was a forger?"

"It looks that way. He had talent, but he wanted more. Probably got a thrill out of fooling people, I expect."

"And his father didn't want anyone to find out."

"Would you? Robson has a reputation. Everyone listens to him when he talks about art. His word can make or break an artist, from what I've heard."

"Yes, Jo has said that too. She thinks people listen to him too much."

"Well, they're not likely to do that now, are they, Miss Bridget?"

Moberly had seen her safely into Mrs. Bagley's care and had left for the station to help with the notes on Robson. Esther had hurried Bridget into a hot bath while Annie fetched her some brandy. Jo helped Bridget into bed and sat with her.

"I feel awful I wasn't there," said Jo. "It never occurred to me that Cecil's father would come after you. I had no idea James Robson was involved. I was stupid not to see it."

Bridget was getting drowsy and just gazed up at Jo, grateful to have her as a friend.

"We did a good job together, Jo," she said. "You couldn't have known. Neither could I. A man of Robson's stature . . ." and then she was asleep.

Jo turned off the light and went to her own room, but she found it hard to fall asleep.

Bridget had spent Monday baking bread and pie pastry and cake. Mrs. Bagley had been happy to help her in the kitchen and to let everyone know they would have a special guest for dinner. Esther, now experienced at purchasing French claret, volunteered to buy some on her way back from her father's shop. Annie bought some flowers once she left the clock shop, and Mabel, who had spent the day designing boys' magazine puzzles in her room, helped set the table. When Moberly arrived at seven, the women were all home and had many questions for him.

"How did you know Bridget would be in the shop?"

"How did you know someone would attack her?"

"Did you know it was James Robson?"

"How did you get in without anyone hearing?"

Mrs. Bagley herself seemed to be all smiles, busying herself with getting dinner ready and listening to the chatter, but beneath was a sadness. She had almost lost one of her girls. These women worked out in the world, supporting themselves, and yet that world was full of people who could harm them. She had heard of James Robson, of course. Everyone had. Was there no way to tell when influential men like him were mad? She was grateful that these days, most of the men she encountered were grocers and tradesmen, coming around to sharpen knives or clean the chimney. She knew to be firm with them. Some were persistent, knocking at the door every day until she gave in and agreed to hire them. She'd had to show more than one the door and let them know she meant no when she said no. But she'd never had to stand up to someone as powerful as James Robson.

Moberly was enjoying the dinner enormously, surrounded as he was by intelligent young women. He seems so very nice, Mrs. Bagley thought. Since he was here, he likely wasn't married, but Bridget had said he had a daughter. So perhaps he was a widower. She liked seeing a man at her table, especially one with a steady job, a reliable man with a kind heart. And like everyone in the room, Mrs. Bagley was tremendously grateful to him for rescuing Bridget. And they were of an age. She wouldn't mind having him come around again.

Gradually the conversation turned away from the previous night's adventures. The women shared their working lives, talking about customers and trends and trade. They discussed the people who were trying to make changes in the city, like Clementia Taylor, whose salon in Aubrey House, Kensington was open to all. She was considering starting an Emancipation Society to continue the fight against slavery. There was talk of women petitioning for the national vote, and the women's rights conventions being held in America. Over dessert, criticisms began of the new Hungerford Bridge, which was being rebuilt even though it had been perfectly fine as it was, and why would anyone want to tear down something built by Isambard Brunel anyway?

At one point during the lively conversation, Moberly caught Mrs. Bagley's eye and smiled. She lowered her eyes and hoped she wasn't blushing.

The Rossetti family was preparing to be photographed by their friend Charles Dodgson, and Jo was sketching the proceedings.

"Look toward the camera, please," said Charles, as he adjusted the lens.

Rossetti stared at him, his hat in his hand. "I am looking toward the camera."

"So am I," said Christina. Her dark eyes stared vacantly in that direction. William, stroking his beard, wandered around the group, looking bored.

"Everyone, please?" Charles looked through at them. Frances glanced around at her three children instead.

The leaves were scattered all over the yard, after a half-hearted attempt to clear them from the scene. 16 Cheyne Walk had a lovely garden, but the steps down into it had been chosen for the photograph. The Rossettis had lived there a year now, adding many bohemian touches but little elegance. Christina wanted to sit on the ugly steps. It was hard to argue with poets, thought Jo.

"I've decided," said Christina, "that I'll look off into the distance, past Mother. That will show my profile to best advantage."

"And I'll look at you looking off into the distance," said Frances. "That will show mine."

"Why does Gabe have his hat and I don't?" asked William, kicking leaves with his shoe. "Are we outside or inside?"

Charles began to wonder whether he should have agreed to this at all and glanced over at Jo for support. Jo kept her head over her sketch so she wouldn't laugh. William took his place next to his mother.

"All right," said Charles, "hold!" He took the picture, shook his head, then began changing the plate.

"I'm going in to get Maria and the table. We need one with her," said William, heading in to the house.

"Fine." Charles mopped his brow and sat down under the tree, shaking his head at Jo. She smiled sympathetically at him. Rossetti came and flopped down next to them.

"How's the story going?" asked Rossetti.

"Story?" Charles looked confused.

"About the little girl, the one who follows a rabbit down a hole."

"Oh, yes. I've got most of the chapters together. It's coming along. I don't think I should publish it under my own name, though."

"Because of your position, you mean?" Rossetti laughed heartily. Maria looked over at them as she came carefully down the stairs slowly in her full skirt. William was behind her with the card table.

"Well, yes," said Charles, "I'm an Oxford mathematician. And the Liddells are in the peerage. I don't want to make anyone look foolish."

"Right," said Rossetti, slapping his hat on the ground as he got up. "I think it's silly."

"What is?" Charles looked up at him, shading his eyes against the sun coming through the leaves.

"All of it! Peerages, Oxford, damned foolishness. Write what you want, and be proud! No Rossetti would write under an assumed name."

"Yes, well that's why I'm photographing you, instead of the other way round."

"Back at it, then," said Rossetti. "Christina wants more with Mother in them." He winked at Jo.

Charles Dodgson photographed the Rossetti family in their garden at Cheyne Walk, but in October.

"Because, as I read in a book on Mary of Modena, it is easier to get forgiveness once a deed is done, than to ask for permission doing it." The book Jo read was one in a series on the queens of England, written by Agnes Strickland. The line refers to the retelling of a story from the Earl of Peterborough about the Cardinal Barberini. He helped arrange the hasty marriage of Mary of Modena to the future King James II, even though the Pope was against it.

Giovanni Morelli was a Swiss Protestant and Italian nationalist who developed a technique for determining attributions for old art works using the method described in the novel.

Samson Light was studying for the University of London examinations for a Bachelor of Medicine. The University permitted external students from anywhere to study privately and take the examinations for a degree.

The Royal School of Mines, where Samson takes Tommy to use the microscope, was in Jermyn Street. Built in 1851, the building is now Waterstones Books, Piccadilly.

T. H. Huxley, professor of natural history, was a scientist, educational reformer, and proponent of Darwin's theory of natural selection. He developed the science curriculum for the Royal School of Mines, which became the Normal School of Science at South Kensington, and ultimately Imperial College.

Regent Circus, where Bazalgette takes Jo into the sewers, is now known as Oxford Circus.

In 1853, Roger Fenton became official photographer to the British Museum, starting with Assyrian cuneiform tablets and moving on in due course to sculpture and carved reliefs—which he preferred to take in broad daylight on the Museum's roof.

Charles Street, where Jo is supposed to call to find another of the photographed women, was the home of Elizabeth Siddal's family and where she was born.

Bibliography

Dalziel, George, and Edward Dalziel. *The Brothers Dalziel: A Record of Fifty Years' Work 1840-1890*. London: Methuen & Co., Ltd, 1901.

Desmond, Adrian. *Huxley: From Devil's Disciple to Evolution's High Priest*. Reading, Massachusetts: Perseus Books, 1997.

Edge, Sarah. "The City, Photography and Relations of Looking." In *The Extraordinary Archive of Arthur J. Munby*. Routledge, 2018.

"Giovanni Morelli." Accademia Carrara, n.d. https://www.lacarrara.it/en/the-collection/collectors-2/giovanni-morelli/.

Hudson, Derek. Munby: *Man of Two Worlds*. John Murray Publishers, Ltd., 1972.

Kelly's Post Office London Directory. London, 1862.

Ladies' Sanitary Association. *The Sanitary Duties of Private Individuals : Especially Separated and Distinguished from the Sanitary Duties of Government ... and to Be Applied by Every One to Himself in His Own Business or Position in Life*. London: Ladies' Sanitary Association and John Morgan, n.d.

Loudcher, Jean-François, and Luc Cerruti. "History of Sticks (Canne)." ResearchGate, 2008.

Loudon, I. "Why Are (Male) Surgeons Still Addressed as Mr?." *British Medical Journal* 321,7276 (2000): 1589–91.

Mayhew, Henry, and John Binny. *The Criminal Prisons of London and Scenes of London Life*. London: Griffin, Bohn, and Company, 1862.

Quill, Sarah. "Lighting up the Darkness: The National Gallery, London." In *From Darkness to Light: Writers in Museums 1798-1898*. Cambridge: Open Book Publishers, 2019.

Royal Institute of British Architects. *Papers Read at the Royal Institute of British Architects*. The Institute, 1862.

Shepherd, F. H. W., ed. *Survey of London*. London County Council, 1963.

Simons, John. *The Tiger That Swallowed the Boy: Exotic Animals in Victorian England*. Farringdon: Libri Publishing, 2012.

Smith, Charles Saumarez. *The National Gallery: A Short History*. London: Frances Lincoln Limited, 2009.

Smith, Stephen. *Underground London: Travels Beneath the City Streets*. London: Abacus, 2004.

Stanley, Liz. *The Diaries of Hannah Cullwick, Victorian Maidservant*. London: Virago Press, 1984.

Acknowledgements

Thanks to my mother, who cared about the characters; David and Taylor and Sarah, who read and listened; Jenny and Payton and Erika, who edited, and John, who commented; and Jane who asked to read it. My gratitude also to Laura Noble at the National Gallery Research Centre.

About the author

Lisa M. Lane is a historian and author of *Before the Time Machine* and *Murder at Old St. Thomas's*. Born in England but living in California most of her life, she is fascinated by the relationship between historical research and fiction. When she's not researching and writing, she can be found pontificating about online pedagogy, gardening in root-bound soil, or watching classic movies.

The typefaces used for this book are Cormorant Garamond by Christian Thalmann, Switzerland, and Libre Baskerville by Pablo Impallari, Argentina. Provided by Google Fonts.